OPHELIA JAYE

CONTENTS

For anyone who has ever felt afraid to try.

THE SKY was still tinted grey and black as we pulled up to the departure terminal at the airport. The rain still hadn't stopped. I placed one of my mid-calf black leather boots outside the door of the taxicab, trying to ensure that I didn't accidentally misstep and trap my foot between the curb and the vehicle.

"Have a safe trip, sweetheart." the driver said, winking at me in the rearview mirror.

"Um, thanks," I muttered in reply, not wanting to be rude even though "sweetheart" had been the least offensive of the ways he'd addressed me this morning. There was *brown goddess, Nubian queen,* and lest we forget, *hot chocolate* right before we'd hit the on-ramp for Highway 401. I also didn't miss the way he stared at my ass before he exited the car to come around and help me take my bags out of the trunk.

Why did he park so far away from the curb? I didn't have the energy for this today. It was just another one of the many annoyances that plagued me this morning.

Thanks to a late-night thunderstorm and subsequent power outage, my stupid alarm clock didn't go off. Plus, I didn't have time to grab anything to eat on my way out of the house.

Now I was late, wet, and hungry while standing at the curb for Priority Fast Track bag check-in.

At least I had done something right by bidding to upgrade to business class at the last minute and pre-registering for curbside check-in service. I was so excited when I saw the airline's email confirming that I'd won with my low-ball bid. Not having to lug heavy bags around the airport as I navigated the summer holiday rush was a godsend.

And this was only the first of three flights I had to endure today.

I was leaving from Toronto to fly into Calgary, Alberta, direct. Then, backtracking across the country from Calgary to Saskatoon, Saskatchewan, where I'd be driven four and a half hours north to Wakepa Lake. Then, I'd fly in a small, chartered aircraft to my final destination, a small town in Northern Saskatchewan called Dènaud, named after the river running through it, by settlers during the late nineteenth century. It boasted a population of six-hundred-and-thirty-four people.

Now, as to why I was bringing my *cityfied* self to these rural parts unknown, well, that was going to take a little longer to explain.

The short answer was that I'd been working on my master's thesis at the University of Guelph, in a university town just outside of Toronto, on and off for the past two-and-a-half years. Academic fatigue had long set in, and my patient thesis advisor, who had been understanding with me throughout my journey, told me in no uncertain terms that I was running out of time to complete my graduate studies before she retired. She warned me that I'd be switched to another advisor and would essentially be starting from scratch regarding a relationship, which I did not want to do.

This trip would give me the final piece of research necessary to complete my Masters of Political Science degree and finally move on with my life. I'd gone straight from an undergraduate to a graduate program because I just wanted to get all my academic pursuits out of the way. That way, I'd thought, I could jump right into my chosen working field and change the world.

But, as they say, *When man plans, God laughs*. During a brief break from my first year of my comprehensive exams, my father passed away. It hadn't been completely unexpected. He had cancer. But that rock of a man had been *dying* of cancer for damn near two decades until about a year ago and exactly two days before Christmas when his body just gave up.

I was in Belize visiting my mom and her new husband when it happened. I was all my dad had, and I wasn't even there when he'd taken his last breath on this earth.

My mom had flown back with me to help me plan for the burial and funeral. No two people had a less acrimonious divorce than my parents. So her wanting to be there for me as much as for him just felt right. They'd been helpful to each other in life like that, so it only made sense that they'd be that way to each other in death. Unbeknownst to me, my dad had already spoken with my mom about his final wishes for his funeral and burial months before his passing. He even picked out the suit that he wanted to be buried in. "Something warm if it's winter," my mother told me he said. My mom actually joked about cremating him because my dad had died so suddenly without giving us a chance to say goodbye. It was probably the only time I'd laughed during the whole ordeal.

Once we'd held the funeral and said our goodbyes, he was interred beside his late sister, my aunt, who'd died of breast cancer in her early thirties. Cancer has been a *shrew* to my father's side of the family.

After the funeral, my mom wanted me to travel back to Belize so she and my stepdad could take care of me. But the independent streak that I'd been born with, and that my mother nurtured, won out. I stayed on my own in my dad's home, the house we'd moved into after the divorce. It reminded me so much of him, and I was convinced I'd imbue some strength from him by being there.

But my father's death had broken me for a while. I'd taken the rest of the term off just to grieve him. I occasionally kept in touch with my academic advisor to ensure she knew that I wanted to complete my degree. I wasn't a quitter.

One day that spring, I finally peeled myself out of my depths of sadness and monotony to return to a fraction of myself again. And each day thereafter, I felt a little more returning until I ended up here, on my way to God's country in Northern Saskatchewan.

I was going to be researching electoral processes in rural settler townships to study the effect, if any, of elections in this area of the country.

Although it might seem boring to some, it was my treasure trove. I loved all things political science and studies of how societies worked together or apart. It had taken several months, practically half the year, to receive the proper approvals to get this trip and study to materialize.

I was meeting two other graduate students from other universities whom I'd only communicated with through email on this research. Clearly I wasn't the only nerd interested in this area of focus. Political participation and understanding the institutions and laws that govern it are the substantive basis of my thesis. I also delve into several more nuanced arguments around structure and leadership in my research, which will pair well with the area focus of the other two graduate students. They each are performing a unique examination of municipal elections, too.

My cousin Sheree thought I was crazy to make such a long journey in the name of academic research. Especially since it meant I wouldn't be spending the summer months club-hopping and trying to find a husband. Sheree was man-crazy, and being on the cusp of turning twenty-nine had only made her more insane—she couldn't abandon the idea of being married or at least engaged before thirty.

I'll tell you, we made quite the pair when heading downtown to Toronto's nightlife. She was 5'4" and thin as a rail. I was nearly 5'10" and curvy. And because neither of us shied away from heels, our differences were even more exaggerated.

And while she'd spend the nights collecting phone numbers and Instagram handles, I avoided the glances, dodged the handsy ones, and pretended to be a foreign exchange student who didn't know English when guys approached. And sometimes the latter got me into trouble with the more aggressive men. But nothing my cousin Sheree couldn't handle on my behalf. She was pint-sized for pleasure but vicious at defending her family, she'd joke.

I liked men, loved them. I just didn't want to get entangled with one while finishing my degree. I was only twenty-three years old. There was plenty of time, I kept telling myself, no matter what my cousin said about staying on the shelf too long.

Sheree thought this trip could allow me to become a little more experienced in the dating department. So she'd packed a sex care kit for me and shoved it in my suitcase the night before I left. I didn't even bother opening it. Sheree would have included only the most lude and ludicrous items anyway. I vowed to throw it away upon arrival.

Now awaiting my travel companions in the Calgary airport, I busied myself with my portable keyboard and tablet, trying to complete the mapping of my summer writing and interview schedule in Dènaud. I was nothing if not prepared.

"Verity?" A smooth male voice made its way into my head.

I looked up from my screen into the greenest eyes I'd ever seen. Couple the eye color with two deep-set dimples, and all at once I lost my train of thought and, apparently, my ability to speak.

"Are you Verity?" The handsome man asked again.

I could manage only a nod. And I kept nodding until he stretched his hand to me in greeting.

Knocking down my tablet, I almost lunged for his hand, gripping it with two hands instead of one like a normal person.

If that weren't embarrassing enough, he was obviously amused by my enthusiasm and encircled my two hands with both of his while his lips upturned into the widest smile. Up until that moment, I didn't think he could get any cuter.

"May I?" he asked, once we got the alien handshake under control.

"Of course, please sit down," I said, finding my voice,

pointing to the seat directly across from me. He didn't take the seat and instead occupied the seat beside me. Who *is* this man?

"I'm Adrian Howard from UBC. We've been emailing back and forth a bit."

"Yes, Adrian. It's nice to meet you in person finally. I'm Verity Reynolds. How was your flight?"

"Oh, I was visiting a friend in Jasper, so I actually just got dropped off at the airport not too long ago." He smiled again, and I think I could feel my uterus contracting.

"Cool," I said, trying very hard to sound *cool*.

"And you?"

"Flew in from Toronto. Yep, actually almost missed my flight." I shrugged my shoulders in reaction to how his eyes widened. Were his eyes that green because his hair was dark or— *shit, snap out of it—oh wait, he was looking at me like he's expecting an answer to something.*

"I'm sorry, I missed your question." I fumbled out the words.

"Not a question, really. Just an observation. You're really pretty."

Yep, I was definitely going to need to change my underwear at this rate. What the hell was wrong with me? It was like I was going into heat. I didn't even really know what to say, and the expression on my face probably showed my surprise.

"Sorry, I'm a little forward sometimes," he said. "I was a

human scientist for a few years when I decided to pursue this degree, so I guess studying people has removed any good social graces from my system. I also like focusing on human reactions." That last sentence he said with a wink.

I didn't know what any of that meant, really, but I wasn't going to ask for clarification. When I still hadn't spoken, I thought he might get uncomfortable, but instead he looked intensely at my lips.

Now, as a black woman with many years on this planet, I knew that my lips were one of my best features. So full and soft that I only needed a bit of clear lip gloss to make my looks pop. That and a touch of mascara, and it was a whole look. Also, I've been told often that my lips are very *kissable*.

He was still looking at my mouth. Oh my. I could feel that a re-application of gloss was necessary, my lips weren't as sticky as I liked them to be.

Realizing what I was doing, I stopped rubbing my lips over each other.

"How far along are you in your dissertation writing?" I asked. *Smooth change of subject, Verity.*

Adrian looked unfazed but willing to humor me. I couldn't help but return his smile, too. Something magnetic about his energy pulled me in, lowered my usually solid defenses. We kept ourselves entertained with this little game of cat and mouse until it was hard to distinguish who was the cat.

That was when our final travel companion, Megan Grayson, arrived.

Megan was all bubbly energy, from a small town herself. She made no bones about the fact that this was only her second plane ride in her entire life, and she brought a sweet, effervescent energy to our little group. She was the youngest of six older siblings and had a suitcase packed with "prepared meals and thermal underwear" by her nervous parents.

Apparently, she'd been the only one who didn't transition smoothly into her family's farming lifestyle and left home to attend university under the guise of studying veterinary science. It was the only way her parents would let her leave home. Obviously, there was shock and disappointment when she graduated with a political science degree. Eventually, she'd won their support for her life's dream of graduate school and law school.

I sat beside Adrian on the plane because Megan wanted to change seats in favor of my window seat. Adrian had offered to switch me to the window instead, but I'd politely declined. No way was I going to be encased in this flying tube between a window and his body, which was making my body do strange things. But as we ascended, I silently wished I could've gazed out the window instead of sitting there twiddling my thumbs.

"Gum?" Adrian offered. "Helps with the ears." He smiled as if sharing some secret wisdom. I popped the spearmint stick into my mouth but noticed he didn't take any gum for himself.

"I'm gonna get some shuteye." And with that, he was out like a light.

Weird. I could've sworn he was flirting with me earlier.

I didn't expect him to finger me on the plane or anything, but I thought we'd at least have some type of conversation.

Perhaps I wouldn't need that sex care kit after all.

CHAPTER 2

Verity

MEGAN accidentally locked herself in the on-flight lavatory about halfway through the flight to Saskatoon. Even with the flight attendants' reassurances that it was an issue with the lock itself and not some defect on her part, Megan was so thoroughly embarrassed that she refused any drink or snack service for the rest of the flight. And she'd barely spoken to either one of us. Obviously, she also didn't visit the facilities again until we landed.

Once we did land, however, she nearly bowled us both over, running towards her relief in the terminal bathroom.

Otherwise, the trip to Dènaud had been uneventful, except for the solitary moose we saw crossing a highway as we drove to Wakepa Lake. I did get some looks of interest as we perused the gift shop at the lone stop at the gas station where we filled up, but I chalked it up to people's curiosities.

Our third and final plane ride that day went off without a hitch. And I usually stay clear of propeller planes, particularly ones that land in the water. Come to think of it, I don't remember anyone mentioning that part when I made my travel arrangements.

We were greeted at a landing dock by a nice older woman, whom the pilot called Tabitha, and her golden retriever named Gray.

"Now look at all of you. Oh, I can't tell you how happy we are that all of you decided to make this trip up to our little slice of heaven. Everyone in the community is super excited to meet you!" Tabitha was practically jumping up and down as she spoke. I watched as the wind played with some grayish tendrils around her face.

Adrian offered his hand to her first, but she knocked it aside and walked in to bear hug him. She had a roundish figure but was much shorter than Adrian, so her head only came up to just below the middle of his chest. Her messy bun of gray and white strands bobbed up and down against his snug-fitting T-shirt. If he was uncomfortable, he didn't let on. He used his arms to kind of encircle her and tapped around her with his hands instead of hugging her back. *Mental note: Either he's a psychopath or isn't big on being touched.*

Megan didn't have any issues with personal space, likely because she had so many siblings. She had no trouble matching Tabitha's energy, hugging her closely, and they both laughed together upon release.

When Tabitha turned towards me, I knew better than to offer her my hand, but I was hoping for something a little less extreme than a bear hug—just something in between.

But Tabitha didn't get the memo and nearly squeezed the life out of me. I tried to return her embrace with as much fervor as I could, but three plane rides and a four-hour drive had drained me. She got what she got.

Because it was summertime in Saskatchewan, the days were much longer. Although we'd been traveling all day, the sun still shone down on us.

Tabitha's dog seemed a little curious about the three of us. He sniffed our luggage pile like a customs and immigration dog, trying to detect narcotics and weapons. *Geeze,* I wondered if any of my various facial or body creams had spilled out into my suitcase. But soon enough Gray turned his attention from the suitcase to us, or rather *me*.

"Good doggie," I said nervously as I stepped closer to Adrian. In a matter of moments, I had tucked myself behind his entire body to shield myself from Gray's prying snout.

Adrian seemed amused and kept moving around slightly to leave me more exposed. But when I put my hands on his waist, he stilled instantly. The outline of his T-shirt hadn't done him justice. If I weren't so focused on keeping Gray from making a meal out of me, I would've splayed my fingers over his hardness.

"Don't worry, he doesn't bite, dear," Tabitha said while her focus was clearly elsewhere. *Yep, that's what everyone says about their dog until it bites someone.*

"I'll protect you." Adrian smiled over his shoulder as he looked into my eyes with something more than just mirth.

I couldn't help but smile back, given my strange situation, but I couldn't have been more thankful to Megan who dropped to one knee to call Gray over. He bounded happily off towards her, but not before he placed a small inquisitive lick on my leg. Regretting wearing a skort instead of jeans, I watched the wet spot slowly dry.

Realizing I was still attached to Adrian, I quickly let him go and put a little distance between us. I noticed that he was looking at the wet spot as well. *Did he just lick his own lips?*

I wasn't a huge fan of dogs; growing up my only pet had been a budgie. Dogs were too much maintenance, and there really was only room enough for one high-maintenance creature in my dad's household, which was me. I could see my dad's wrinkled forehead and smiling face as he watched me reorganizing my closet or the contents of my bathroom vanity for the umpteenth time. I was a fan of style and order, convinced the two could live harmoniously together with enough attention to detail. Did that make me crazy? Probably. But who cares?

"Headley, are you coming over for the cookout tomorrow, too?" Tabitha said, motioning to our trusty pilot.

"The wife has me doing some things around the house, and then I've got another flight in the afternoon to Bridges Bay.

So I'll try, but can't make any promises," he said as he unloaded the last of our luggage from the plane with Adrian's assistance.

"No worries. Tell Marigold I said hello and kiss that sweet little baby in her tummy for me. I'll save you all some plates." Tabitha offered as Headley made his way back into the pilot seat.

I hadn't realized that he would be dashing off so soon. I scrambled for my purse to try and offer him some cash as a tip. I had no idea how you were supposed to tip your pilot, but it worked easily enough when a taxi driver unloaded your bags for you.

"Just your thanks is plenty. You all take care." He waved as he closed the cockpit door. I felt a little foolish as I turned around to face Tabitha and the rest of my travel mates.

"City folks." I heard Tabitha mumble under her breath, but she had a huge smile on her face as she shook her head.

"Great first impression," Adrian remarked as he reached down to grab my suitcase. He was smiling, too. Or was that a smirk?

"It's all right; I can do it myself." I hurriedly tried to take the handle stand away from him without success.

"Oh, darling, just let him do it. Chivalry isn't dead, right, handsome?" Tabitha winked. Was she flirting with Adrian? She had to be at least in her late forties or early fifties-she was graying, but I'd say it was premature because her skin looked age-free. But I guess, with his looks, he'd be used to things like that.

Megan grabbed her hiker's backpack and slung it over her shoulder. Clearly she knew how to pack for the trip to Northern Saskatchewan.

I had a rolling suitcase that was bright orange and so glossy that the water around the dock we were standing on reflected on the sides of it. Then I had my purse and a large tote carry-on. I'd been tempted to carry my designer tote with me but figured that it'd probably make me seem even more out of place way up here. So I grabbed some non-descript tote from a vegan accessories shop in downtown Toronto, figuring that I could help the planet at the same time as indulging in my joy of shopping.

Adrian had been commandeered by Tabitha, who had her arm looped into his as they strolled towards a green 4 x 4 parked just ahead.

"I'm glad that I'm not the only one who gets embarrassed sometimes," Megan said as we sat next to each other in the back seat. I gave Megan a smile, glad to see that she had finally resumed speaking to us after her little in-flight incident. I shrugged my shoulders. "Happens to the best of us."

This loose bond that Megan and I created by feeling foolish kept us laughing and talking in the backseat all the way to our accommodations.

Approximately thirty minutes later, we pulled up a long

gravel driveway to a large farmhouse. It had blue and white shutters, bright white wooden sidings, and a wraparound porch that looked like it was straight out of the Deep South. Gray jumped out of the truck bed and sprinted past us to the back of the house.

Grateful that I'd switched into my cross-trainers, I stepped out of the car, trying not to slip on the gravelly surface. I looked around and was pretty much in awe of the place. Not the house specifically but the land surrounding it. This must be what they call an acreage. It was massive. As far as the eye could see, there were huge swaths of land in every direction. The forest seemed to edge towards us a little closer in parts, but it was true what they said about Saskatchewan: you could see your dog running away for two weeks. And it was breathtaking. There weren't enough adjectives in the English language to describe how perfect the landscape was.

So enraptured by my surroundings, I nearly missed Tabitha's welcoming speech: "…became known as Clarence House. And it'll be your home for your stay here in Dènaud."

I'm sorry, what did she just say? We were going to stay in the farmhouse? I'd sworn that my confirmed travel arrangements included a stay at the town's only inn—some kind of chalet.

"I can see that puzzled look on your faces. Well, the Snow Chalet had some bad flooding during our last rainfall. Poor Marybeth. It's a family-owned business, you know, and she sure was looking forward to the income from your stay. But it couldn't be helped and won't be fixed for a few months. So we scrambled to find some more suitable accommodations for you guys." Tabitha looked at us, three weary travelers, with sympathy in her eyes. "I promise you it will be just as nice as the Snow Chalet. And here you can be much closer to nature."

I didn't know what type of "nature" she was referring to, but as beautiful as this place was, the farmhouse looked a little rundown upon a closer look. I was looking forward to a hot bath and some warm, clean sheets. Maybe even a fluffy down comforter and regular housekeeping. I knew it would be a different experience for sure, but I hadn't expected to live on a farm, literally. Come to think of it, I hadn't even seen the barn yet. *What exactly did they farm on this land?*

"You'll each have your own room instead of you ladies having to share." Tabitha offered as a consolation.

My eyebrows raised. Yet another thing that had been left out when I'd made my original travel arrangements. I really needed to speak with the university about this.

"Enough said! I'm sold!" Megan practically yelled. Then thinking better of her response, she turned towards me sheepishly. "Sorry, but I have so many brothers and sisters that I had to wait until university to get my own room, and even then I had a roommate who I shared the kitchen space with.

I really wasn't offended at all. Being in my own room

was what I was expecting, so to hear differently made me wonder what else on this trip was going to be a surprise.

Adrian had thus far been quiet, apparently finding enough amusement in my facial expressions. His gaze was a little unnerving. We'd barely spoken more than a few sentences to each other outside of just the basic chatting that one does when traveling long distances with another person: I'm hungry, are you? You should get some rest; it's gonna be a long drive. Are you sure you don't want any gum?

I mean he'd called me "pretty" and then basically clammed up on me. *Weird.* Perhaps he wasn't interested in me at all and had just been making polite conversation—all questions for another day. I was exhausted and needed to get settled into my room. Besides, I wanted to let my mom and Sheree know that I'd arrived safely.

"Come on. It'll be great. Let me get you guys set up here." Quite frankly, Tabitha sounded like she needed convincing as well.

We left the heavier bags in the truck and made our way up the front porch. Each creaking step communicated the age of the house.

Just as Megan had crossed the threshold behind Tabitha, who had to use her shoulder to push open the front door, I heard barking coming from around the side of the porch. *Oh no! Was Gray coming to finish what he'd started?*

Adrian's taller frame blocked my view, and he thought I'd keep moving forward. So when I stopped short, startled at the barking, Adrian's momentum hadn't stopped, and he ended up bumping into me kind of hard. My body lurched forward, but I felt his hands immediately at my waist to stop me from falling.

Looking up, I only had a few short seconds to return Adrian's smile before Gray was at his back. Up on his hind legs, Gray could've been mistaken for a human being, trying to push another person out of the way. Adrian moved his shoulder back until Gray fell back on all fours. But the barking didn't stop.

To a more informed person, Gray was probably not growling, just barking loudly. But to my untrained ear, coupled with my discomfort with dogs generally, it just looked to me like he had added Adrian to the menu.

I didn't see what Tabitha or Megan were doing because my focus was suddenly drawn to a tall stranger with broad shoulders making his way toward us with an even gait.

"Gray. Down," the stranger said. No shouting—just two simple words—but the command was effective. Gray immediately sat on his hind legs, then lay down on his stomach with his head over his front paws. The once menacing beast now looked like any tamed animal.

Drawing my focus to the owner of that voice, I realized that a large, pulled-down Stetson still hid the person's face.

"Noah, you're here!" Tabitha exclaimed excitedly. Until

now, I hadn't even been aware that she'd made her way back onto the porch.

The stranger hit one of his boots against the other as if he were trying to get something dislodged from it. And then he looked up. His lips came into view first, right after his chiseled jaw with a spattering of stubble.

Oh.

He was chewing on something—a piece of straw or hay. It looked cliché, but it was the sexiest thing I'd ever seen in person. I also noticed a small bump on the bridge of his nose. It had been broken at some point but had since healed. I couldn't quite confirm the color of his eyes from this distance, but I knew that they were a combination of at least two colors.

"Come up. Come up and meet everyone." Tabitha exclaimed, waving the stranger forward.

I realized that Adrian still had his hands around my waist as I felt his grip tighten. Almost possessively.

As the man with the Stetson approached the front steps, he removed his hat to reveal his mop of red hair. Upon closer inspection, his sideburns, which went up the sides of his face into his Stetson, were neatly trimmed. But the mane atop his head was unruly and desperately needed a cut.

The porch was narrower near the steps, but when I tried to reposition myself to give us all room to meet the new guy, I felt Adrian try to pull me closer to him.

"This is Megan, Adrian, and Verity." Tabitha introduced us by waving her hand towards each person.

Megan looked starstruck and almost missed the new guy extending his hand towards her. She finally grabbed it with a little more gusto than she'd probably intended. Adrian eyed him a bit and gave him a firm handshake that lasted a bit too long.

I'd finally managed to push myself free of Adrian's grasp to take the hand extended to me. The stranger's hands were warm and calloused. His hand lingered around my own even after I'd begun to loosen my own grip. I was finding it difficult to tear my eyes away from his gaze as he towered over practically everyone on the porch. He was similar to Adrian's height and stature but clearly had a body developed over years of hard manual labor instead of a gym. *Believe me, there was a difference.*

"Noah Sawyer, Miss. It's a pleasure to meet you. Welcome to Clarence House, my home," he said while still holding my hand.

Oh my. I'm in trouble.

VERITY

AFTER BEING SHOWN to our rooms, I desperately needed a shower—or rather, a showerhead. Orgasm was a sure-fire way to release the tensions from the long day of travel, not to mention my surprise attraction to the hot cowboy hosting us during our stay in Dènaud.

At home, I only used a standing shower, so I'd angle the faucet head underneath me and temper the movement of my body to achieve the best results. But this bathroom had a huge clawfoot tub that was solid white with golden feet. I'd never seen anything so ornate, and quite frankly, it seemed a little out of place in such a classic-looking farmhouse, but who was I to complain?

In fact, all the little decorative touches in this bathroom had an expensive feel to them. It was no wonder that the front steps creaked so much; they'd busted the budget on the bathroom. There were double oval mirrors above two pedestal sinks. This was the first bathroom I'd seen, outside of a luxury brand catalog, with this type of wallpaper. It had intricate flower designs in black and white that complimented the gold faucets and other gold accents. It was almost as if the bathroom had been made to someone's unique specifications—perhaps a woman, like a lady of the house with high-end tastes—maybe Noah's mother…I hoped.

But, back to what I was doing, it certainly didn't help to think about Noah's mother at a time like this. Instead, my mind retreated to the recent encounter on the front porch. The way he stood and how his eyes traveled the length of me from head to toe, like he wanted to impress upon me the sheer size of him.

I'd completely ignored Adrian, with his hand at my waist. *I was going to have to speak to Adrian about that. He was sending too many mixed signals.*

Noah was at least 6'2" with a muscular build and wide shoulders. He looked as if he gave the best hugs in the world. I felt a warmth creeping up from deep within. Not to mention that I was now spraying the showerhead directly onto my clit, moving it in a semi-circular motion to increase the buildup for climax.

I slid further down in the tub and widened my legs even more. I knew I was close when I felt the familiar tightening in the core of my stomach muscles. One of my legs made it over the edge of the bathtub, and I raised up my hips slightly to meet the steady stream of pulsating water that was thrumming my sensitive bud. The rhythmic motion pushed me further and further to the edge. And just when it seemed as if I wouldn't be able to contain myself, I lowered myself a little deeper in the tub to delay my release.

Why was I teasing myself? Let's get this!

Conjuring up the image of Noah once again, the veins in the back of his large hands as he held my own, I imagined what it would feel like to have that hand encircled around my neck, applying just the smallest of pressures as he moved his mouth over mine. Would his stubble be ticklish or awaken every sensitive point as it glided against my skin?

I was writhing underneath the liquid barrage now. Holding my free hand over my mouth, I stifled a moan as my body lifted as far as it could upwards so that my core could receive its final pounding. And there it was. Pure ecstasy as that familiar height was achieved, and I was sent over it in excruciating waves of pleasure that didn't want to stop.

My body trembled in the aftermath as I tried rather awkwardly to pull my dangling limb back into the tub. I'd tried not to let myself be heard, but honestly, I'd never come that hard from self-stimulation before. I couldn't even remember whether I'd yelled out or not.

As the tingling sensation traveled down my body, indicating my return from bliss, I sat up further in the tub. I hadn't intended to take a bath *per se*, but now that I was there, I figured what the heck.

NOAH

AS SOON AS I laid eyes on her, I knew I would put her in the primary suite with the newly renovated ensuite. A woman that beautiful deserved to be pampered in a most special and unique way, I thought to myself.

My desire for her had been instantaneous. Locking eyes with her had shaken me to my core. Everything about her screamed out to me every desire and want I'd ever had. And I wanted her badly, in a way that I hadn't felt in a while. In fact, if I was honest with myself, I'd never felt this desperate for someone.

The way the setting sun made her dark skin almost glow would stay in my mind for a very long time. It was difficult for me even to tell whether she'd been wearing even the slightest hint of makeup. She had a heart-shaped face with beautiful brown eyes framed by long lashes that I just knew I could get lost in. And when she smiled at me, I became so hard that I felt self-conscious about her seeing the imprint of my manhood in my jeans. Luckily, she'd kept those beautiful eyes above my belt, or it would have been embarrassing for us both.

She smelt amazing, and I was dying to know the name of her perfume so that I could gift it to her over and over again.

Seeing how her travel companion—Adrian, I think his name was—kept his hand on her waist almost possessively gave me only a momentary pause. The way she'd stepped away from him told me all I needed to know about how she felt about Adrian's actions towards her. Adrian was exhibiting desires that weren't being reciprocated. From what I'd heard of the group, they didn't attend the same university, so there was a chance they'd just met. There was no way this guy could be staking some type of claim this early.

When I followed her through the hallway to show the ladies the rooms they'd be staying in, I'd made sure that Verity's was the one closest to my own and furthest away from that guy Adrian. I would've put him on a different floor if I could. *Was it too late to put him in the bunkhouse?* That'd be a bit much, considering that Adrian was a guest and didn't work on the ranch.

I didn't go into the bedroom with Verity, just simply opened the door for her and pointed towards the ensuite prior to leaving her in the room by herself. Even in the hallway, I needed to get out of this confined space with her in it, so I immediately headed for the stables. I needed to go for a ride.

VERITY

THE NEXT MORNING, everyone was gathered at the large wooden picnic table just outside two double doors leading to the kitchen from the porch. Seeing the property from the front on the drive up had been beautiful but looking out over the expansive untouched land behind the house was the definition of breathtaking. From this vantage point, I could imagine what sitting outside and watching the sunrise would be like. As I surveyed a distant tree line over the top of my teacup, I felt a certain kind of contentment. I'd been the first one up this morning, so I quietly made myself a cup of tea, waiting for the others to join.

My self-directed sexual release the night before must have loosened me up more than I'd thought because, although I had intentions of finding a snack before heading off to bed, I'd practically passed out wrapped in only a towel on top of my bed. When I woke up at some point during the night, the gnawing in my stomach wasn't great enough for me to venture downstairs, so I simply lost the towel and got underneath the sheets, revelling in the feel of the soft cotton sheets against my bare skin. I almost forgot about the *whatever*-Chalet.

The night was hot, but with my window open, I'd gotten enough air circulating in my room to give me one of the most restful nights of sleep I'd had in a long time.

"No more coffee?" I turned to find Adrian entering the kitchen barefoot in sweatpants and a T-shirt. He definitely had the cutest bedhead I'd seen on a man up to this point. As he rubbed his face, I rose to join him, walking back through the porch doors and re-entering the kitchen.

"I don't know. I could make you a nice cup of tea. I don't drink coffee, actually."

Adrian looked at me like I'd grown a second head. The corners of his mouth turned upwards, and he squinted his eyes as if trying to figure something out. "Seriously? I don't even think I can look at you right now?"

I shrugged my shoulders and laughed at him. "There's a coffee machine over here, but I don't know how to work it."

Within no time, Adrian had sidled over to stand directly behind me. Reaching above my head, he opened the kitchen cabinets, seemingly searching for whatever elements were necessary to work the machine before us. *Here he goes again.*

I could feel him against my back. His pants material was a poor barrier, and I could feel more of *all* of him against the small of my back. A bit startled, I tried to move out of his way, but then I heard a cough coming from behind us.

Noah stood stiffly, balancing a tray of coffee cups in one hand and a handled paper bag in the other. I couldn't quite place the expression on his face, but if I had to hazard a guess, I'd say he was *pissed*. But the emotion was fleeting as he moved past us.

Placing the tray of black-lidded cups on the island, he tipped his hat towards us before walking with the bag out to the table on the porch. "I figured you guys weren't quite ready to give up certain city comforts just yet, so I rode into town and got some of Dènaud's finest from our café. It's not Starbucks, but you won't find a more quality bean in the entire country."

I ignored the Starbucks comment, and Adrian looked at

Noah skeptically. His eyebrows rose almost into his hairline when he brought one of the cups down from his lips. Adrian simply nodded his approval and started making his way towards the table in search of what goodies Noah had brought for us. But not before he stopped short and grabbed a second cup.

"Verity doesn't drink coffee, so I'll take hers. Wouldn't want this to go to waste."

Noah's gaze fell on me immediately. "I'm sorry. I didn't know. I just assumed…" he trailed off, looking a bit miserable.

"Don't worry about it, truly. I'm totally fine. I just don't like the taste of it," I said with the biggest smile I could muster.

"Good to note. You don't like the taste of coffee. Is there anything else I should know? Are you allergic to any foods?" Now he looked frantic.

This all was too amusing to me. "We've got a long summer ahead of us," I said. "Why don't we learn each other as we go along? But to answer your question, I'm not allergic to anything." I hadn't intended for my response to be as flirtatious as it was. But I stopped second-guessing myself when I saw the look of relief that washed over his face.

Just then, Megan walked into the kitchen with Tabitha, carrying a big basket covered by what looked like a folded picnic blanket.

"Good morning!" Tabitha sang towards us.

"Wow, Megan, what time did you get up?" I asked.

"Around six-thirty," she replied. My look towards her must have said "why?" because she kept going.

"So I decided to walk around the property. Then, I bumped into Tabitha along the way, and she gave me a tour of the grounds. There's a swimming hole not too far away, and the most beautiful horses I've ever seen are in the stables…" Megan just couldn't help herself, describing everything she'd taken in this morning and rattling off all the fun things there were to do. It was almost as if she'd forgotten we came here to work and not to take a vacation.

"Megs reminds me so much of my grandkids," Tabitha said as she unpacked some of the contents of her basket. *Megs? When did these two get so familiar?*

"Grandkids?" I blurted out, instantly regretting my actions and placing a hand over my mouth, but it was too late. "It's just that. I thought you were…you know."

"Younger than I look," she said with a wink. "Don't worry, sugar. I'll take that as my first compliment for the day. Yes, I have two grandbabies now and one on the way." She reached for her phone as Megan and I flanked either side of her.

"That's Headley from yesterday." Megan pointed excitedly.

"Yep. He's my eldest, and he's got one on the way with his wife. They got married not too long ago," she said with pride on her face.

"But he called you Tabitha?" I said, genuinely puzzled.

She shrugged. "I had Headley when I was sixteen years old. So we grew up together, and he's just always called me by my first name."

"Huge scandal apparently back in the day." Noah smiled knowingly. I looked up to see a devilish smile that made him even more handsome—if that was even possible. Our eyes locked, and he winked at me. I quickly looked away.

"I'm nothing if not dramatic," Tabitha declared without a hint of apology. "This town needed something to liven it up," she said, continuing to smile. "And here is my other son, Ogden. He lives in Calgary with his girlfriend and their two daughters, Quinn and Stassie. Hopefully, they'll get a chance to visit while you're in town, so you can meet them all."

Eventually, we all migrated over to the table and dug into the baked treats Noah had brought, along with the Tupperware filled with freshly cooked sausages, eggs, and fried tomatoes. Everyone was eating communal style with their fingers as we were all famished, and everything just tasted so darn good.

"So do you actually use that kitchen, or is it just for show?" I cheekily asked Noah.

"He's a wonderful cook, dear. I just thought I'd help out a bit since this was kind of sprung on him last minute and all."

Noah looked slightly annoyed with the disclosure, but I couldn't tell which had done it: the remark about his culinary skills or becoming a surprise host.

His eyes found my own, and he stared at me intently as though trying to communicate something to me alone. It was a little too intense, so again I broke eye contact and returned to my meal.

"I'm happy things worked out like this. Now, let's get you all fed, and then I'll ride you into town for your meeting with the mayor," he offered.

So it was the latter part.

"Do you think that's a good idea, Noah? I'm already here and more than happy to take them to their meeting," Tabitha interjected. Something passed between them both that made me wonder if there was something more going on. But I brushed it away since we were just there for work—nothing else, really.

But when Noah looked over to me and simply nodded his head, he seemed agitated, which piqued my curiosity again. He stood up rather abruptly and put his Stetson back on his head. I didn't really remember him taking it off.

"All right, I'll be heading out. See you at the cookout this afternoon." He turned, but not before tipping his hat towards the table. "Ladies." He managed only a grunt for Adrian. And then he was gone.

THE RIDE INTO TOWN didn't take too long thanks to Tabitha's lead foot. *How hadn't I noticed it yesterday?* It wasn't as if there was any heavy city traffic. On the contrary, it was an open one-line road from the Clarence House property line to the center of town—nothing but endless fields on either side of the road for long stretches at a time. The nearest neighbor had to be a good distance away by foot because you couldn't see any other homes around from the roadside.

Tabitha didn't take her foot off the gas, literally, until we pulled up in front of an older-looking building with the words City Hall etched into the brick archway above the double-door entryway.

Once inside, the light from a stained-glass ceiling atrium, which looked much newer in terms of the structure's construction age, let in tons of sunlight down onto a beautiful tapestry of colored tile. The design was centered in a circle of solid black tile and featured golden wheat, tall trees, farmland with a barn, and a solo cowboy on horseback. It was a very romantic scene, straight out of a romance writer's imagination.

As graduate students, we were tasked with being the ambassadors of our respective institutions. We all brought with us signed letters from our deans and university presidents. My thesis advisor had included a special note of thanks to our host and the mayor directly. I needed to remember to give the note to Noah when we got back to the house.

Time passed quickly as we awaited the mayor's arrival. Apparently, she'd been called away at the last minute and, according to her assistant, sent her apologies to us for the deviation in her schedule. It worked out since it gave me more time to consolidate my thoughts for the meeting; I knew her time would be precious.

Tabitha promised to wait for us in the building's lobby instead of coming up with us to the mayor's office, which I found a little strange. I knew it was a small town where everyone probably knew each other well, but the opportunity to meet with a leader of your town seemed like a unique opportunity—at least, it was to me.

"I'm so sorry I'm late. My apologies, truly."

All three of us rose from our seats as a tall, dark-haired woman entered the mayor's office's waiting area. She talked and moved towards us as she handed her suit jacket and briefcase to a young man struggling to keep up with her long strides. She looked like an athlete—as tall as a professional volleyball player and just as fit.

She wore a burgundy pencil skirt and a light rose silk blouse tucked into her small waist area. When she came closer to us, I noted that she wore bright red lipstick and a little too much eyeliner, which aged her somewhat. She didn't look to be much older than we were—probably in her late twenties, perhaps. And she definitely had a few frown lines etched into her face, denoting that she was a worrier, as my grandmother would say. There were a great many things on her mind at all times, and she probably had difficulty sleeping well at night.

Why was I making all these assessments and assumptions about this woman I didn't know? Verity, snap out of it!

"Hello, I'm Verity Reynolds from the University of Guelph," I said.

Adrian and Megan introduced themselves, and then we followed her hand direction into her office and sat down in some oversized plush leather seats. For the next forty minutes or so, the mayor provided us with a long, meandering at times, primer on herself and the town of Dènaud.

I'd been right! She was young—twenty-eight years old, on the cusp of twenty-nine. The town's youngest mayor ever. Her father had been the mayor of Dènaud for three terms and was headed into his fourth after a landslide in the last municipal election when he suffered a massive heart attack and died.

Mayor Leona Grant had obtained her master's in Business Administration in the United States and had been back home for just over a year when her father took ill. She'd been working in his office prior to leaving for school and managing his campaign for this last election, so she'd been intimately involved with the campaign and the mayor's office for some time. But she was born and raised in this town, having only ever left once to attend university.

"Wow, becoming the youngest Mayor of your hometown must have been an interesting story. Right?" Megan added the last part when the mayor paused before answering for the umpteenth time. It appeared like she was trying to eat up the time allotted to us by answering so slowly. Or perhaps she was just being careful about her responses. Either way, it did create an air of awkwardness.

"I'm not sure what you're getting at," Mayor Grant answered sharply.

"What I think my colleague meant was that it's impressive that you've ascended to these heights politically at your age." I tried to soothe whatever had ruffled her feathers. Megan's look told me that she was relieved as well.

"I've worked extremely hard to get to this position. So if hard work and determination are impressive to you all, then yes, I'm more than grateful that the town of Dènaud has put their faith in me," she replied.

My curiosity piqued because, according to my research, Mayor Grant had simply assumed the mayoral position upon her father's passing. He'd won the election but hadn't made it to the inauguration by the date of his untimely death. So due in part to the financial burden of running another election, the other candidate had simply deferred to Ms. Grant. According to some local reports, the town had otherwise benefited from the lack of need to recirculate a ballot. It wasn't even clear whether the process itself had been legal, and it was one of the things that I'd vowed to investigate. I would need access to town bylaws and records, though, which weren't easily accessed.

Leona Grant was poised and polite in her dealings with us, but it quickly became apparent why it'd taken so long to get the appropriate approvals to conduct our study in this town. At times, Mayor Grant seemed somewhat suspicious of our choice to come to this town, and her misgivings came across loud and clear, given the way she answered our questions.

In fact, she outright asked us why we didn't choose other towns and didn't seem entirely satisfied with the responses we gave. She was protective in a way that bordered on concealment, which was a bit strange.

"So have you had a chance to see much in our fair town?" Mayor Grant asked while taking the steaming cup of hot coffee from her assistant's hand, who'd just popped up. Her assistant backed away carefully and—strangely—also backed his way out of the office, not once turning his back to us.

Adrian caught my eye and raised an eyebrow. I scrunched

my face slightly as if to say, "Don't say anything." The atmosphere in the office wasn't exactly comfortable, so there was no need to bring up anything else. Besides, Mayor Grant seemed happy that the time set out for this introductory meeting was coming to an end. That thought was confirmed for me when she rose from behind her desk and walked towards us with an outstretched hand. We'd barely had any time to even consider her last question to us.

"Um, not yet, but we just got into town yesterday. I'm looking forward to the cookout tonight, though. Will you be coming?" Adrian asked while standing and taking her hand.

Mayor Grant paused before him as he rose to his full height. In her heels, he had her by less than an inch, and she seemed to like that. She'd been cool with all of us for most of the time since we'd met her, and now she appeared to be warming up to Adrian—literally, as we were speaking.

"I'll have to check my schedule, but if it permits, I may just see you all there." She tried to disguise her interest in Adrian by glancing at both me and Megan while she spoke.

Megan may have been oblivious, but I'd caught it. She was attracted to him. It was hard not to be, really, when he was giving off sexy professor vibes, with frames that I doubted were prescription and the leather saddle bag he'd just hiked over his shoulder.

Adrian didn't seem at all fussed about her paying him

special attention, though. *Strange. If he wanted some excitement during this trip, there was no better conquest than the mayor of the freaking town.* That would be a major feather in his cap. Perhaps I'd underestimated him.

Once we'd finished our goodbyes, the mayor's jittery assistant appeared in the doorway again to usher us back into the waiting area. I'd noted Adrian's hand placement at the small of my back as he followed me out of the mayor's office. Hoping I'd covered my surprise at the familiarity of his touch and that the mayor hadn't seen it.

I didn't know why, but I just felt that I should stay in her good graces as much as possible during our stay. *Let's not do anything to rock the boat.*

***

Back in my room, I was busily trying to fix my hair in the mirror when I heard a soft tapping on my door. I had to wait until I heard it again though, before I moved to open it, not completely certain that someone was even there.

Opening the door, I'd expected to find Megan on the other side. I'd just sent her a text to say that I needed help tying the back of my summer dress. The pattern was a crisscross of spaghetti straps that I called my "help me" dress because I could never tie it by myself. That was also why I rarely wore it, but something about this beautiful land around us and my just wanting to feel pretty made me glad that Sheree had packed it.

Oh shit! I need to call that woman. I'd already texted her and my mother but knew my cousin wouldn't be satisfied with an "arrived safely." I could almost hear the words "this *bitch*" falling from her lips as she read it.

I opened the door and was more than a little flustered to see Noah standing before me in a newly pressed shirt and dark-colored jeans. Up until this point, I'd only ever seen him in clothes that he wore to work on the ranch: a Stetson, naturally distressed blue jeans, and either a white T-shirt or other casual short-sleeved top. He looked good in anything, but this combination made him absolutely mouth-wateringly sexy.

"Oh, um…hi," I managed to get the words out eventually.

He was holding his Stetson against his chest. I got hit with a wave of pine-fresh bath soap and some other musky scent that I couldn't quite place. It wasn't cologne, of that I was certain. Did this man just have his own way of smelling? *Mercy.*

His eyes widened ever so slightly as they left my face and traveled downwards. It was then that I realized that my dress was hanging a little loosely in the front. You couldn't see my breasts, but you could certainly tell that I wasn't wearing a bra.

"Ah, sorry. I didn't mean to interrupt when you're getting ready," he said, bringing his eyes swiftly back up to my face.

Damn. He looked more embarrassed than I did. It almost

made me laugh. In fact, I started to chuckle. Bringing a hand up to cover my mouth, I took a step back into my room without thinking. Noah's eyes lit up, and the blush on his cheeks started to deepen. Then, as if taking my movement as an invitation, he stepped forward into my room.

He stalked me for a couple more steps until I stopped just before the foot of the bed. We both just stood there for a moment. Him staring down at me with a hand at his side. I could see his breathing increase somewhat as his nostrils flared with each breath. It was like I was mesmerized by the rise and fall of his chest myself. Suddenly, I felt a little lightheaded. Like I wasn't completely in control of myself. *Was it getting hot in here?*

Moving both of my hands, I clumsily held up the front of my dress to keep it from falling any further. The action drew Noah's gaze immediately to my chest area.

I took another step back away from him.

Noah matched it and took a step towards me.

I was frozen. Feeling like I should do or say something, but not entirely confident in what that should be.

"Let me." Noah almost whispered.

I didn't know at first what he was referring to. *Let him what? Kiss me? Touch me? Fuck me?*

When I didn't immediately respond, he clarified by reaching out and touching one of the straps of my dress. I had to control the shudder that was forming when I felt his fingers graze my skin. *Oh God. I hope he didn't see that.*

Instead of speaking further, he turned me slowly around until I stood with my back completely towards him. He placed his hat on the dresser. When I raised my chin, I saw our reflection in the standing mirror in the corner of the room. I could see how he scrunched up his face in concentration as he tried to pull and figure out the strings across my back. The look was present on his face for only a moment, though, before his gaze rose to meet my own in the mirror, and I felt the familiar tightening of the dress across my chest and back.

When he was finished, he placed both hands on my shoulders and leaned down until his mouth was right above my ear. "You look gorgeous."

"Thank you." I managed to say after taking in a bit of air. He'd noted that quick intake because I saw a knowing smile creep across his handsome face. His scent and large presence behind me were intoxicating. His hands were slowly making their way down my shoulders to my arms until he took one large hand and placed it at my waist. At this point, my movements were directed purely by my subconscious as I felt myself leaning into his solid frame.

"I love this dress on you." He said as he squeezed my waist with his other hand, pulling me closer to him. It was almost as if he wanted to say the opposite, though—that he'd love this dress off me, too.

I closed my eyes and shook my head a little to clear my thoughts. *What was I doing?*

Already slightly bent, he turned his lips into my hair. It wasn't a kiss *per se*, but there was contact with the skin just below my hairline and above my ear. The tingle it created shot straight down to my core. At this rate, I was going to end up having to change my underwear, which would've been such a shame because it was a matching set. *Oh, shut up, silly girl!*

This man was threatening me with a good time using only words and the slightest touch, and I was barely hanging on. What would happen if something really did occur between us?

The thought hung in the air as we were interrupted by a louder knock on my bedroom door. *Now, that was a Megan-like knock.*

Noah still had his hand firmly on my waist, not moving an inch. I did my best basketball pivot out of his grasp and moved quickly to open the door.

"There you are! I was waiting for you to come and help me with my dress," I uttered a little too excitedly.

"Sorry, I got held up doing my makeup," Megan said shyly, clearly affected by Noah's presence in the room. I've got to get that girl to be more confident this summer as a sort of pet project. It was then that I noticed that she had practically mimicked the heavy eyeliner we'd seen earlier in the day on the mayor and that the lipstick she'd used was two shades too dark for her complexion.

"I can see," I said as I looked at Noah for some reassurance.

"Yep, you look great, Megan. Well, I think I'll leave you two to get ready. I'll be waiting downstairs," Noah said.

With that, he placed his hat on his head, moving quickly past Megan and out the door. I thought I'd caught a smirk on his face as he left. I didn't know whether it was because our brief encounter nearly had my panties drenched or if he was amused at Megan's handiwork on her own face.

Looking over at Megan, I felt a slight pang of guilt. "Why don't we finish doing our makeup together," I proposed.

Megan looked a bit puzzled, but she simply shrugged and let me drag her into my bathroom towards my makeup bag.

I WANTED to be less obvious, but every time I was around her, it was like the north and south poles of a magnet—just drawn to each other. At least that's the way it was for me. I could tell she was interested, but as to how deep that went, I was still in the dark.

Feeling the exact same pull, I stood outside her door last night. She'd turned in early, as did everyone else—not surprising, given the length of her journey. So I missed out on talking with her a bit more once I'd finished up with some provincial representatives from the Agribusiness Commission. My ranch bordered some crown land, and every year around this time, I'd get a visit to ensure that my livestock didn't graze too far onto federally held lands.

That night, I remembered feeling a slight movement of air coming from underneath her door and wondering whether she regularly slept with the window open, or whether she was uncomfortable in her bed. Perhaps the bed wasn't to her liking? *Was she having a hard time falling asleep?*

The thought of her lying sweaty on her bed conjured up

images that immediately made me uncomfortable in my pants. I wanted to check on her. Knocking lightly, I tried not to disturb her if she'd already fallen asleep, and I didn't want to wake up anyone else on the floor either.

There was no movement. Not a sound.

With my hand on the doorknob, I contemplated what it might look like if someone caught me sneaking into a woman's room in the middle of the night. But I got over it by convincing myself that I only wanted to make sure that she was all right.

Thankfully, none of the doors in my house squeaked, save for the room that I put Adrian in. I wanted to be completely aware of all his comings and goings. Especially if he'd intended to go anywhere near Verity.

Turning the handle and pushing the door inwards, I called out to her with a soft voice, not wanting to startle her. I was still behind the threshold and only holding the door open slightly to let her maintain her privacy.

But once again, there was no reply.

There wasn't a chance that she'd gone off somewhere on her own in the middle of the night, was there? City folk can be adventurous for all the wrong reasons and ignorant of real and present dangers all around, especially on a ranch.

I took one step into her room, and I stopped breathing. Verity was indeed in the bed, lying on her stomach with the side of her face resting halfway between two pillows. Her naked back was completely exposed, as she must have kicked away the comforter with only the flat sheet draped haphazardly across her body. One of her legs was completely covered but the other was dangling precariously off the side of the bed. If it weren't for the moonlight illuminating her room from the open window, I wouldn't have been blessed with such a view.

My mouth went completely dry. The suppleness of her skin called to me, as she was beautiful all over—at least everything that I could see.

I only intended to confirm that she was in the room. I wouldn't have opened her door if I hadn't had thoughts that made me have to check on her.

And now I was standing here, salivating over her state of undress, and wishing that I'd been an invited guest rather than what felt like a peeping Tom.

My hand ran down my face as I began to retreat. And I had almost started to close the door when she moved slightly but suddenly.

Shit! How was I going to explain myself if she woke up? But she didn't awaken. She was just shifting positions to be more comfortable. But it also meant that I was treated to the view of the fleshy but firm side of her breast.

Now, I truly felt like a piece of garbage. I had to get out of here—and quick. Backing up, I pulled the door back into place. After checking that I hadn't been seen, I half-walked, and half-ran back to my own room.

I had to take two cold showers that night.

***

The following morning, I thought I'd get a head start as I figured they'd most likely all sleep in. And despite my actions the night before, I was focused on being a good host to my guests. So heading into town to grab coffees and some light grub for them made a world of sense.

But when I'd returned to Adrian crowding Verity and his pronouncement that she didn't drink coffee, my mood plummeted. I so badly wanted to learn things about her—what kind of music she liked, what her favorite foods were, what made her happy, and all the things she didn't like so that I could do everything in my power to avoid them. And yet, here was this guy, who'd only met her in person a few hours before, telling me what she did and didn't like.

My self-worth was salvaged somewhat with the way she'd tried to reassure me that my mess-up hadn't been one at all. It renewed my desire to pursue her. So much so, that I'd volunteered to drive them into town to meet with the mayor. Thankfully, Tabitha had brought me back from the brink.

I didn't want anything to get in the way of Verity and me having a "good start." I wanted to see if I could steal some one-

50

on-one time with her before we all met up later that afternoon for the cookout.

I'd figured that even with how long it could take a woman to do her hair and makeup and get dressed, it was still reasonable to knock on her door around thirty minutes before we were scheduled to leave. What I hadn't taken into consideration was that each person is different. Especially women. They were all different.

So when she opened the door looking radiant, but with her summer dress hanging loosely from her chest, I was once again reminded of just what a different type of woman she was.

Verity stood in front of me fully clothed, but all I could think about was stripping her bare and running my tongue over every inch of her beautiful body.

"Ah, sorry. I didn't mean to interrupt while you're getting ready," I said and immediately took in the way her face looked. Every inch was a vision to look at, and if she'd been wearing any makeup, I certainly couldn't tell. Her hair was a mass of curls, with several tendrils hanging sexily around her face, only enhancing her features. Her lips had no artificial color on them but were glistening, looking so soft and inviting. *Wait, was she checking me out?*

Breathe, dammit.

I couldn't stop staring at her face; the only distraction was the sight of her dress straps falling slowly. Something inside of me wanted to reach out and pull them the rest of the way down, so I could land kisses on the places where they'd been.

She took a step backward as she brought her fingers and my eyes to her falling dress. I was instantly reminded of the soft, round mounds I'd seen the night before. I wondered what they felt like to hold. To squeeze. *Were her nipples ultra-sensitive? Or could she take a bit of pain?*

I was hypnotized by my thoughts, so when I saw her take a step backward, my instinct was to get closer. Then, when she did it again, I needed to touch her.

If I didn't get a good hold on my thoughts, I was going to end up having to explain my erection to her and whoever else was in the house because I was sure I wouldn't be able to get it down the way things were going. And I wasn't some prepubescent boy who lacked control of his own body. In fact, I enjoyed exercising a lot of control. Especially in moments of intimacy, and of course only with the consenting, right person.

I was going to start making her uncomfortable soon. If I was being honest, it was already a bit awkward, so I did the next best thing. "Let me," I said, noticing immediately that the wheels in her head started spinning. *She was a thinker. I liked that.*

I realized only then that the burnt orange and bright yellow colors of her dress made her skin even more appealing to me. She was soft and had curves in all the right places. With her back to my chest, I quickly figured out the machinations of tying it; thank you, 4H club. I made sure to meet her eyes in the full-length mirror. My actions were slow and deliberate, trying to prolong the moment for as long as possible.

"I love this dress on you." My hand had drifted to her waist, and I was now pulling her back further into me.

If the look I'd given her just a few moments ago wasn't enough to show her that I had more than a passing interest in her, then what I was about to do surely would seal it. Leaning down, I placed my mouth on her just above her ear. I inhaled her soft, flowery scent.

I'd wondered where she might be sensitive, besides the regular parts typically associated with having sex. And now I knew that I could make her melt like this. She didn't know it yet, but this was dangerous information for a man like me to have.

This was just enough for now. Tasting her would've been heavenly, and I desperately wanted to feel the warmth of her skin with my tongue. But I didn't want to scare her off.

Just then, a ridiculously loud knock echoed throughout the room. It was almost as if the person on the other side had wanted to take the door off its hinges. Never removing my hand from her waist, I wanted to show whoever came through that door that I had certain intentions where Verity was concerned.

But as if she knew who was there already, Verity moved out of my grasp too quickly. And I was somewhat thankful when I saw Megan bound into the room looking oddly familiar. *Did*

I could pretty much tell that she had some type of crush on me, and I didn't want to put her and Verity in an awkward situation. Once I'd made things clear with Verity and determined where she stood, perhaps, she'd have some insight on what to do with Megan. But for now, it wasn't my problem.

After exchanging some niceties, I grabbed my Stetson and made a quick exit to leave them to finish getting ready. There'd be more time to get to know her better I reasoned.

And that's all I wanted to do.

NOAH told us, as we drove in his truck, that the cookouts in Dènaud were kind of famous around these parts and attracted visitors from neighboring towns as well as the nearby First Nations' reservation. He cited how enhancing relations with the First Nations community had been a personal mission of the former mayor's office and the mayor himself.

A singular water source was shared between the town's population and the reservation's inhabitants. After a fire badly damaged the high school on the reservation, most First Nation high school-aged students attended high school in town. So there was more than a vested interest in the communities surrounding Dènaud. In fact, there was also a stalled effort to build a casino nearby.

We were headed to Tabitha's farm, which was a few miles away. I, having chosen to sit in the back seat with Megan and her bundle of nerves, caught Noah looking at me from time to time in the rear-view mirror. It wasn't as if he'd been hiding it. I began to get a little concerned that he would become too distracted on the road, so I stopped meeting his gaze and concentrated on the scenery passing by and Megan's commentary.

"Does everyone here where a cowboy hat?" Adrian had inexplicably added a bit of a drawl to the last few words of his query.

Where did he think he was? Texas?

Noah seemed to be ignoring the teasing tone from Adrian and answered simply. "Not everyone. But when you're working hard all day out in the sun, you need proper protection."

Adrian could've left it at that. *But no.*

"I bet the ladies love it. You must have girls from all over beating down your barn door," Adrian added flippantly.

Oh, brother. Insert eye roll here. I couldn't figure out why Adrian was being such a jerk to Noah. He'd opened his home to all of us, fed us, and now, for crying out loud, he was even chauffeuring us. I needed to say something, but I wasn't quick enough.

"I wouldn't know anything about all that," replied Noah. "I prefer one woman. No girls."

I'd been ready to chastise Adrian when I heard Noah's reply and couldn't help it when my eyes sought the source. Sure enough, Noah met and held my gaze in the rear-view mirror for a couple of seconds longer than I thought that someone with their foot on the gas pedal should.

Thankfully, we'd come to a stoplight and not only did Noah keep his eyes on me through the rear-view mirror, but he reached up and tipped the mirror downward so that I could get a glimpse of the smile across his lips.

The movement of the mirror had also given Noah a better view of my neck and shoulders, but I was only focused on his mouth. *Those lips.* I felt a tingling within remembering the way he'd brushed them against my skin earlier.

If anyone else in the car had noticed his actions, they weren't saying anything. Adrian had thankfully been muted at least for the time being.

Megan shifted every few minutes in her seat as she tried to get comfortable in the dress that she'd chosen to wear after seeing what I was wearing. I tried to convince her to wear only what made her feel the most like herself, but she ignored my advice completely on her attire. So here she was, trying to pull down the dark-colored dress and messing with the scooped-neck collar in the back of the truck. Megan was already beginning to perspire a bit. At least she'd let me fix her makeup.

"We're here," Noah said as he pulled to a stop on the side of a long, winding driveway.

Noah opened the door for me first and offered me his hand as I stepped out. After thanking him, I moved to let go of his hand, but he didn't release it. Instead, he extended his other hand to Megan until she landed with a hop on the ground.

Intertwining his fingers with mine, I looked up at him with a questioning glance. His response was just another one of those smiles that I was getting a little too used to. It was also at that moment when I realized that he'd already let go of Megan's hand.

"Oh my goodness! It's all so beautiful!" Megan squealed as she trailed beside us around the truck.

I pivoted towards Megan and began to walk forward. The subtle result of that was the release of my hand from Noah's, but not before he let a single finger trail down the inside of my palm. My body's reaction was instantaneous. I hoped that no one else saw me shiver. *Noah probably did.*

I looped my arm into Megan's, and we both made our way up the driveway towards a large field filled with lots of townspeople, more cars and trucks, and several long picnic tables packed with food. We left the men to bring up the rear.

"You're finally here!" A tall, leggy blond figure ran past Megan and me at breakneck speed.

I reasoned that it must have been someone who knew Noah because Adrian hadn't been in town long enough. And sure enough, once we turned around, we saw the woman jump on Noah. He caught her with ease. Then after a longish embrace, he set her down gently on her feet.

We were all staring at the scene unfolding before us. Noah had to bend down to pick up his Stetson, which had been knocked off his head. Adrian looked at me with raised eyebrows before turning his gaze back to the young lady. Taking her in, she was less of a young woman and more of a girl—a very young girl, actually. She couldn't have been more than fourteen or fifteen, but she was taller than Megan and me. She fit right in between both of the guys as she kicked the dirt from her cowboy boots. *Where had I seen that before?*

"Everyone, meet Callie. Callie, meet everyone."

She gave us all the once-over before settling her sights on me. Rushing over to us, I worried that she'd topple us with the same velocity she'd used on Noah. I braced myself for the crash, which never came. Instead, she wrapped us both up in a tight hug. First Megan than me, much the same as Noah had done to her. *Who was this person?*

She took a little longer with me and kept a hold of my hand as she began to speak.

"So you're Megan, and that means you must be Verity." But she drew out the syllables of my name as she spoke for emphasis.

"Calls," came the deep timber of Noah's voice. Damn, he needed to stop doing these little things that made my body do little things. I squeezed my legs together and took a couple of deep breaths.

"It's nice to meet you," I stammered. With all those loose nerves, I was beginning to act like Megan.

"Oh, it's especially nice meeting you, Verity." Again, with the drawn-out syllables. *Was I missing something?*

"Okay, that's enough. I think I hear your name being called," Noah interjected.

"Brother, I don't hear a thing," she countered, with as much sass as she could muster.

Brother? As in Noah's little sister or just "brother, brother" like "wassup brotha"? Look where you are, I reminded myself. And then, rolling my eyes, I landed on it being the former.

"Is this your sister, Noah?" Megan piped up.

"Unfortunately," he said, touching the brim of his hat.

Callie had still refused to let my hand go. I didn't want to just drag my hand away from her, but I wondered what she was up to. She seemed to be ignoring his response as she turned her attention to me.

"You're really pretty," she said.

"Ah, thank you. You're very pretty, too," I responded, feeling a sudden warmth spread up the back of my neck.

"Don't you have some other people to harass…I'm sorry, I mean greet." Noah was beginning to laugh now.

"Actually, you're too right. Booker and Cole would just love to meet these two pretty ladies. Why don't I just escort them over to the dance floor and do some introductions, eh?"

Megan perked up at being paid a compliment, and Callie already had her arm around both of our shoulders, turning us towards the crowd.

I caught the look in Noah's eyes as we were escorted away. He looked a little upset, but Callie dragged us away so quickly I could only manage a brief look back at him.

She was much stronger than her age would suggest, probably from being raised on a ranch. Megan and I found ourselves being carried away by sheer force that was difficult to stop. Before we could count to ten, we were both standing in a line for food and our backs to where the guys had been. Looking around, I noted that she hadn't actually taken us to the dance floor or over to anyone named Booker or Cole, for that matter.

"I thought you both could use some grub before we danced the night away. Are you originally from Toronto? Do you have any siblings? Is this your first time staying on a ranch?"

"Whoa, whoa," I said, raising both hands. "You've got to slow down a bit. Let us take it all in."

"Sorry. I get a little excited when there's someone new in town. And typically, it's just more male ranch hands who are here for a season or two and then gone. We never get any new girls around." I could tell by her emphasis on the word "never" that she was going to be particularly excited around us.

"Well, to answer your question, I'm from Toronto. Originally. And I'm an only child, but I've always dreamed about having siblings. And yeah, this is my first time on a ranch." Thinking that I'd answered all her questions, I turned to Megan to let her hit some out for a while.

"Excuse me before you answer," she said while casting a glance towards Megan. "Um, are you single?" Callie directed her question to me without a hint of reservation.

"I…I, um…"

"Don't have to answer that." And again, there was that deep voice that made my body do involuntary things.

I felt a hand on the small of my back just as I thought I'd lost my equilibrium from the suddenness of her question. I wasn't expecting that at all. I'd barely turned when Noah stepped up beside me. There'd been some room between me and Megan, which he now occupied.

Looking sternly at his sister, Noah's hand began to move slowly in a circular motion that soothed me all at once. But I was slightly startled at the intimacy of his touch, especially in public, so I tensed up. When he responded by halting his movements, but spreading his palm on my back, I took a quick peek in front of him and beside him. Megan didn't seem to see what he was doing to me, but Callie did. Her eyes were as round as saucers.

"Ah, brother, I think your hand, um…"

"That's enough, Calls. I'm serious." He interrupted her and put a halt to whatever she was getting ready to say. There was a brief stare down, and Callie was not backing down.

"Noah?" came a voice from off to the right side of our little gathering. All our heads turned at the sound as the mayor walked up to us.

Noah moved his hand from the small of my back then, bringing it around to encircle my waist. I wanted to move, but he held me in front of him as we all turned to face her approaching figure. Mayor Grant's eyes went straight to my waist as my brain was still trying to process all that was happening around me.

I was no longer concerned with whether Megan could see Noah's hands on me or what Callie had been up to with her questioning. But as Noah pressed his fingers softly into my waistline, the person I most wanted to question was *him*.

"Mayor Grant," Noah replied, tapping his Stetson with his free hand.

I couldn't tell if the young mayor's expression was one of exasperation or disappointment at Noah's words. Perhaps she didn't care about his words at all because she still hadn't really taken her eyes off Noah's hand at my waist.

"You look so lovely, Mayor Grant," Megan added, seemingly oblivious to the awkwardness. "Verity and I were actually going to follow up with you about spending some time in your archives if that's all right with you."

Queen of distraction! Thank you, Megan!

Ignoring his hold on me, I wanted to back up my colleague on that request. "Oh, yes. We weren't certain whether we needed to make an appointment through your office," I added.

It seemed to work as the mayor's focus left my waist and

returned to our faces. "Sure, I'll let my assistant know you'll be in touch."

Perfect. I couldn't believe how easy that'd been. I thought for sure it would be another set of delays to get access to anything related to the town records. Perhaps her being distracted had worked in our favor after all. But I was still being nagged by what we may have stepped into between the mayor and Noah. I didn't want to speculate on anyone else's relationships, but I certainly didn't want to get caught up in some messy drama either.

"Noah, could I get a word?" Mayor Grant asked, already turning her back to walk away from us. *Sheesh, she didn't even say goodbye or see you later.*

"Oooohhh. Someone's in trouble."

"Callie, stop." The rebuke from Noah was sharp. And it held a warning. Callie seemed to be able to sense that she'd already pushed him too far and immediately halted her musings. But she didn't miss out on the opportunity to stick her tongue out when he turned away from her.

"I'll be right back," Noah said, leaning over to my ear and placing both hands on my waist. He gave me a gentle squeeze before walking off toward the mayor.

I got over being startled quickly enough to turn towards Megan, but her attention was being held by something else.

"Mmm hmm," Callie hummed as I turned to where

Megan's gaze was locked, just beyond Callie's shoulder. "That's Booker and Cole. Come on, ladies, let me introduce you to the twins."

NOAH

"I DON'T THINK we have anything to discuss, Leona." I sounded a little harsher than I'd intended, but I was just trying to get back to Verity before my sister introduced her to half the town. I hadn't announced it or anything, but my little sister could tell that I had more than a passing interest in one of our new lodgers.

Callie lived in town with my aunt Peg while our parents were out of town for the season. She could've stayed with me at Clarence House, but everyone knew that Callie needed a bit more supervision than I would've been able to give. I could be an overprotective big brother when I needed to be, though, and that was another reason she preferred to stay by our aunt's.

Standing here to be lectured by Leona was bordering on annoying. "You know it's not such a good idea to get involved with people just passing through our town, Noah."

"I'm not sure what you mean."

"I mean, that woman. Verity. What do you even know about her?"

"I'm sorry. How is this any of your business?"

"I, I just care about you. Still."

I rubbed the back of my neck as I watched the twins stand so all the ladies could sit. Well, at least they were acting like gentlemen. *For now.*

"Leona, we're not together anymore. And if I recall, that was your decision. So, why don't you just let me be, and I'll stay out of your way as well?" Touching the brim of my Stetson was my sign to her that the conversation was over. But she reached out and held on to my arm, stopping my attempt to walk past her.

"Just because we're not together anymore doesn't mean that we can't be civil towards each other!" She couldn't have meant to raise her voice like that. She looked around nervously as if she, too, had the same thought.

I didn't really have anything more to say, but I figured there was no point in making the situation worse.

"Leona, I respected your decision then, and I truly want you to be happy. I'm a big boy, and you don't have to worry about me. All right? Now enjoy the cookout."

This time, I really did walk away from her. Not looking back, I headed straight for Verity.

VERITY

THE TWINS, as they were so aptly called, were identical. The way they spoke and dressed, and even their mannerisms as they both cleared a spot for each of us to sit down beside them at one of the larger picnic tables. Each one looked as if they'd stepped right out of a magazine shoot. *Was brooding and handsome a prerequisite for being a cowboy in this town?*

Already straddling the picnic bench and raising to their full height, they touched the brim of their hats. Since we arrived, I hadn't met too many people who were six feet and above, but these two had to be hovering around the same height as Noah. In fact, there was a slight resemblance except for their blonde hair.

Callie sat across from us as both Megan and I were sandwiched between both brothers.

"Guys, this is Megan, and this is Verity." Once again, I didn't miss the emphasis on my name.

"Pleasure…" said one.

"…is all ours," finished the other.

I couldn't call them thing one and thing two, so I'd need to sort out some way to tell them both apart.

"And you are?" I offered up my hand to shake the hand of the twin closest to me. He turned my palm downwards and laid his lips gently on the back of my hand.

"Cole." His eyes were sparkling and seemed to light up as he took me in.

Megan was being charmed by what must have been Booker then. I could feel her blushing beside me as she leaned a little further into him.

"So, what have you ladies seen in our little town since you arrived?" Booker asked, leaning over the table in front of Megan.

"Just the mayor's office so far," Megan chirped.

"Ah, well, that's no fun," Cole scoffed and then smiled at me. He still hadn't put my hand down. *Why was everyone so touchy-feely?*

"Yeah, we can definitely do better than that," Booker stated in agreement.

"I don't know, guys; I think that Verity might already be spoken for," Callie quipped, not hiding her mischievous little grin.

I threw a questioning look across the table but kept it playful by smiling at her. She wasn't exactly the easiest person to read. Besides, her brother didn't have any claim on me. *Why should he care what I do or who I do it with while I'm here?* As if on cue, though, I felt a hand on my shoulder from behind.

"Verity, can I talk to you for a moment?" Noah lowered his hand to take mine and began helping me up from my seat. It certainly didn't seem as if he was giving me a choice.

"What cuz…no hello or how yah doing?" Cole threw his head back trying to contain his own laughter. There was an inside joke that I wasn't privy to.

And I wasn't sure if I liked being completely in the dark. *And the twins are their cousins? No wonder they all sort of reminded me of Noah.*

"Boy, that was quick. I thought you'd be in hot water for sure," Callie added, which made both twins even more animated.

But one look from Noah, which I caught as I was being pulled up to my feet, cut them all to the quick. The laughter stopped immediately, and the mirth was replaced with an awkward silence.

"Too soon, I guess," Booker offered before extending his hand to Megan. Come on, beautiful. Let's dance." Without so much as another word, Megan trotted along behind Booker's long-legged gait towards the area where quite a few people were dancing to a live band.

"*Et tu mademoiselle?*" Cole turned with a huge grin on his face to Callie.

"*Mais oui!*" She almost shouted and raced off in the same direction as the others before Cole could stand fully to his feet.

Cole rolled his eyes after her and touched the brim of his hat when his gaze went from his cousin to resting on me briefly. And then he also walked away.

It was just the two of us standing before each other then. I suddenly didn't know where to look. I caught the mayor staring at us through the corner of my eye before Noah brought his finger to the side of my jaw and turned it towards him.

"Let's go for a walk."

I simply nodded my response. He was our host, after all,

and I guess our semi-tour guide. Although the twins' offer had its own appeal, too.

After we'd been walking for some time, I noticed that we'd separated ourselves from the rest of the cookout attendees, having wandered over to a quieter side of the farm.

The fields extended all the way around us, for what seemed like miles and miles, seeming to end only at the edge of the sky. It must have been amazing to go to sleep with this view each night and wake up to it each morning.

"Absolutely stunning." The words fell out of my mouth like breath over my lips.

"Very." I turned to Noah when he spoke, and his eyes were riveted on me. We were standing near each other but not touching, but somehow, I could tell that he wanted to touch me.

A few more moments passed before either of us said anything. I was the first to look away. The intensity of his stare was a little too much.

"Noah, I hope that we didn't get you into any trouble with the mayor earlier," I said first.

Noah's face scrunched up in a funny but cute way before he removed his hat to run his hand through his hair. And then he gave me a smile that nearly took my breath away.

"Leona and I used to be in a relationship. We were together for a couple of years before she went away for graduate school and then again briefly when she came back to town to work with her father before he passed.”

I knew there must be more. He may not have wanted to share more, but I knew there had to be more. Although, I wasn’t even clear on why he was making this kind of disclosure to me.

“She pulled me aside to ask if anything was going on between the two of us,” he said finally.

Pause. Silence. I didn’t know what I was supposed to say at this point.

“Ah, why would she…” I didn’t get to finish speaking as he immediately dropped his head and kicked at the ground before pushing a bunch of air out through his lips.

“I guess I haven’t been making myself clear enough.”

And before I had a chance to decipher the meaning of his words, he took one step towards me. His large frame blocked out my view of the goings on at the cookout and brought his body so close to my own that air couldn’t have passed between us.

I felt every vibration rolling off his broad chest as he hummed before me. In fact, it started off as a humming sound but developed quickly into more of a low growl before he took my chin in his hand and titled my face upwards. Looking into those eyes, I was finally able to see the blueish orbs with a hint of hazel right around his irises. I hadn’t really looked deeply before, but my own breathing was accelerated now. Almost matching the rising and falling of Noah’s chest.

He’d barely touched me, and I was already headed

towards being an absolute mess. The hairs on my arms were standing at attention, and I could feel the goosebumps rising along my skin. Was he going to kiss me?

It looked as if it was taking all his self-control not to make physical contact with me. But I could also tell that he was only a few moments away from losing that battle.

He'd been dropping hints for the past couple of days, but I hadn't wanted to misinterpret things. But with this disclosure about Mayor Grant and the way that others around us had been carrying on, perhaps I was the one who was failing to see what was right in front of me.

But then the question was, did I even want this? I was here for my education. And even if I'd thought about "treating myself" as Sheree called it, I wouldn't want to do something so frivolous with someone like Noah. He was different.

So what do you want, Verity? It was too soon to take advice from my heart, I reasoned, and my head was at least resigned to the fact that whatever happened, it couldn't be trivial.

So I raised up on the tip of my toes slowly, trying to lessen the height deficit. I didn't have to wait long or at all. Noah met me during my upward movement and encircled one arm around my waist while bringing the other to the side of my face.

And when our lips met, it was nothing short of fireworks. I don't know what I'd been expecting, but it certainly wasn't the toe-curling kiss I was receiving. And he was just on the outside, sucking my lips gently at first and then increasing the intensity as he maneuvered his head to draw the most from me. I felt lightheaded. If this was my reaction to him being just on the surface, how was I ever going to survive him placing his tongue in my mouth for a deeper kiss?

Thankfully, he had mercy on me, and I was lowered back down on my heels.

"Wow," I hadn't meant to say that out loud and my hands immediately flew up to cover my mouth.

Noah slowly lowered my hands and brought them down to my sides. With that smile, he knew he was a wonderful kisser.

"Verity, would you let me take you out to dinner?"

The way I was feeling, I really could only manage to nod my head in the affirmative in response, but that wasn't going to be good enough. I couldn't play it cool at all since that "wow."

"Yes, I'd really like that."

IT'D BEEN SEVERAL DAYS since the cookout, and the amount of work that Megan, Adrian, and I had to complete in preparation for our municipal records review and subsequent meeting with the mayor had been nearly overwhelming.

At the last minute, the mayor finally acquiesced and agreed to let us into the municipal archives to gather some data. But Mayor Grant hadn't made it easy. So we'd been struck by a deluge of paperwork, including a non-disclosure agreement that we had to forward to our respective universities so that all parties were informed and consented accordingly.

I secretly wondered whether we would've been made to jump through all those hoops if Noah hadn't publicly staked his claim at the cookout. Even after the atmosphere-shifting kiss, he'd outright refused to let go of my hand as we walked around so he could introduce me to the other families in attendance. I swear, I must have met half the town.

And since then, nothing.

Tabitha would come for us each morning to transfer us to and from town as we needed, but Noah had been completely

MIA. He'd mentioned something about attending some rodeo or horse show in a neighboring town, but I didn't think we wouldn't see him at all. He'd come home late every night but was gone long before any of us woke up.

I looked lazily at my cellphone, which was bouncing erratically on the arm of the rocking chair I was sitting in on the porch.

"Hello," I answered.

"Took you long enough! How come you haven't been answering any of my calls?" Sheree wasn't an early riser, so the fact that she was calling me at this hour must have meant that something serious was going on.

"What's wrong?" I didn't try to hide the panic in my voice.

"What's wrong is that you haven't been answering any of my calls," she replied. I could almost see the look on her face; somewhere between Heath Ledger's Joker and a toddler on their first day of daycare. She missed me but was ready to draw blood.

I moved the phone to the other side of my face before responding. "Sheree, sweet cousin of mine. What can I do for you?" I let all the sweetness drip from my every word.

"Number one, stop rolling your eyes."

And I was rolling them. "How did you…" she cut me off.

"Because I know you, little cuz. And two, what are these images you keep sending me?"

I had to remind myself of what I'd sent to her because it'd been so long since we last spoke. Then I recalled that I'd sent her some pictures of the sunrises and sunsets I'd been enjoying since my arrival in Dènaud.

"Aren't they beautiful? I thought you'd enjoy seeing those." I wasn't offended or anything, just amused that she seemed so perturbed that I'd sent them to her.

"Ma'am, I don't want to see sunrises unless you can tell me that you and that cowboy watched it together post-coital. And the same goes for those sunsets. Keep that soft *shit* to yourself and give me the real, raw. Now go!" She was deadly serious, too.

I burst out laughing, so hard that I almost lost control of the chair I'd been rocking back and forth in all this time.

"Sheree!" I feigned shock.

"Um, mmm. I'm over here just waiting."

"Well, I don't have anything like that to share with you."

"Yet? I feel like there was a 'yet' coming."

I was shaking my head before I realized she couldn't see me. The Wi-Fi outside of the house wasn't strong enough to support a video call, so we had to go old school.

"I told you. It's not like that." I was beginning to tire of this line of questioning, especially since I was a little disappointed that Noah hadn't prioritized planning what was supposed to be our first date.

"Something's up. I can smell it."

I looked into the cellphone screen briefly before returning it to its perch between my shoulder and my cheek. "Smell? You can smell it, can you?"

"Like I said, I know you. But whatever, you don't have to share it now. You will, though."

"And how can you be so certain of that? I don't tell you everything that happens in my life."

There was an audible sigh on the other end of the line. "Oh, please. I bought you your first sex toy; you came to me before having sex for the first time with your little boyfriend; I explained how you orgasm from fingerplay and cunnilingus; and who taught you those 'Superhead' moves on a banana that one family trip…"

"Okay! Okay! Stop!"

"Stop what?" came a male voice from behind me. I nearly jumped out of my seat as I watched my cellphone fall to the ground. But Adrian's hand stopped its descent.

I looked up at him and could almost hug him for not letting my screen get cracked. Then I remembered that Sheree was still on the line and that his presence had precipitated the cellphone drop. I reached for it in his hand, but he held on to it like he'd discovered a new game.

"Adrian. Can I have my phone back, please?"

He looked at my open palm and then at the cellphone, and then he just smiled. "Sure, but I want something in return."

"I don't have time for this, and I'm not finished with my call. So give it here."

This time, I stood up, and although I didn't match his height, I still tried to impress upon him that I wasn't in the mood to play around. But that didn't seem to deter him at all.

"Say yes first," he said, putting the hand containing my cellphone behind his back now.

"Adrian! This isn't funny."

"I'm not trying to be funny. I'm trying to ask you out."

Up until this point, I'd been moving towards him, trying to figure out how to take my phone back from him. But his declaration stopped me right in my tracks.

"What? Are you serious?"

"Why do you have to say it like that?" he said, sounding a bit wounded.

I had to gather myself together for a moment. "Sorry, it's just I'm a little surprised. Can you give me a minute to finish my call and then we can talk about this?" I could see the myriad of possible responses running through his mind as he tried to decide whether to give up his leverage and return the phone to me.

Ultimately he did just that and stepped back inside the screen door. When I was certain he was no longer within earshot, I returned the phone to my ear.

"Guuuuuurrrrrllll! Was that him? The cowboy?" Sheree was a little too excited.

"Ah, no. No, that was not. Listen, I've gotta call you back later."

"I'm boyfriend number two, oooohhh!" Sheree started singing the chorus of Pleasure P's hit song "Boyfriend Number Two." I was so through.

"Bye." I hung up before she could get to the second chorus.

Walking timidly back into the house, I didn't immediately see Adrian anywhere. Releasing a little air from my lungs, I felt relief that I wouldn't need to be confronted with this development so soon. I shouldn't have relaxed.

"Done with your call?" Adrian asked as he walked towards me from the kitchen, throwing an apple up and down in the air. "Ready to talk?"

"Where's Megan?"

"Ah, deflection. Nice one. That's gonna leave a bruise." He smiled at me and took a bite of his apple. I gave him a puzzled look.

"My ego," he said plainly.

I nodded my head in realization of what he was saying. "Adrian, I didn't think that you…" But he didn't let me finish.

"Now, you're not playing fair, Verity, I saw you first."

"What's that supposed to mean? You saw me first, so what, you get first dibs or something?"

It only took him a few strides to make it so that he was

standing directly in front of me. He didn't touch me, but the proximity was intimate.

"Don't do that." His eyes closed to slits before he reopened them.

I tried holding his gaze, but it was clear he had no intention of backing down. Then he did touch me. He used one finger to push a curl of mine and dragged his finger along my neck. I couldn't help but shudder. And to that, he just smiled.

"Ready to head out? Our ride is here!" We both turned at the sound of Megan's cheery voice. And she wasn't alone, as Booker trailed behind her through the porch door. *Had they been out there the entire time?*

Booker gave Adrian a wary look, which Megan seemed to be completely oblivious to as she grabbed my arm and pulled me out the door.

Tipping his hat to me, Booker stared at me as I passed by him for a little longer than I was comfortable with.

"Morning," he said to me after a brief while.

I simply smiled my greeting back to him, but I noticed that he butted in behind me as we went through the door, cutting off Adrian from following me.

Oh, this ride into town will be fun.

VERITY

BOOKER'S TRUCK had a backseat that could comfortably hold three or even four people. I happily assumed that Megan would be riding shotgun, especially given that she'd practically skipped over to that side of the vehicle. But before she could open the door to hop in, I saw Booker whisper something in her ear.

For a fleeting moment, I caught a look on Megan's face like she'd smelt spoiled milk. But a second later, it was gone, and she moved to hop into the back of the vehicle. Adrian was already halfway seated in the back, so the only seat left for me would've been the front seat.

I gave Megan a look that begged the question, "What the hell, dude?" I mean, it wasn't exactly a well-kept secret that she had feelings for Booker. And for at least the duration of the cookout, they'd been inseparable. And if their showing up together this morning was any indication of things, I was certain that Booker was reciprocating.

So it begged the question: Why was she in the back seat? And to put the icing on the cake, Booker was holding the freaking door open for me. I stole another look at Megan, but she simply returned my look of curiosity with that same sweet smile as she always did.

"Perhaps the boys can sit up front then?" I made a last-ditch effort to leech the awkwardness out of this situation. But to that, Booker simply placed a hand on my arm and pulled me gently towards the already open front door.

"If we don't get on the road, you guys are going to be late." He said with a wink.

I give up.

The ride into town was far less eventful than I'd thought it was going to be. Adrian and Booker didn't say a single word to each other, but Megan and Booker stayed animated throughout the entire ride.

Trying to get a word in edgewise with those two was like throwing a pebble into the ocean. Their range of topics hit everything from the weather to the upcoming new movie releases of which Dènaud was getting none because the only screen they had in town was an outdoor movie theatre. And it was only licensed to run the movie Twister.

Questions abound as to why a small town would even want to play a film with the singular premise of a small town being destroyed by a tornado. But there were quite a few things about this place that were doing my head in, the least of which was their choice of movie theatre showings.

When we pulled up to City Hall, I noted that while

Adrian had hopped out quickly, he'd still been unable to beat Booker who opened the doors for both me and Megan since the cab had suicide doors. Booker escorted us only to the foyer, so the three of us made our own way to the mayor's office.

"So nice to see you all again," Mayor Grant addressed us while standing at her assistant's desk. "Have you all had breakfast yet? I thought we could chat over a cup of coffee, at least."

Raising her eyebrows hopefully, Adrian was the first to answer. "Of course. We'd love to."

I wouldn't "love to" anything. I was a nerd at heart and just wanted to get stuck in those archives before too much time had passed. After all, we'd only been given a limited amount of time to go through a voluminous number of records. Was this some type of stalling tactic on her part?

But as she walked in step with Adrian before us, I wanted to take a more positive view of the entire thing. Her body language today was far less tense and distrusting than it had been on our first meeting.

During breakfast, she went out of her way to ensure that Megan and I were included in all conversations, even smiling with me at several points throughout. Perhaps I'd judged her too harshly. This may turn out to be all right after all.

"So, Verity, I'm sure that you're anxious to finish up this little detour in life and head back to the big city, right?"

Well, so much for that.

But before I could answer, Adrian piped up on my behalf. "This is the first trip for all of us to Dènaud. I can't speak for Megan, but I've never been this far north in Saskatchewan before. Beautiful area, though."

Inside, I felt like a tea kettle that was just beginning to boil. I hadn't missed the underhanded meaning of the question she'd directed only at me.

"And what about you, Adrian? Do you have any plans?" Her body language was less hostile as she leaned closer to Adrian and waited for a response while drawing her coffee spoon from her mouth with a pop.

Surely Adrian wasn't oblivious to the way the mayor acted around him. It wasn't even borderline; she was full-on flirting every chance she got. But whatever helped us get closer to our goal of getting more access to people and records. Yes, that's right. I was more than willing to offer up Adrian on a silver platter if it got us what we needed. Well, maybe not quite. He was my colleague, after all. His well-being while we were in this town and for the duration of our work together was also my primary concern.

However, Adrian was a big boy and clearly didn't need anyone to take care of him. Adrian smiled, and it was the first time that I'd seen him even remotely uncomfortable.

It was time to put an end to this.

"Mayor Grant, we can't thank you enough for your offer of breakfast, but given our tight time constraints, I think it'd be best if we got to the record storage area."

I didn't wait for her answer, as I'd already pushed back my chair and was rising to a standing position. Giving both Adrian and Megan an encouraging eyebrow raise, they followed suit in getting up from the table as well.

Perhaps out of frustration or sheer embarrassment, the mayor didn't waste any time standing either. Declining our offer to pay, she handled the bill and then escorted us back to City Hall and its security desk, which was just to the side of the foyer.

"And remember, you're our guests here in Dènaud, so whatever we can do to make your short stay with us more comfortable, please don't hesitate to let us know."

And with that declaration, she turned on her heels and left.

***

The municipal archives were partially accessible through an encrypted database in the computer room of the public library, which was just a couple of doors down from City Hall. The rest of the records were housed in a building located in a small field behind the library and contained actual physical copies.

We started at the library, and a couple hours before it was

scheduled to close we migrated over to the building that looked somewhat abandoned. Adrian had his fill by 6:30 p.m. and had been desperate for a dinner break. Not wanting to waste more time, I decided to stay behind to continue going through the files.

I couldn't convince Megan to stay behind either, so when I promised Adrian that I wouldn't work past eight o'clock, they both finally left, and I grabbed a sandwich from the vending machine at City Hall.

The building wasn't big at all, but because it was packed from floor to ceiling with loose files and old banker boxes, it seemed cavernous at points.

I'd lost track of the time, but after my umpteenth time stretching my body, I noticed that the one blacked-out window that had a small scratch in its black paint no longer let in any light.

Standing on my tiptoes, I could barely see any of the streetlights. It was pitch-black. Looking at my phone, I wondered why I hadn't been receiving any reminder texts or calls from Adrian or Megan. Then I noticed that I didn't have any bars—*damn this city and its dead zones.*

With a sigh, I began packing up my things before heading over to the sole exit. But when I tried the doorknob, it seemed to be locked. *Strange. It hadn't been locked when we'd entered and not even when I'd returned with my vending machine dinner.*

I pulled on the door a few more times. And then wrapped

my closed fist against it as well.

"Shit."

Taking my phone out, I moved around the room to see whether I could catch a signal and call someone to get me out of there. But no such luck. And then, as if that wasn't bad enough, all the lights went out at once.

"Wait. What the hell?" I whispered only to myself.

There was no light at all except for a tiny sliver coming from the scratched-up window. And it was eerily silent.

Come on, Verity. What can you do to get out of this?

I'd begun to give up on ideas when I suddenly heard what sounded like someone talking at the window. Slowly, I moved towards the sound.

"She did it. She did. She did it."

It sounded like a man's voice, but it wasn't making much sense at all. And the person, whoever it was, was almost singing the words.

I was probably going to end up getting murdered, but I went for it.

"Hello?" I said, as close to the window as I dared. In truth, it was less of a window than a small square with a windowpane in it. It wouldn't have been possible to get through that space unless one was the size of a child, and if there weren't any bars on it. Which there were.

"Hello?" came the answer back, almost like an echo.

"I'm a student and I'm stuck in here. Are you able to unlock the door, or maybe go get me some help?" I pleaded.

"Hello?" This time the voice sounded like it was mocking me.

Case closed. I'd rather sit in this mildew-smelling, dark space until morning than continue communicating with whoever was on the other side of that window.

Moving away a little more quickly this time, I put my back against the wall on the other side of the room.

NOAH

I'D GOTTEN A TEXT from Booker during my drive back to Dènaud. Thankfully, the horse trailer I was pulling was empty since I'd had a very successful day selling the two mares I'd taken with me. There would typically be one other person with me on this drive, but it was only a couple of hours away, and I was winding down my trips for business. So I decided to go solo and give my guys a break.

I also had one person in mind with whom I wanted to spend some more time. We were well overdue for our first date, but this block of business trips couldn't be avoided.

When I saw Booker's text, though, I realized that my mistake was not being clearer with Verity about how long I'd be keeping up this pace and that I was really looking forward to taking her out. I was breaking all sorts of speed limits to get back home to her.

But when I'd called down to the bunkhouse, I'd been told that only Megan and Adrian had returned. And now Verity wasn't answering any of my calls. *Was she upset with me?*

"Pick up the phone, Verity." I punched the screen in my truck again, but this time, it didn't even ring. Just went straight to voicemail. "Fuck!"

I'd *fucked* this up royally. And now that joker, Adrian, was slithering in where I'd left him a wide opening. Pressing my foot down further on the gas pedal, I silently hoped the trailer wouldn't unhitch as I picked up speed.

VERITY

I HADN'T CLOSED MY EYES, but I could feel the heaviness of my eyelids. There was no longer anyone talking outside the building, but I'd watched enough horror movies to know that didn't mean whoever it was had left.

So when I heard someone fiddling with the lock on the door outside and rotating the knob, I pushed myself up the wall a little too quickly. Looking frantically around in the blackness, I'd thought to flip on my phone's torchlight, but it died long ago.

I only had my bag to defend myself. Whoever was coming through that door was going to get it right upside their head. *I refuse to get murdered tonight.*

When the door flung open, a figure stepped across the

threshold. I was already mid-swing when a flashlight illuminated the face of my savior instead of my killer.

"Noah!" I screamed as I launched myself into his broad chest.

I COULDN'T get out of that building fast enough and practically crawled up Noah like a koala climbing a tree.

"I got you. I got you." Noah's arms were so solid and all-encompassing. If it was even possible, I think he was holding me closer than I was holding him. And the way he kept repeating those words into the side of my head felt like the only comfort I'd ever need. It was very nearly the sweetest thing I'd ever experienced.

We stood like that for what seemed like an eternity, but it only took a few minutes for Noah to have me safely ensconced in the cab of his truck.

With my forehead pressed against the window, I could only watch as Noah argued animatedly with the security guard who I remembered from the City Hall foyer earlier.

Oh, how I wished we could just get out of there and head back to the house. Now that I'd been released from this ordeal, all I wanted was a hot bath and a good night's rest. I didn't even have the energy to do anything about my stomach, which had started growling at me. I guess the de-escalation of the stressful situation had returned some of my senses to me.

Come on, Noah. I didn't want to argue with the man who'd just saved me, but I was anxious to leave this place.

I was about to put my hand on the door handle when I noticed some flashing lights and sirens approaching.

What the hell?

***

So not only had the cops arrived on the scene, but a very dressed down Mayor Grant was also getting out of her car to approach the formerly deserted area where I'd been trapped for the past few hours.

I thought I was going to die of embarrassment. *How had this spiraled out of control so quickly?* Slumping down slightly in the cab, I tried to hide my face from a small group of onlookers who had now gathered a short distance from the truck.

Then I heard a tapping sound on my window.

Startled into an upright position, I turned my face towards the person beside the glass next to my head.

"Adrian? What are you doing here?"

He didn't just answer me, but also opened my door and pulled me into a full-on embrace.

"Oh my God! I'm so glad you're safe."

"Yes, I'm fine. But, what…"

"Booker drove us out of town for dinner and we got a little caught up before heading back. But when we arrived and didn't see you at the house, we just figured you'd lost yourself in the work. I never thought that you'd be in any type of danger. *Fuck,* Verity, I'm truly sorry."

"It's not your fault," I said while tapping my fingers against his shoulders. The hug wasn't completely unwelcome, but I didn't want to muddy the waters where Adrian was concerned.

He seemed reluctant to let me go until I gave him a few more reassuring pats on the back and a smile. Adrian released me just in time for me to see Noah charging towards us with what I could only describe as an angry cowboy walk—or just an angry walk, period, even without the cowboy part.

"And where the fuck were you this entire time? I thought you all were supposed to be working in there together." Noah was pissed. And I couldn't tell whether it was all directed at Adrian, only for this incident, or whether there was something else going on.

"Noah, it's all right. It isn't his fault. It's nobody's fault. It just happened."

But Noah looked unconvinced, and I needed something or someone to intervene in this dick-measuring contest that was about to kick off because Adrian didn't look like he was going to back down at all.

"I was the one that called the police," Adrian said with measured breaths in between his words.

Noah seemed to only be getting madder. I placed my hand on top of his bicep and used a gentle rubbing motion to try and bring down the temperature. It seemed to be doing the trick until Adrian opened his mouth again.

"And besides, it's not like you've been around much these days. I'm surprised you were even able to tear yourself away from your precious horses to give a *shit* about Verity's wellbeing."

Noah moved first, and I felt myself being propelled forward into Adrian's chest as I tried to block Noah from getting into his face. There would've been more of a tussle except for the fact that I was between them with my hands pushing against Adrian's chest. But Adrian just wouldn't learn. He placed both of his hands over the top of mine and stepped back so that I had no choice but to step towards him.

That snapped Noah out of it briefly, and he grabbed me around my waist to pull me fully into his chest. I braced myself to meet his chest, but his arms encircling my waist controlled my backward movement and tempered the impact.

Not taking my eyes off Adrian, I knew from his body language that he was going to do something stupid, so I pulled my hands away from him and placed them firmly on Noah's arms.

"Stop it. Both of you. Please. I can't do this right now." The plea was all it took. That, and the mayor's interjection.

"Is everything okay here? Noah? Verity, are you all right?" she asked.

Noah didn't respond to her, and something inside of me felt a little uneasy at her inquiry into my state of being. But my mother hadn't raised a wretch, so I found my good manners.

"Thank you, but I'm fine. I must have forgotten that the door was locked from the outside or something. I should've been paying better attention really."

"Um, Verity, the door wasn't just locked…" But one look from Noah, and she didn't finish her sentence.

"Let's talk about this later, when you've eaten and gotten a chance to get some rest," he said instead, already turning me away from where we were standing.

I didn't have the energy to argue with him. So when he pushed me towards the open door of his truck, I didn't hesitate to use his assistance to get in. Closing the door firmly behind me, I couldn't hear the words that he'd said to Adrian. If the look on the mayor's face was any indication, it wasn't polite. But instead of re-engaging, Adrian seemed to back down and walk away.

When Noah jumped into the truck beside me and started it up, I glanced once more at the building. The police and security guard were still on the scene.

"Don't I need to speak to anyone? Like the police or

something?" I wasn't really offering, but my mind was telling me that because I was the cause of this commotion I should be more helpful somehow.

"Not now. Later. Let's get you home."

I loved the way that sounded. And I loved it even more when he placed his large hand over mine and began caressing the palm of my hand with his fingers.

***

I showered with as hot a temperature of water as I could stand, rethinking the bath because it would just take too long.

Noah had tried to get me to eat something in the kitchen before heading up to my room, but I didn't have any appetite after all. I'd simply try again in the morning.

I had no idea how Adrian had gotten back to the house, but I'd heard his door slam down the hall when he'd finally gotten in. *That poor doorframe.*

Rifling through the skimpy negligées that Sheree had undoubtedly packed for me, I wandered instead towards the armoire in the corner of the room. I needed something a bit comfier and cozier than lace and silk.

The mirrored doors creaked a bit as I opened them. I half expected moths to fly out, but instead, I found several big T-shirts neatly pressed and hung up on hangers, as well as those longer-sleeved shirts that Noah wore around the ranch daily. The smell of him washed over me, making me press my face into all the fabrics within.

Choosing a white T-shirt, I dropped my towel to the floor and pulled it over my head. The warmth and feeling of being protected was instantaneous. And as if answering my second question, I reached up and pulled down some soft plaid pajama pants. Thankfully the pants had drawstrings that I could cinch at my waist, but my body was still overwhelmed in his clothes. I'd never felt more comfortable than when I crawled underneath my duvet with them on.

After about thirty minutes of trying to fall asleep, I realized that something was missing. I was in his clothes, but they were a poor substitute for the man himself.

So when I found myself knocking softly on his bedroom door barefoot and swimming in my choice of night clothes, I started to question my sanity.

But when the door opened fully and Noah appeared before me shirtless and wearing nothing but his boxers, any thoughts I had in my head of a return to sanity completely disappeared.

I WAS still trying to come down from the eventfulness of the night. Verity was back home, safe in her room next door. I'd been sitting in the dark in my own room, trying to get my head together, when I heard her turn off the shower.

She didn't want anything to eat before, and I didn't want to pester her about it. I could only imagine how scared she must have been locked in that building all by herself with no lights and no way to get word out that she was in trouble.

As soon as I'd heard back from Booker that the trio had gone to dinner in nearby Lake Wittier without her, I knew that there was something extremely off about her not being at the house when they'd gotten back.

The security guard on duty at City Hall confirmed that no one was left in the building except the cleaners, but he'd recalled that someone matching her description had been let into the archives building next to the library.

I dragged him over there physically and ended up snatching the keys out of his hands when he tried to give me some song and dance about needing to get clearance before unlocking the door. I could've torn it off the hinges, but I didn't want to scare Verity more than I assumed she already was.

I felt completely justified in my actions when I felt her clinging to me for dear life after she had run out of the building. Once she was safely sitting in the truck, she'd regained some of her equilibrium, so I thought I could question the security guard about how she became locked in there in the first place.

The circumstances of the whole situation just seemed fishy to me. The door had not only been locked but also barricaded shut with concrete blocks. We'd set to work removing them quickly when we'd discovered them like that, but when the security guy suddenly stopped before opening the door once we'd cleared it, I saw red.

I didn't leave until he felt the entire weight of my rage. I only drew back somewhat when the police arrived on the scene, so they could finish off where I'd left off. They had more than a few questions for this dude, too.

Fearing that I'd left Verity for too long, I was just about to head back when I saw her in Adrian's arms.

The time for words was over at that point.

***

I hadn't expected to hear another peep from anyone in the house for the rest of the night or, rather, until early morning.

Listening for any movement in the next room, I'd convinced myself that Verity had fallen asleep. So when I heard the faint knock on my door, I didn't bother to make myself decent before answering it. But there she was.

"Hey," I managed to say the word, but in my head, I'd forgotten how to speak.

"I'm, I'm sorry. I can't sleep."

"You don't have to explain anything. Let me just…" I turned around quickly and reached for my jeans, which were on the floor next to the foot of my bed.

Turning my head slightly towards her, I could see that she was still standing on the other side of the threshold. *Was she waiting on an invitation to come in? No, I couldn't do that.*

I'd only had a few moments to drink her in but seeing her standing at *my* door in *my* clothes had sent a shock right through the middle of me. *Fuck me.* She wasn't wearing a bra. I could tell by the outline of her breasts and the way that her nipples were tenting underneath the cotton tee.

No, she couldn't come into my room.

As I rummaged around for my T-shirt, I glanced back at the doorway, and she was no longer there. My head swung around so fast that I nearly missed her standing just to the right of me with her back up against the wall. She looked scared. Adjusting the hem of my T-shirt I walked slowly towards her.

"Come here," I whispered as I opened my arms to her.

She stepped into my embrace without making a single sound, but I couldn't miss the release of air as she wrapped her arms around my waist. Resting my chin on the top of her head, I gave her a few kisses.

"I don't think that I can be alone," she murmured. Her voice muffled as half of her face was pressed into my chest. She smelled so good. Like a fresh shower, but also like the way the air smelled after the rain.

"You don't have to be. I'm here." Tightening my hold on her I eased her back so that I could look down into her face. I placed a kiss on her forehead. She took a deep breath. And then she tilted her head upwards, momentarily dislodging my lips from her skin. I simply straightened my back and went back to kissing her forehead again.

But when she pulled her head down slightly and then returned her gaze up to mine, I sensed something shift. We stood there staring into each other's eyes for a moment. I could hear my own breathing now.

When she parted her lips suddenly, it took everything in me not to mash my mouth into hers. Instead, I dipped down towards her face, searching her eyes for any indication that she was resistant. I found none.

When our lips were a mere breath apart, I watched as she closed her eyes. And that's when I kissed her.

It was slow and gentle at first. Then the intensity picked

up as I sought entrance to the place behind her lips. I hinted at my intent by nipping and using my tongue along the crease of her mouth. She opened her eyes, and I could swear that I heard her moan somewhere in the back of her throat.

Oh, how I wished I could've swallowed that for her.

Bringing one hand up to the side of her face, I caressed her until only my fingertips were on her skin.

Then she let me in. It was a subtle shift at first, but I could feel her lips move to welcome me and I took full advantage. Using the palm of my hand once again, I turned and held her face in place so that I could go as deep as possible.

My knees nearly buckled as I tasted her. Her saliva mixed with mine was like the headiest drink I'd ever tasted and that was saying a lot because I was a scotch man. And fuck *the rocks*, I took it straight.

She was affecting me the same way right now and it was truly doing my head in.

Lowering her hands to the top of my jeans, I thought I'd have a stroke if she went anywhere below my belt. Thankfully, she kept her hands resting there, but I was struggling with not touching her more intimately now that the kiss was heating up.

I was trying to take my cues from her and to listen to what she was saying with her body, and right now all that she was communicating to me was that she was enjoying this kiss. *Fuck, so am I.*

But were we ready for anything more at this point? I hadn't even taken her out like I'd originally wanted to, and now we were locked in a *tongue of war* inside my fucking bedroom.

I was so glad that I'd decided to get dressed before she came fully into the room.

If someone was going to regulate this situation, I guess it was going to need to be me. Pulling away from the kiss first, I tempered the move by trailing soft kisses along her cheek and down her jawline to her throat. I hoped this move said, *I would rip your clothes off right now and fuck you senseless, but I don't want just a quick roll in the hay with you.*

She meant more to me than that.

When she buried her face in my chest and went back to squeezing my waist tightly, it felt like she was grateful for the slowdown as well. She wanted my comfort and my protection.

I couldn't believe I'd come this close to messing things up with her. If I didn't take it slow, then how was I going to make it last? I knew exactly where we were going to start: our first date.

"Why don't we go to the kitchen? I'll make you some hot chocolate and tell you my plans for our first date," I said, and the smile that lit up her face couldn't have been more radiant.

Grabbing her hand, I led her out of my room and away from my bed. I'd have her in it soon enough, but on both our terms, when we had time to really consider the choice we were making together.

***

The sun was coming up. My body just instinctively knew when it was dawn. It came from years of living and working on a ranch. I'd be halfway done with my chores under my father's era. But looking over at the woman lying in the crux of my arm, I knew that I could never be anywhere else this morning.

After the hot chocolate last night, I convinced her to eat a little something before I returned her to her room. But instead of letting me leave, she'd held my hand and wouldn't let go.

"Do you want me to sleep with you tonight?" The question itself was innocent enough, but there really wasn't a less provocative way to deliver it.

But I knew we were in tune with each other when she replied with a strong "yes."

So I slept on top of the duvet, fully dressed, while she cuddled up beside me underneath it.

Watching the steady rise and fall of her frame was hypnotic. So much so that I failed to see those beautiful big brown eyes staring right back at me until she made a little coughing sound.

"Good morning," she said.

"Hi, Beautiful."

With that response, she tried to hide her face in her pillow, but I reached for her and turned her around to face me.

After a few seconds of silence, she spoke. "Thank you for last night."

"You don't have to thank me for anything. I'm only glad that I could get to you."

A questioning look flitted across her face briefly. "Do you want to get up and head down for breakfast?" she asked.

"Mmm, not really," I replied truthfully. Lying there beside her was everything to me. The only way that it could've gotten any better would be if I'd been underneath the covers holding her body next to mine.

The air between us shot up a few degrees before she rolled out of the bed and stood up. I took that as my sign that this bliss was over for the time being. And if that didn't do it, the heavy knock on the door certainly did.

I watched as Verity walked over to the door wearing my clothes. Even though they were at least three sizes too big for her, she looked incredibly sexy. Best of all, because she was wearing my clothes, she'd smell like me. It was the next best thing to touching her.

Okay, I need to get up now.

Verity opened the door, and Megan rushed in like a cold breeze. "Verity, oh my God! What happened to you last night?"

At that point, I was in a standing position, but I didn't

care if Megan knew that we'd slept in the same bed. And clearly, neither did Verity, as she didn't even bother to check my positioning before opening the door to her.

"I'm fine. I'm okay," Verity said, her voice muffled from Megan squeezing her in a tight embrace.

"Oh, Noah." Megan had finally noticed I was in the room.

"Ladies. I'll run into town and grab some coffee and bites. I won't be long," I said as I moved past Megan, who had somehow found herself further inside the room than Verity.

I mouthed the words "You, okay?" to Verity as I took a finger and stroked the side of her face. There was no way that she could've mistaken the intimacy in the touch, and I wasn't hiding it for her or for Megan.

She nodded and raised her hand to meet mine. Lingering for a moment, the message was clear: She was feeling something for me, the way that I was feeling something for her.

And with that I did a shallow bow as I headed out the door, closing it behind me. Turning around in the hallway as the door clicked, I nearly bumped into Adrian, who was making a beeline for what I could only assume was Verity's room.

Hell no.

"The ladies are talking. Why don't you and I take a ride into town to get them breakfast." It wasn't meant to be a question, and from the look on his face, I could tell he knew that.

The macho in him didn't want to run away from a challenge, so instead of trying to get past me he simply nodded in agreement.

It was time we had a man-to-man chat about some things. Motioning with my eyes, I let him go ahead of me down the hall.

JUST as we stepped outside onto the porch, Adrian turned abruptly, standing inches from my face. We weren't the same height, and the differential was more pronounced with us standing so close. I didn't think he'd be stupid enough to throw a punch, but my body immediately loosened, and I stood ready for anything. He didn't speak, just stood there with both of his hands at his sides, trying to hold eye contact with me.

And I wasn't budging.

I could tell that he'd probably been in a fight or two before because of the way he was holding himself. But I knew he wasn't made for this. I'd grown up on a ranch and handled animals that weighed north of a thousand pounds. Not to mention the fact that I'd done the amateur boxing circuit in my youth. And some things you just never forget.

But I was a big believer in the saying, "However you bring it to me, is the way I'll bring it to you," so if what he needed today was getting his ass handed to him, I'd be more than willing to oblige.

After a few moments, I was getting ready to end the great stare-off on my front porch when I heard someone drive up.

"Gentlemen, gentlemen!" Booker's voice cut through the tension in an instant. Adrian backed away from me.

"Everything good cuz? All friendly and such?" Cole added, only a few steps behind his brother having jumped out of the passenger side.

"Of course," I responded, placing my hat on my head and taking a few long strides over to my truck.

I had a rethink about carting Adrian into town with me after all. And I wasn't interested in socializing with these two busy bodies either. I knew that Booker had probably come to see Megan, which meant they'd be sticking around for a while, and I didn't need to worry about Adrian interfering with Verity.

"I'll be back." With that, I sped off down the driveway, making sure that my rear tires spun out, leaving an excessive amount of dust and kicking up stones in their wake.

***

A couple of days later, I found myself sitting outside the mayor's office waiting for an audience with her along with several other townspeople. The group, included one of the officers who had responded to the distress call the night that Verity was locked in that building.

At first, I didn't want to attend. Leona and I had a history, but that wasn't the reason why. I thought it strange that the person who had suffered the most that evening hadn't been invited to this little gathering. I became even more suspicious of the motivations behind this meeting when I saw Hex Tanner, a member of the county's wealthiest family, arrive just seconds before Leona ushered us all into her office. There were only three leather seats facing her desk, so of course I stood. Leona gave me a look that I didn't care to interpret before taking her own seat.

"I'm sure you all have the same concerns that I do about what happened a few nights ago to one of our town's guests. Now Bryan, is it true that your officers haven't been able to put together any leads?"

"Yes, Madam Mayor. We've been canvassing the area for any witnesses, and thus far, nothing. And I've had my best people working on this, of course—it would be an utter shame for Dènaud to be known as someplace that's unsafe for tourists."

I hated the way that Bryan spoke. It was nasally and he always gave off the impression that he was trying to cover up something. A terrible attribute for the town's police chief.

"She's not a tourist," I corrected. Leona's gaze immediately went to my face, but then she cleared her throat and continued.

"I think Bryan was just trying to highlight that she's not originally from Dènaud. He didn't mean anything by it," Leona said, tapping her finger impatiently against her desk.

I didn't have anything further to add, so I didn't.

"Should we be at all concerned that these graduate students are picking apart our municipal records? I mean, what on earth are they even looking for?" One of the townspeople in attendance spoke up and then immediately looked at both Hex and Leona. It was a slight movement, but I'd caught it.

In response to this statement, I couldn't help but roll my eyes. But I must've done something audible as well since everyone in the room was now looking over at me. From my place, leaning against the window, I pushed up into a standing position.

"Are you kidding me? Their research has been in the works for months, and they jumped through all the hoops you put before them to get the proper access. And what, now you want to question their motivation? Verity was intentionally locked in that building that night!" I could feel myself getting angrier.

"Now let's not jump to conclusions," Bryan tried to interrupt me.

"No, no…*let's*. There were cinder blocks against the door that had to be removed to even get to the locked door. How, how is that not intentional?" I was practically shouting at this point.

"Noah. There are aspects of the investigation that are still unknown to all present in the room, so I'd appreciate it if you'd calm down and be a little more circumspect in your commentary," Leona cut in, trying to regain control of the conversation. "You were invited here because you are their host and undoubtedly have a vested interest in keeping them all safe."

"Why wouldn't they be safe here, Leona?" I snapped.

The room went completely quiet. Perhaps it was the familiar way in which I'd just addressed the mayor in her own office, in front of all these people. But at this point, I was feeling a bit reckless. We lived in fucking Dènaud for crying out loud, not some big scary city. Things like this shouldn't happen in our town. And for Leona to insinuate that Verity and her colleagues might somehow be in danger…I could see the precipice that I was about to be pushed over.

"Perhaps we could have the room for a moment, everyone. Just a few minutes," Leona asked with the sweetest smile she could conjure.

And then, one by one, the audience of six moved out into the reception area. Everyone seemed in a hurry to leave except for Hex, who looked as if he'd never been told what to do a day in his life. That statement was probably true. I knew for a fact that he was a major supporter of Leona's mayoral appointment and had been an old friend and financial supporter of her father's public life as well. Hex and his family businesses had benefited bountifully from those relationships.

When the office was just ours alone, she rose and strode over to where I was standing. She came a little too close to me, and it took everything in me not to back away.

"You were always like this."

I looked at her with a puzzled expression. "I don't know what you mean," I countered.

"Handsome and noble to a fault."

"I'm not sure what my looks have to do with this." I was getting more annoyed by the second. And when she made a move to put her hand against my chest, I immediately removed it and placed it back at her side. I could tell she didn't like that.

"Don't let any feelings you might have for her muddy your thinking. She put herself in danger by being in that storage space well after hours. I mean, look how much time and other resources we've already wasted on this investigation. She wasn't hurt in the long run, so why are we still worrying about it?" Raising her hands in exasperation, she moved to sit on the edge of her desk.

I couldn't believe what she'd just said. "Leona…" but she didn't let me finish.

"Look, don't get upset. I just meant that she's all right now, isn't she? I mean, there isn't a need to make this a bigger deal than it needs to be."

I'd had quite enough. Placing my Stetson on top of my head, I barely nodded in her direction as I made my way to the door. I wasn't going to wait around to hear the rest because it was clearly not going in the direction of finding out the truth about what happened that night. I just had to make sure that it didn't happen again, and if that meant sticking close to Verity, then that was what I was going to do.

I ignored the looks that I got from Hex and the police chief as I stormed by them. Something felt off about this entire situation.

***

I'd promised that I'd be waiting in the receiving room for her by 5:30. I wanted to take her for a drive first and show her some of my favorite places in town before going to the next town over for dinner. If things went according to my plans, I'd show her the best of what Dènaud had to offer and hopefully make her fall in love with this place.

Thankfully, the twins had gotten both Megan and Adrian out of the house for the night, so there was no one to disturb us.

I'd poured myself a scotch neat to try and calm my nerves as I paced a little in front of the window. I looked at my watch—5:29. Then I heard a series of soft clicks, the sounds of Verity coming down the staircase. She came to a stop after the final step, and I heard myself take a deep breath. Seeing her, I almost dropped my glass on the floor, barely able to place it down properly on the nearby table.

"You look...wow!" My brain needed oxygen. She was wearing a soft, flowing yellow dress that hugged her curves with small flowers and an embroidered hem. My grandmother was a master embroiderer, and the design that bordered her dress looked intricate and hand stitched. Coupling the dress with a light silk shawl and gold strappy heels, she looked picture-perfect. I'd never seen anyone look so beautiful in a dress that was so simple. It was almost as if her body shape and other physical attributes enhanced the dress rather than the other way around.

"Noah, please, stop looking at me like that," I heard her say.

But I couldn't. I was mesmerized. Walking towards her slowly, I held out my hands to her and reveled in the feel of her softness when she placed her smaller hands in mine. Drawing them to my chest, I stole another few moments to just take her in.

Tonight was going to be our night. It would be special, and I'd make sure that she enjoyed herself and that it was something she'd never forget.

Feeling a sudden pang in my chest, I realized that I wanted this to be the beginning of something. Verity was only supposed to be here for a few months, and then she'd be back to her life in Ontario. But I wanted—no, I *needed*— something more.

"Are you all right? Where'd you go? Lost you for a moment," she smiled as she spoke, while her loosened curls hung just over her shoulders.

I began shaking my head. "No, I'm right here." I

desperately wanted to add something more to that statement, but I didn't want to push. Besides, I didn't need words. I could show her. Placing a kiss on her cheek, I pulled her towards me so that I could rest my hand on the small of her back as I escorted her out the door.

Let it begin.

THE WONDERMENT in my voice couldn't be hidden. We'd been driving for about twenty minutes or so when he turned his truck into what could only be described as a hidden oasis.

"This is so beautiful, Noah. I never knew that a place like this could even exist."

Reaching up to the sky, the trees looked as if they were hundreds of years old, anchored to the earth by their massive trunks. The lower branches bowed towards the ground like a weeping willow. But these were no delicate branches. It was an entire sea of strong and thick trees that seemed to be out of place and in stark contrast to the plains around them. I'd never seen trees as big as this outside of the redwood forest in California, and that had only been on TV.

"I'm glad you like it," he replied somewhat sheepishly.

"Like, no, I love it," I said, turning around in bare feet while my dress twirled around me.

When Noah had suggested that I remove my heels, I didn't even hesitate. Being the gentleman that he is, he tried to pick me up first upon opening my passenger-side door. But as romantic as it would be to be carried in his solid arms, I was no Miss Priss. I softened the refusal to be carried by stealing a kiss, and I could still see the color in his cheeks from it. His lips were soft and I could taste the drink that I'd seen in his hand earlier.

We'd been walking hand in hand for a while. I loved the feel of his fingers between mine and the soft ground below us. He'd also removed his boots, leaving them behind somewhere along the path we were following.

Taking a deep breath, I noticed that even the air felt cleaner. I was in awe because this forest seemed to just come out of nowhere. The road leading to it was flat lands as far as you could see right before the turnoff. But once we drove off the paved road, we immediately found ourselves inside this canopy of trees, which blocked out most of the evening sun. Yet it wasn't dark; rays of light pierced the thick cover of leaves.

"How did you find a place like this?" I asked him, not having fully turned around to face him. I felt a slight pull against my forward movement, so I turned and smiled at him.

"I grew up in Dènaud, remember? So I know all the secret places." He paused for a moment before continuing. "But this place is something special to my family. My dad brought my mom here when they were dating, and my grandfather did the same thing with my grandmother years before."

That caught my attention. "So there's some kind of generational pull to this place, huh?"

"I guess it's a beautiful place you bring someone when you feel like they're someone special."

I don't think anyone had ever said something so sweet to me, outside of my own family. It felt like a moment to say something equally wonderful, but I was still trying to take in everything he said. *Stop overthinking, Verity. This is a first date.*

"Come on, there's more," he said, drawing me out of my thoughts.

I couldn't imagine anything more amazing than what we'd already seen so far, so when we came to a clearing a few steps away from the path, I took my free hand, the one he wasn't holding, and placed it underneath my own chin to close my mouth.

"Noah." It was the only word that came to mind, and it left my lips as a whisper.

Before us was a pond, the clearest body of water I'd seen outside of the Caribbean Sea. There was no sand surrounding it, just a grassy edge that slipped underneath the water. The temptation to run my feet through the water was too much, and as if reading my mind, Noah pulled us both into a shallow area a couple steps from a small man-made dock. If there had been a canoe or any type of boat tethered to it, I would've had to pinch myself because, surely, I was in a movie at that point.

Dipping one of my bare feet into the water, I broke the water's mirror-like surface.

"Ahh!" I yelped as my body absorbed the shock of ice-cold water.

"I know. It's warmer towards the center, but you'd have to swim out there." His look towards me was filled with heat.

I saw the glint in his eye that promised mischief, and truthfully, the idea of skinny dipping hadn't escaped me either. But when he backed away from the water's edge, I knew we'd have to keep that for another time. Besides, I was excited to see what else he had in store for our date.

It felt like a perfect moment for a kiss, so I couldn't help but feel slightly disappointed when he didn't give me his lips.

On the way back to the truck, we found his boots right where he'd left them. The trek back to his vehicle, along with our wet feet, meant we'd picked up a lot of forest ground debris on our soles. Not wanting to bring the dirt inside with me, I tried dusting it off with my hand until he stopped me. Disappearing briefly to the back of his truck, he returned with a bottle of water.

"Great idea," I said, reaching for it. But Noah held it just out of reach, putting it on the hood before turning to pick me up.

He placed me inside the truck, my legs dangling over the side, out the open door. Then he slowly pushed up my dress. He left a trail of goosebumps wherever he touched. My dress balanced easily above my shin. Running his hand down my leg, I became so focused on how my body reacted to him that I almost missed when he retrieved the water bottle and emptied the contents over my feet and ankles.

Not only did he pour the water over my feet, but he also caressed each of my toes with his fingers to ensure they were cleaned. It was the most sensual thing anyone had ever done to me. We were making a lot of firsts tonight, I thought to myself.

"How am I going to do the same for you?"

"This isn't about me. Let me take care of you tonight. We'll worry about me another time." And with that, I relaxed my body into the passenger seat and watched him complete his task. He dried my feet with a soft towel that he just happened to have on hand before sliding my heels back on, one by one. My feet were tingling. Just like another place on my body.

When he took my hand over the center console again and began to drive away, I wished for him to bring me back to this place *very soon.*

***

"Wow, your dad sounds like an amazing man."

We'd finished with our appetizers, and I was just finishing my story about how my dad had scared off a childhood bully of mine in the fifth grade.

Noah leaned towards me, deeply focused on every word.

"Yeah, he was great. You would've really liked him." I took a sip of my dirty martini. A bit strong, so I was nursing it.

122

"Do you think he would've liked me?" Noah looked so scrumptious before me in his dark pants and dress shirt.

He could've worn what he did every day, and he'd still have been the best-looking man for miles. Nothing compared to his masculine presence in a room. I'd seen the looks he received when we'd entered the restaurant. Every eye was checking him out, from the hostess taking us to our table to the waitress serving our drinks. And not to mention any other female diners we walked past. Even now, while eating, I'd catch an eye or two peeking our way.

"I like you, so he would like you." That settles that, I thought. But talking about my dad had brought back a lot of memories that I'd kept buried. And I could feel a heaviness beginning to form inside of my chest.

"Hey." I felt his hand on the back of mine. The warmth of it drew me back to the present. I got lost in those eyes of his. And then he smiled.

"Sorry to interrupt," the waitress said, almost looking apologetic, "but the gentleman at the table over there would like to send over a bottle of champagne."

Noah didn't respond right away but turned his head to follow her head movement after a brief pause, almost as if he already knew who the waitress was talking about. There was an older gentleman I'd never seen before, but I did recognize the woman he was with, Mayor Grant. The two looked as if they were having an intimate dinner of their own.

"Tell him no thanks for us, but thanks," Noah responded dryly before returning his gaze to me.

"Um sir, if I, um…" the tiny waitress looked absolutely terrified for some reason. She was stuttering her words and glancing back and forth between our table and theirs.

Placing my other hand over the top of his, I tried to take away some of the tension. "Champagne sounds yummy," I offered while giving the waitress a reassuring smile.

"Fine," Noah said. But clearly, it wasn't fine with him.

Does he still have feelings for the mayor or something? Clearly she's moved on, though. Weird, I thought she'd been flirting with Adrian.

Before I could get too settled in my thoughts, I felt a presence approach our table. "Well, how are you both this evening?" The man who'd sent the champagne was standing just to the right of me, but I noted that the mayor had not followed.

Noah didn't immediately respond and didn't look as if he was even going to.

"I'm Verity Reynolds. It's a pleasure to meet you," I said, extending a hand to him, trying to break the awkward silence.

"The pleasure is all mine. I'm Hex Tanner, the owner of this fine establishment. How has your meal been so far?"

"Oh, it's been wonderful. And thank you so much for the champagne. You shouldn't have," I said, looking at Noah, who'd apparently gone mute.

"It's a welcome to our town. A beautiful bottle for a beautiful couple," he said before bending to kiss my hand.

I was probably a little too eager to pull my hand out of his grasp and hoped he hadn't noticed. But something about the way he'd approached us and the way Noah still hadn't uttered a single word made me uneasy.

A movement out of the corner caught my eye. The mayor had stood up abruptly, thrown her cloth napkin on the table, and stormed out the front door.

"Well, it seems that's my cue. Until next time. Noah," he said, pausing briefly to get some acknowledgment from Noah.

"Hex," Noah answered without lifting his head.

I watched as Hex walked after the mayor, with her assistant popping up out of nowhere to trail them out the door.

***

The drive back was a little less animated. I guess we'd said all that we wanted to say about ourselves at dinner. The meal itself was amazing and rivaled some of the fine dining meals I'd had back home. But there was no escaping the damper that had overtaken the mood after Hex had left our table. And we didn't end up drinking any of that champagne. It was rolling haphazardly in the back seat beside the bag with our leftovers.

"I had a wonderful night," I said, reaching out to touch Noah's arm.

I saw his jaw unclench slightly, and eventually, he offered me another one of his beautiful smiles. "It was great." Taking that same hand, he pulled it up to his lips.

And we stayed that way until we were almost the whole way up his driveway. But the flashing police car lights made us sit up a little straighter.

"What the hell?" That was all I heard Noah say as he pulled his truck to a stop in front of the house.

"What's happening?" I said, more to myself, as we were both in the dark about what we had come back to.

I already had my hand on the door handle when I felt his grip on my thigh. "No, stay here," he declared before exiting the cab and making his way over to where the police were standing. I had every intention of staying put until I saw Adrian sitting on the steps of the porch with a folded-up cloth to his lip and what looked like a black eye.

Before I knew what I was doing, I'd jumped out of the truck and was running towards him.

"Shit" was all I heard Noah say as he tried to grab my arm as I ran by him.

LOOKING to get some information about the bizarre scene in front of me, I exited the truck and approached the officers. "Goodnight, officers. What seems to be the problem?"

"Night, Noah. Sorry to disturb your evening, but there was an emergency call from your landline about possible intruders," said the young officer, holding a pen and pad as he spoke.

"Intruders?" I almost didn't believe what I was hearing.

I was just about to press him for additional information when I heard the cab door of my truck door open. I'd just turned my back for a moment when I saw Verity practically sprinting in her heels towards the house. I wasn't fast enough to grab her as she made a beeline right for a figure slumped on the front steps.

So I took off after her and was a moment behind when she finally came to a complete stop. Placing my hands on either side of her arms, I tried holding her in place against me.

"What's going on?" I said as I looked over her shoulder at the person. But Verity hadn't minded or just didn't hear me as she bent down to take a seat beside a bruised Adrian.

"I'm fine. Thanks for asking," he said wryly, massaging his jaw with his free hand.

"Adrian. Oh my goodness. What happened to you?" My body tensed as she reached out to touch Adrian's shoulder and his face where it wasn't busted up.

"Ah, nothing. Just a warm Dènaud welcome from some local youths, I guess," he seemed to shrug while answering.

"You saw who did this to you?" I dug a little further. This was just too confusing. Things like this didn't happen in Dènaud. People in this town didn't even lock their doors.

"Saw them? There are two of them in the back of that squad car. One of them got away," he said, pointing with a hand that had some red and pink scratches on the knuckles.

Seems like whatever happened to Adrian, he'd made sure that the other person didn't get away unscathed. The tiniest piece of me developed a bit of respect for him, but as I watched Verity sitting beside him, it all but evaporated.

I turned to the police car and couldn't make out the figures in the rear. I wanted to go over there and get a better look at who could've done this, but I found myself rooted to the ground, not wanting to leave Verity as Adrian's nursemaid. But she'd already begun to ring out the cloth, which must have been filled with ice, and was reapplying it to the side of his face.

"Oh my God! Where's Megan?" Verity shouted.

"And where the hell are Booker and Cole? I thought you

guys were all out together?" I added, a wave of fury hitting me.

"We're right here, cuz." Cole appeared with Megan right behind him, holding an additional bag of ice.

Verity rose to place her arms around Megan. "Thank God you're all right."

"Booker's already down at the station," explained Cole, "but I didn't want to leave these two alone until we'd heard from you. We figured you'd be on your way back."

Thankfully, one of the other responding officers was making his way over. "Noah, there are two young males already in custody, but we'd like you to come down to the station to see whether you could 'ID' the third," the officer said while looking directly at Adrian.

"Officer, don't you think that he should get some medical attention first? Perhaps go to the hospital?" Verity chimed in.

I couldn't wash away the feeling rising within me as Verity went into "caretaker" mode for Adrian. I guess I shouldn't have expected anything less because, after all, they were colleagues and probably friends. But as much as he looked like he needed to be checked out, his proximity to her still irked me.

"I'm sorry, miss. Of course, Mr. Howard, if you'd prefer that we visit the emergency room first then…"

But Adrian interrupted the officer before he could finish his statement. Standing up with a little assistance from Verity, he pushed himself down the rest of the steps and the walkway.

"Nope, let's just get this over with," he said, visibly leaning on Verity for support.

I wanted to reach out to her and pull her back or suggest that he travel there on his own, but Adrian had been attacked in my home.

I watched helplessly as Verity got into a separate cruiser with Adrian for transport to the police station.

***

We'd had this amazing evening, and then I'd come back to all-out chaos in my home. And to top it all off, Verity had completely ditched me and wandered off with Adrian. If I'm honest with myself, that's not entirely a true statement, but that's how I felt.

Cole and Megan rode with me to the station, and we all piled into a waiting area.

"Noah, I got back down here as soon as I could," said Chief Miller. "Thanks for coming in this late in the evening." He wasn't dressed in uniform and looked, quite frankly, like he'd just rolled out of bed not too long before meeting us.

"Chief, what's going on?" I couldn't take this anymore. I needed answers.

"Well, it seems that a few ranch hands from the neighboring town paid Clarence House a little visit tonight. But I guess they weren't expecting anyone to be at home, so when your cousins and Adrian came upon them, a small fight broke out, and here we are."

"Wait, the town over? What the hell were they doing here?" I couldn't hide my impatience. And I needed to get Verity out of here and back home where I could keep her safe.

"We're still trying to ascertain that now. From what we can tell, they're pretty much drifters who got some work locally and then ended up at your house expecting to rip you off and leave town."

That made absolutely no sense. I was shaking my head before I even realized it. "Chief…" I managed to get out, but then he was called away suddenly by an urgent phone call.

Looking around at everyone in the waiting area, it was clear that I needed to wrap this up as soon as possible. So, taking matters into my own hands, I approached the officer at the front desk.

"Dan, do you think it'd be possible for us to do this in the morning? I mean, it's Saturday night, and you guys don't intend to release these guys until court on Monday, right?"

I'd known Dan for some time. He was an old friend of my father's and had watched me grow up. But he was looking nervously around before he answered me.

"Look, Noah, I'm not sure I should even be telling you this, but those men aren't drifters. They're hired hands, seasonal workers over at the Tanner Ranch. One of them told me on his way down to the cells that he'd been offered money by someone to start a little trouble at Clarence House." His voice was barely above a whisper, and he was looking over the side of his desk to make it seem like he wasn't even speaking to me.

The revelation hit me hard. If Hex was involved with this, I was going to kill him. What good reason could he have for interfering with Verity and my other guests? I mean, what business was it of his that they were in Dènaud in the first damn place. He didn't even live in this town.

Before I could question Dan further, he nodded in the direction of the chief who was approaching us.

"Like I said, Noah. We're doing the best we can. But we'll let you know if anything comes of this." The chief rambled on as if he'd been talking the entire time.

It sounded like I was being dismissed, but I'd been told to come to the station for identification purposes. Perhaps Chief Miller had forgotten, or he really was the idiot I thought he was.

"We've got the lineup ready, sir, so we're ready whenever you are chief," a young officer said to me.

The chief gave a look that was half astonishment and half annoyance. *This idiot really didn't know what was going on in his own station.*

"Yes, of course. Let me escort you and Mr. Howard to the room."

Adrian was already halfway up to where we were standing, having probably overheard his name being called.

Giving Verity a reassuring look, I followed the chief further into the station.

***

After giving Booker a good telling-off for being the one to run down the third perpetrator before handing the guy over to the police, I made sure that he and Cole got off safely before heading back inside.

Megan had made it an early night, and with all the excitement, who could blame her?

I delivered the two extra-strength Tylenol that Verity had requested for Adrian and was relieved when she finally headed back to her own room instead of keeping vigil by his bedside as she had been since we'd returned from the police station.

The men they'd caught wouldn't give up any further details, not even the one who had already confessed to Dan. They clammed up quickly, and I had to wonder why. All they'd say for sure was that they'd received a few hundred dollars from someone, but they couldn't identify the source of their payment and had likely been taken advantage of themselves.

But it was clear from their limited statements that they hadn't intended to hurt anyone, and from their appearance, they wore the worst of this night. Booker and Adrian had apparently waled so badly on them that at least one would need medical attention before the night was done. Watching them from behind the two-way glass, I felt sorry for them. They were clearly out of their depth, barely adults themselves, and they looked terrified.

The prosecutor wouldn't look the other way on this one, so they were going to be charged with something, but seeing as how they were the ones who took the brunt of the injuries that night and had no adult criminal records, they'd receive a bit of leniency.

In the end, I'd never been so happy to get out of a place and get home.

***

"Not at all how I expected this evening to end with you," I said to Verity as she stood in the frame of her bedroom door.

The lamplight behind her gave her an almost ethereal glow. She was no longer wearing her shawl, and the sleeves of her dress had become bunched up on her arm. Using only my fingers, I slowly drew them down. She shivered visibly at my touch.

"Are you cold?" I said, stepping a bit further into her room as I began rubbing my hands up and down her arm for warmth, or so I told myself.

"A little." She smiled as she replied. "Mmm, Noah?"

"Yes." I was now standing directly over her with my head just above hers. I inhaled before closing my eyes.

"Would it be too much trouble if I wanted to sleep beside you again? Tonight?"

Oh, so there was a less provocative way to say that phrase. But I couldn't help the smile that spread across my face, and I looked directly into hers so that she could see it.

"It's no trouble at all. I'll come back once I've showered and changed."

"Uh, wait. I meant that I'd come to your room."

I think my heart just stopped.

"Are you sure?" I asked. We'd slept just fine together that one night.

She just nodded her head affirmatively. "I want to sleep with you tonight in your bed."

And if I'd had any doubts at all about the wiseness of having Verity sleep in my room, they completely evaporated as I opened my bedroom door to her later that night. This time, she wasn't wearing my oversized T-shirt or pajama bottoms.

VERITY

I HAD BEEN standing in the hallway for less than a few seconds when I felt both of his hands on my arms, pulling me into his room. Expecting to end up against his chest, I was a little relieved when he kept me at arm's length while closing the door behind me. But that feeling left me as soon as I watched his eyes roam all over my body.

The negligée I was wearing wasn't see-through, but it didn't leave much to the imagination in terms of showing the outline of my shape. I coupled it with the matching loosely fitting silk robe that I left untied.

I heard the soft click of the door closing and almost lost my nerve. When I'd conjured up this bright idea to seduce Noah, I'd been going off the reactions I noticed with him every time I was near Adrian. He'd watched me closely but hadn't interfered in my efforts to help a friend who was obviously hurt and in need of my attention.

But we'd had such a one-of-a-kind day together, and I truly didn't want it to end the way that it did. Who could've predicted how this night would unfold?

So I wanted to regain some control over it and inject some of my own agency into how things progressed between us.

It was a fifty-fifty shot really that this type of forwardness, as they say, would even appeal to a man like Noah. From the very beginning, he seemed to be a straight shooter without any airs about him. If he wanted something, he was clear. And if he didn't want something, he was equally transparent.

All the signs tonight—and since the first day we'd met—suggested that he was not only interested in me but really cared about my well-being. Now I didn't want to be so presumptuous as to believe he had any other intentions towards me besides cultivating a mutual attraction, but we'd been headed somewhere prior to tonight's unnatural ending, and I was curious to explore it.

"Come here," he said.

Oh my. I took one step towards him and then another.

The timbre in his voice created a wetness between my thighs that was immediate. If I had any doubts about the sagacity of my approach, the way he was looking at me was all the affirmation I needed.

Taking a few steps closer to him, I was able to take in more of his scent, which had struck me when he initially opened the door. He was no longer wearing his outfit from earlier, so I assumed he had taken a shower, as I had. Getting the grime off from sitting around that station must have been a priority for both of us.

I could see that the hair that licked the nape of his neck was still a little wet. Small beads of moisture were also on his forehead, just by his hairline. It could've been from the shower or perhaps a little sweat.

Feeling the sharp tingles rising inside of my own chest, I wondered if he was as nervous as I was. If he was feeling any trepidation, he wasn't showing it on the outside except for that little bit of perspiration.

It was almost as if he took over from my initial exertion of courage in even showing up like this at his bedroom door.

Taking my hand, we walked over to the bed together and sat on the edge.

"I don't have this all planned out," I smiled nervously.

I trembled when he took his other hand and used his fingers to trace down the side of my face and neck to my shoulders.

"We don't have to do anything you're not ready for."

I could see on his face that he liked the way my body was reacting to his touch. But I still couldn't tell if he was getting more excited. Noah was keeping his cards very close to his chest, probably so he wouldn't scare me.

We sat in silence for a little bit longer. Sitting underneath his gaze was making me feel hot all over. He had a way of observing me without letting on that he was doing so.. It was the sexiest thing.

Leaning forward, I kissed his lips. I closed my eyes, so my only sense of direction was the warmth of his breath on my upper lip. He'd taken a drink before I'd arrived. I could smell the smokiness of the scotch. As soon as our lips touched, he reached a hand around my waist and pulled me closer to him.

At first, I thought that perhaps he was going to let me initiate all the first moves to make sure that this was what I wanted, but I was mistaken. Taking me in both arms, he boosted me onto his lap in one swift motion. And then he really started to kiss me.

"Mmm, ahhh," I managed, in addition to grabbing some breaths. Then, without unlocking our mouths, he slowly pushed my robe off my shoulders. I shrugged out of it with little effort as it fell someplace beneath me.

He'd been the one holding me up to this point, so I took both of my arms and encircled his neck as I tried to draw him into an even deeper part of my mouth.

I wished I was straddling him instead of sitting sideways across his lap. The erection that was rubbing up against my bottom was just begging for attention. Although I could tell that he appreciated my strategic placement of it just below my entrance, there was something dissatisfying about not being able to rub myself back and forth over it.

Putting both of my hands on his shoulders, I pushed down and adjusted my knee to signify a change of positioning, but Noah placed both hands firmly on my upper arm and held me suspended above him.

He pushed his forehead against mine as our lips parted again. The panting and heaviness of our breathing patterns were the only things either of us could probably hear.

"I want you. God, I want you so badly. *Fuck*," he almost hissed. Then I watched as he squeezed his eyes together.

It felt like an inopportune moment for a "but," but that was exactly what I felt was coming. Straightening myself, I moved slightly to try and climb off him, but he held me even tighter.

"Noah," I gasped when his fingers began digging into my flesh a little too hard.

He immediately loosened his grip but still wouldn't let me go. "Vee, you don't know everything about me yet. I can't do casual with you." The use of a nickname initially threw me, but the ending revelation had my stomach in knots.

There was so much promise held in that moment between us, and I'd be lying if I didn't say that it scared me a little. I knew that Noah was an intense guy, but I was still at a loss for what he wanted or what he thought I wanted from this. I wasn't naïve enough to think that I was just in his room tonight to sleep with him without anything else, and clearly, he was having those types of thoughts, too.

I'd made the decision to proposition him because I wanted him. And now he was making me uncover more of the *why* for my being here. *Was I ready for that? Was he?*

NOAH

I FUCKED UP. I could tell the moment that the words left my mouth. She'd tried to get herself down, but I couldn't help but hold her closer to me. If I didn't start spouting off at the mouth, I'd be tongue-deep in her sweet juices right now.

My hands were burning from wanting to discover every part of her body. I wanted to put my fingers in her most intimate places and watch her writhe beneath me as I made her cum repeatedly. Then I'd hold my fingers to my nose and inhale her sweet scent deeply right before I licked each finger clean while she watched. And then, when it was finally time for me to pierce her with my dick, I would observe that gorgeous face transforming incrementally as she took every single inch of me.

I just couldn't keep what I was feeling from her. Even as crappy as the day had ended, our time up to that point had been everything that I'd wanted it to be. It was even better than I'd expected.

I knew that Verity wasn't a woman who would decide to sleep with a man without careful consideration. And I'd never hid my intentions from her, even if I'd never been more explicit than at this moment. And I wanted all of her, everything that she would give me.

I also wanted more. Because, yes, I was greedy. I didn't want her to be with anyone else but me. I wanted her all for myself. And I needed her to know this part of me, particularly when it comes to her because I was falling in love with her.

Was I selfish for wanting to know more about how she felt before moving forward? Hadn't we both been flirting our way to this point?

She may not have realized how much power she already had over me. *So what was I going to do now?* As if in answer to my internal thoughts, Verity put pressure against my hold on her to complete the motion that she'd been in the midst of when I decided to have a moment of clarity. She lowered herself down onto my crotch slowly, never breaking eye contact with me. And then she kissed me. And it felt like she was drawing from my very soul. The connection made first with our lips, then her breasts pressed up against my chest, and finally, her warm core over my erection, was taking my literal breath away.

She didn't have to say in words what she was communicating to me by her touch. And if I didn't already feel it, she said it.

"Make love to me, Noah."

NOAH

I FELT like I was going to combust. Hearing her say those words made me even harder. She was already crushed against my chest, but I needed to be closer. I wanted her to feel all of me at once. So placing a hand underneath her butt cheeks, I first squeezed and then lifted her up so that I could rise to my feet still holding her. I kissed her with a ferocity that I'd never had with anyone before, and when I lifted her, I swallowed the sound she made.

We both needed to breathe, but I felt out of rhythm momentarily as I wanted to consume all of her. I was completely enraptured by everything about her: the way she felt in my hands, the feel of her body pressed up against my chest as I lay her down on her back, and the soft mewling noises she made as I explored her mouth with my tongue.

So that we could both catch our breaths, I released her mouth from mine and raised up to stare down at her. She was exquisite. My eyes roamed down her body. Her breasts were teasing me behind their silk prison, and I was desperate to free them. Just thinking about sucking them made my mouth water.

Seeing where my eyes were focused, I saw Verity's eyes widen. *Good.*

I wanted her to have a little trepidation. Making love to her meant that she would see my complete and utter bare desire for her. All my desperation to please her. But also, that I needed her to yield over control to me so that I could fulfill the hedonistic urge within.

Tonight was about her.

Sliding on my knees off the bed, I lowered myself so that my head was positioned at the base of her thighs. Verity had already begun grabbing the sheets into clumps around her as I slowly pushed the material, she tilted upwards to expose her pussy to me.

Thank fuck.

She wasn't wearing any underwear. I'd assumed as much when I noted the wet spot on the front of my bottoms. I took a moment to take in all that I was being treated to. Her dark folds were bare except for a small runway of hair that stopped just above her core.

I could tell that she was growing more aroused by the size of her swollen bud, so I brought my head closer and tasted her. Verity's response was audible when she bucked beneath me. Holding on to the top of her thigh, I put my tongue and lips to work teasing her. Putting one finger inside of her, I quickly added another to help stretch her out.

"No…ah, ah, Noah…" She moaned my name as her hand found the top of my head. Her attempt to guide me only made me want to do more, so inserting a third finger into her I increased the pressure within until I'd found that spot that made her want to scream.

We were in the furthest room and down a considerably lengthy hallway, but if she'd yelled out, there was no way that the others on the floor wouldn't hear her. *Note to self: make love to her somewhere that she can scream her lungs out.*

She was close, I could feel her walls tightening around me. There needed to be just one more thing. Her head was completely thrown back, so she had no idea what I intended to do when I reached up her body and pinched one of her nipples.

"Ahhhh!"

Jackpot. Now I knew how sensitive those buds could be.

I'd slid my arm underneath her thigh seeking out her nipple, so when she began closing her thighs in against my head, I kept up the pressure on as her whole body spasmed.

"Noah! Oh my…I…"

That's what I liked to hear. Every unintelligible word uttered reassured me that I was doing what I'd set out to do.

She'd ended up with her legs draped down my back and hitched over my shoulders. But as she tried to bring them down, I held her in place, sucking every drop of her juices with my tongue and lips.

When I finally lowered her back down to the bed, her limbs were still trembling.

VERITY

WHEN I'd opened my eyes again, I was looking up into the astonishing multi-colored orbs of this man who had just devoured me. And he looked as if he wasn't finished yet.

There was no hiding the bulge being restrained by his clothing. And when he caught me looking down there, he simply wiped his chin and lips with the back of his hand. I felt my pussy clench.

Rising on his knees, I felt the bed dip down even further as he pulled his shirt over his head with one hand.

My negligée was all the way up around my waist, but I couldn't help but to push my hands towards the muscles that rippled their way down his chest. He was hard everywhere. But a lingering question remained, and I got my answer as soon as he started pushing downwards on the waistband of his pants. The bottom matched the top.

I saw his widening smile as his dick was revealed. He should smile, the man had been blessed. I watched how it moved between his strong thighs. I was going to be impaled on that soon, and I couldn't wait.

He moved over me to grab a condom from the nightstand and went to tear it open with his teeth.

I'd wanted to pleasure him like he'd done to me, but I'd been clear from the start at who was in charge this night. *I'd get my opportunity.*

When he put the condom on, I thought it was a forgone conclusion what would happen next as I spread my legs beneath him. But he only lowered himself and positioned his dick right at my entrance. *Was Noah a tease?*

I raised my pelvis upwards to meet him and try to force the connection. But that only made him pull back and smile down at me. Pulling me up into a sitting position, he waited as I adjusted my legs until I was perched above his dick.

But if I had any thoughts of controlling anything, that all went out the window as he took my nipple into his mouth. Sucking and flicking it into a hardened state with his tongue, I was slowly losing my mind.

In one swift movement, he pulled my garment off with a little help from me. Then he positioned me over top of him and lowered me down until I had taken in every sweet inch of him.

We sat there for a moment with me fully seated on his cock. I could feel him growing inside of me and it was all at once deliciously painful.

I desperately wanted to move.

And the next thing I knew, we were.

The pace he set was slow at first, but he quickly ramped up the speed until all you could here was the slapping sound that was made each time I descended onto him, and of course, the juiciness of our connections.

This time I really was going to have to scream.

And I did, right inside of Noah's mouth.

***

I was spent and incapable of coherent function. The warmth of his body behind me and the strength of his arms pinning my back against his chest were the only thing on my mind. My body felt as if it didn't have any joints, and I wanted nothing more than to spend the rest of the day in bed with this man.

"How are you feeling?"

"Good, so good." I whispered back.

"Just good?" And I could feel his smirk behind me. So, turning around in his arms, I pushed myself up so that our faces were at the same level.

Instead of answering me, he inserted his fingers between my legs and pulled them towards him. There was no mistaking the wetness that he'd touched. Couple this with the fact that my entire body shivered in response to his touch.

"No, I think I have my answer," he said.

I kissed him and then snuggled my way into his chest.

This was bliss and I wanted to experience it for as long as

possible. But when I heard a soft wrapping against the door, it seemed as if fate had other plans.

I looked up at Noah, but he simply placed a finger against his mouth before delivering another kiss to my lips.

"Yes?" He couldn't quite hide the annoyance in his voice, but I could've sworn that I heard him chuckle.

I poked him in his ribs.

"Um, sorry, I was trying to check on Verity, but she's not in her room." We heard Megan's timid voice from behind the door. My eyes widened as I looked up at Noah. But he seemed to be completely at ease.

"She's fine. She's with me." He answered in the most nonchalant manner. My mouth hung open, but Noah simply turned his body to look at the time on the clock sitting by his bedside.

"Oh, oh…okay," Megan replied.

I mouthed the words *oh my god*, but he was undeterred.

"All right, goodnight." This was the only thing that came out of his mouth before he flipped off the light by his bed and pulled me into an even closer embrace.

I was too stunned to say or do anything. I guess Megan knows that I sleep in Noah's room now.

"GOOD MORNING," I said, taking one more nuzzle into his chest before pushing myself out of the bed. We were going to head back to the archives today, and I was determined to get in early and leave well before dark.

Noah drew me in closer and began to leave small kisses on my forehead, then down the side of my face and on my neck. When he made it to my lips, I playfully placed a hand over my mouth and shook my head.

"I don't care," he said, with all seriousness.

I shook my head again but hadn't put down my fingers.

"Verity," he warned.

So I tried to turn to leave the bed, but he was too fast and had me pinned underneath him before my foot could even think of touching the floor.

"Ah!" It was the only sound that escaped my mouth before Noah's lips crashed down on top of mine, capturing me in a fire-starting kiss.

I thought I could get away with just the kiss and then explain to him that I really had to get my morning started, but as

I brought my arms from around his neck and put my hands on his shoulders, I felt him begin to grind himself in between my legs.

He was so hard. And my mind began to spin at the possibilities.

I recognized that I had commitments to my colleagues too, although I was going to try and convince Adrian to take the day off, but my pussy had needs too. And right now, she desperately wanted to take care of that hard-on attached to the sexy cowboy between my thighs.

"Noah." It was more of a plea to stop tormenting me with his body. But he completely ignored me and set about what he was doing with a little more intensity. The condom package tore with ease as he put it on in one swift motion.

His fingers had found their way down the side of my body and were hovering just over my hipbone. *Noah was a tease.* Then he inserted all three at the same time, slowly to give me a chance to adjust to them being in there. All the while, his mouth never left mine save for me calling his name that one time.

Every moan that escaped was reverberating within the cavern of his mouth and he was loving it.

I was too.

The fingers were setting a dangerous pace that would have me shuddering from my release very soon. And I thought that was the plan until my greedy cowboy did something unexpected. Removing his fingers in one quick movement, he pushed his hand underneath my bottom. Then he flipped me onto my stomach and brought his body weight down on top of me, with my breasts being crushed into the mattress.

If I'd lost some of my breath it wasn't because he was on top of me, it was how easily he changed my position in the bed. Lifting and turning me like I was weightless. I almost came right then and there.

"Hmmm….mmm." I heard him grunt sexily as he filled me up and my walls stretched to accommodate him. He immediately set about thrusting deep and fast into me. The patience he'd exhibited with his fingers was long gone.

"Ahh… fuck, you're so tight. I'm gonna cum."

Maybe it was his size or how expressive he was being about what he was feeling, but I came in spectacular fashion while screaming into a pillow. Noah was seconds behind me as he grabbed me around my waist and raised me slightly to deliver a few more deep pumps before letting us both fall to our sides.

"I think you might be the actual death of me," he said through his raspy breaths.

I laughed as he tightened his grip around my waist and pulled me closer to him. "Don't say that." I replied in a teasing tone.

As he pulled his dick out of me, I missed the fullness. He began kissing a trail down the back of my neck, and I realized he wasn't completely erect; but it wasn't soft either. *If I don't move,*

I'm going to be trapped with my legs spread for the rest of the morning. Not a bad thought at all, but I really needed to get this day started.

"Noah?"

"Mmm." It sounded as if he was already falling asleep.

"I need to go back into town today."

I felt him tense up slightly. "It's Sunday morning, everything is probably closed. But if you tell me what you need, I'll see if I can get my hands on it."

"No, you're sweet, but…Megan and I are supposed to go to some buildings today."

He rolled me onto my back and positioned himself over top of me, but this time it wasn't with the intention of driving me wild with his pleasure stick. I tried not to get distracted by his muscular arms positioned on either side of me, caging me in.

"What are you talking about, Verity?"

"Well, we have research to conduct and since the buildings are public access during the week, we requested to go today so that it would be quieter, and we'd be able to get a ton of work done." The words were falling over my lips, but a part of me was a little annoyed that I even felt I had to provide an explanation.

"What buildings are you talking about?"

I was trying to find a spot on the ceiling above his head that I could focus on because it would be hard to look him directly in the face.

"The library, city hall, and the archives." I whispered that last part.

"No," he said as he rolled off me and stood up from the bed. He was standing in all his muscular nakedness, and I was finally given the chance to check out everything that had been hidden underneath his clothes. Sure, I'd caught glimpses last night, but it had been only the dim lamp lighting between us. This morning's natural sunlight was a much better highlighter. And oh man was the sunlight *giving* today.

I was staring so long that I'd almost forgotten that he'd told me "No" until he put his hands on his hips.

"No? Noah, I mean," I said, getting out on the other side of the bed while dragging my gaze away from his thighs and what was dangling between them.

I was trying to uncover where we'd thrown my robe last night. Finding it underneath a pile of his own clothes near the foot of the bed, I quickly donned it and was tying up the sash when he walked up to me. Still naked.

"Verity, come on. There's gotta be another way to do this. You were trapped in that building, don't you remember?" He was sounding a bit frantic now.

"Yes, I remember. How could I forget? That's why we're going there in the morning, and then we'll do as much as we can before dark. We could use a ride, though." I tried to change the tone of the conversation because I really didn't like the direction it was heading.

Leaning up on my tip toes, I placed a peck on his lips and let the fingers on my right hand graze his Johnson. But that only made him sterner, if anything. "This isn't a joke, Verity. Something bad could've really happened to you that night."

"Like what? Noah, honestly, I'm over it. It was an unfortunate mistake that I got locked in there by accident, and I think we must let it go. It's no one's fault."

There, sales pitch done. I started for the door but then turned back, remembering that my negligée still hadn't made an appearance.

"It wasn't an accident," he blurted out.

I paused my search and turned towards where he was standing. He was pulling up his jeans with one hand and had the other on his shirt. "What did you just say?"

"I said, it wasn't an accident. None of the things going on in town since you've all arrived have been accidents."

"What do you mean, Noah?"

"Adrian and Booker startled some wannabe burglars last night here, but turns out they were hired to, I guess just to scare you guys. And the night that you were trapped in the archival building, there were cinder blocks placed against the door."

My hand reached for the mattress as I lowered myself down on it. I needed a moment. "But why would anyone care about us in this town?"

"I think it has something to do with the work that you're doing. Looking at the past election and such." He sat down beside me and pulled my hand into his lap.

I was shaking my head. "I still don't understand why anyone would care about that. We're not trying to make any trouble for anyone. We're just studying government structures and procedures. It's all benign. And besides, it's only in the name of academic discussions. There was no government overthrow being planned." I laughed. There wasn't much else I could do but laugh.

"Look Verity. I don't want you to put yourself or Megan or even Adrian in harm's way. Let's just let things blow over and then perhaps you can get access to the records you need some other way, later."

"Noah, I'm on a timeline. I mean, I have a deadline for my dissertation to be completed, and then I have to go back to Guelph and prepare for my defense. I'm sorry, but I can't put off my plans just because a few people in town have misplaced aggression towards what we're doing."

He was silent for a while and just kept touching the back of my hand in his. "I feel so stupid."

"What, no, no you're not. Noah, it's beyond sweet that you want to protect me, but I'm a big girl. And I came here in pursuit of an academic goal. You don't know me that well yet, but trust me, you don't want the version of me that would compromise on that."

He was looking at me now. Directly in the eyes and unwavering. "You think this is just about protecting you? Verity, I'm not quite sure where your head's at with what's developing between us, but I'm beginning to understand more of where mine is."

I suspected, but I didn't expect that he would blurt it out like that. The difficulty was that I didn't yet know how to explain what I was feeling. And I didn't know how to even tell him that.

So I sat staring at him until he began to slowly remove his hands from my own.

Oh no.

VERITY

TWO WHOLE WEEKS. That's how long it'd been since Noah and I had slept together. It wasn't as if there wasn't enough going on in my life to keep me busy, but now I was actively contriving ways to avoid running into him on a daily basis. Most times it was easy enough because he was typically up before dawn and didn't come back to the house until late in the evening.

Megan, Adrian, and I had been to the archival building at least three times during those couple of weeks, and we'd gathered so much data that we needed to take the last few days to revise and weed out extraneous information.

"I'm hungry, tired and I need to get laid," whined Megan.

Oh yeah—that was another thing that seemed to have transpired with the passage of time. Megan had awaked her inner sexual self and was now vocal with nearly anyone who would listen that she was getting some on a regular basis. Booker, with the extra pep in his step and frequent visits to Clarence House late at night, was suspect *numero uno*.

"Good for you. I'm glad that someone is experiencing a

sexual renaissance in this little town." Adrian said rather drily.

"Aw, don't worry, I heard you'll be getting some soon yourself." Megan offered without a hint of shame.

I exchanged an awkward look with Adrian as if he was looking to me to provide some solution to some unanswered question hanging between us.

"What?" I said looking straight at him.

"Not her, silly. She's already getting her engine checked. That engine light has been off since…" I covered her mouth before she could finish. That was the other side effect of Megan getting it in; she was suddenly spewing out the worst metaphors ever. *Why couldn't this woman just get some good dick and keep her mouth shut like a regular person?*

The way that Adrian was looking over at me I could tell that I hadn't stopped Megan's diarrhea of the mouth fast enough.

"You're sleeping with him?" Adrian nearly shouted.

"I'm not answering that, Adrian." I began packing up my things. Booker would be by shortly to pick us up and I didn't relish having this conversation carry over into the ride back.

"I can't believe you." And with that Adrian stormed out of the building, leaving me and Megan to reassemble all the files strewn across the desks that we'd been using throughout the day.

"I should leave you in here by yourself and let you do this alone," I shot at Megan. But she simply shrugged and smiled in that way that made it impossible for me to stay mad at her.

Besides, it was none of Adrian's business what I did anyways. It wasn't like we were together or anything.

I know that he'd expressed an interest in me, but I hadn't reciprocated. In fact, he was on my list of people that I was avoiding in that house unless it was related to our research. So that meant declining two offers to go for an evening walk, one request to take me to the drive-in, and countless rejections of being asked to work together inside of my bedroom.

Things were murky at best between me and Noah, but I didn't want to muddy the waters even further by leading Adrian on. *I thought that I was being so clear with him. Sheesh.*

So after Booker dropped us back at Clarence House and he and Megan scuttled to parts unknown, I was ready for a hot bath and an early night. And that's exactly what I'd expected until I heard a soft knocking on the bathroom door.

Dammit, I'd just gotten the water to the right temperature.

I pulled open the door expecting to see Megan's face but was taken aback when I saw Noah standing there with his hat in his hand by his side. For some unknown reason, my hand immediately flew up to pull the sides of my robe closer together over the top of my chest.

If Noah had noticed, he didn't lead on.

"I wanted to stop by to let you know that I'm going to be away for a couple of nights."

"Oh. Oh okay. Is there anything you want me to do while you're away?"

He raised his eyebrows at the question. "Like…"

"I don't know. This is a pretty big ranch."

He started laughing. Now ordinarily I would've been pissed when someone was clearly laughing at me and not with me, but I hadn't heard him laugh or seen him smile in so long. *I missed him.*

I'd left the water running so there was a good level of steam in the air around me. Most of it was escaping into the hallway through the open door as I stood there before him.

"Hold on a sec. Let me just turn off the water." Turning without closing the door, I went over to the tub and had to bend at the waist to close the faucet.

I heard a low rumble coming from behind me and then as I reached for the other tap, I suddenly felt large hands gripping my hips. Rising back up to a standing position, my back almost fell into the broad manscape which was Noah.

I didn't stop him when he lowered his fingers towards the hem of my short silk robe. Nor did I resist when his other hand inched across my waist. He encircled my body entirely and pulled me roughly up against his chest. My heart beat so rapidly, I could've sworn that Noah would feel it too.

I heard him make a hissing sound when I began rubbing my bottom against the zipper of his jeans.

"Verity." It didn't sound like a question as it leaked through his lips as a whisper.

"Want me to stop?"

With my back to him, I brought my arm up so that I could hook my hand around the back of his neck. Now there wasn't even a sliver of space between us.

The arm pinning me against his body had gone seeking a nipple underneath my robe, and when he found it, he rolled it between his thumb and forefinger with a little too much skill. I felt the wetness growing in between my thighs. If he kept this up, I was going to need something to brace myself with.

"I just want you," he said, descending his lips onto my neck like his life depended on it.

I was so caught up in the way his fingers were teasing my breast and the finger that had just entered me, that I didn't notice when he'd somehow pulled the sash to my robe, letting it fall like a feather to the ground.

I mourned the loss of the finger inside of me, but it didn't go very far as he added another and gently stroked my folds, spreading my juices.

He played me like an instrument, strumming me like he had a roadmap in his head of how to give me pleasure. And when I felt him begin making a small circular motion on my clit, I knew we needed to either switch locations or he needed to get in this damn bathtub.

NOAH

I JUST wanted to see her. Touch her. Hold her. It'd been killing me, this awkward dance of avoidance we'd both been doing. I knew that she was trying to spend less time in spaces where she knew I'd be. But she wasn't completely to blame, as I'd been keeping my distance too.

No matter how busy I got on the ranch, I would always make time to see her, so there was no excuse. I'd perfected the art of not being seen by her when I sought her out. But I had one final trip to Lake Waters to pick up a couple horses we'd purchased, and I just needed to see and speak to her before I left.

I'd intended to wait until she was free in one of the common areas of the house, or even to knock on her door, but when I heard the water running in the bathroom, I knew that she was going to be in there for a while. Then she'd probably just head off to bed, and with me leaving before dawn, I knew we'd miss each other.

It was a bad idea, but I just couldn't help myself. I'd knock lightly, I told myself. And if she wasn't decent, she'd just say so, and I'd asked to speak with her when she was finished up.

But she'd opened the damn door, and she was standing there, in a robe. In *that* robe, from *that* night.

I could've made it out of there, but when she turned around and bent over to turn off the tap, I'd lost the ability to speak. The garbled murmur that came out of my mouth sounded like some wild animal.

She wasn't wearing any panties.

Perhaps with the humidity in the room, she hadn't felt the coolness against her private parts. Or maybe that was the view she'd meant for me to see. My feet moved before my brain could catch up, and that's what brought us up to this point, with my finger teasing her clit trying to make her cum.

And she was close. I could tell. We'd only spent one night together, but her body was so attuned with my own that I felt like she'd been created just for me. And I very much wanted all her orgasms to be mine.

Placing one then another finger inside of her, I kept up the pressure on her clit. I was applying pressure to the pubic bone with the palm of my hand as I thrust my fingers in and out of her.

"Noah…ahhh." She shuddered against me as her orgasm took over, and I felt each tremor as her channel choked on my fingers.

When it felt like she was ready, I turned her around in my arms so that she could watch me draw both fingers across my bottom lip and insert them inside of my mouth.

"Mmm, you taste so sweet."

I had her complete attention now. Even if she hadn't been

able to clearly communicate her feelings about me, the way her body reacted to my hands was practically translucent.

Ready to help her return to the bathtub now that she was stark naked and thoroughly fingered, my head almost imploded when she lowered herself to her knees in front of me.

"Vee…"

"Shhhhhh" was all she said. Then she unbuckled my jeans and made quick work of my zipper. Sliding my pants down along with my underwear, I felt relief at no longer having my erection constrained.

But nothing could've prepared me for the warmth of the inside of her mouth. I could tell at first that there was a little trepidation on her part about whether she'd be able to take in all of me completely, but that was quickly dispensed with as she rolled her tongue up from the base to the head.

I knew that she was tasting precum with her tongue now because my dick was so rigid that I could see the veins as she sucked back and forth on my shaft. Watching the way her head moved each time she took me in was almost rhythmic. And when she grabbed the base and applied a slight pressure to it, I knew it wouldn't be long before I exploded. I made a move to lift her up, but she wasn't having any of it.

"I'm gonna cum, Vee," I said through gritted teeth.

And I did. And it just kept coming. I surprised myself with just how much, but the even greater surprise was that even when there was none left, she didn't stop sucking.   She swallowed every last drop.

I think she truly is going to kill me.

Verity: Sheree?

Sheree: Bitch, it's six AM!

Verity: I got your bitch, hussy

Sheree: anyways, wassup?

Verity: I did IT last night

Sheree: need a little more than that

Verity: That thing you taught me to do

Sheree: ???

Verity: With my mouth and tongue on someone

Sheree: 👀👀 BITCH!!!!!?????

Sheree: 🍆💦

Verity: Never mind 🙄

Sheree: We need to talk!!!!!

Verity: I said never mind....

Sheree: VVVVVeeeeeerrrityyyyyy!!!!!!!

Verity: FINE....I'll call later this week when things slow down a bit

Sheree: 😜 DON'T 4Get!!

Verity: 😘 love u cuz.....xoxoxo

***

"Hey, baby." Hearing my mother's voice was a soothing balm I never knew I needed and I loved that she'd usually pick up my calls after the first ring.

"Hi, momma."

"What's wrong? Why do you sound like that?"

I was hoping that I'd gotten the sleep out of my voice before making the call, but apparently, I hadn't. And I was nursing a little cold that I'd picked up from God-only knows where. Probably sometime during the weeks we were holed up in those drafty buildings, completing all our research.

I'd been feeling under the weather for the entire week that followed, and even after taking some scary looking

168

concoction that Tabitha brought over last night, I was still feeling a bit rough.

"Oh, it's nothing. How are you and Manuel doing?"

"He's fine. We're both missing you though. Are you going to come out and visit us anytime in the near future sweetheart?"

"I will. I will. Just need to finish up here, and then I'll try and come out and see you right after my defense.

"Well, we're both so tremendously proud of you. And you know your father would've been too."

"I know, momma."

"Verity?"

"Yes, momma?"

"Is there something else going on with you?"

I sighed. There was no keeping any type of secret from her. It's why we'd ended up at odds so many times when I was younger because she'd *tell* me rather than *ask* me what I was hiding. So forget sneaking out to go to parties or messing around with boys—my mother had a radar for BS and concentrated all her abilities on me.

Thankfully we'd grown closer to each other since that time, especially after I moved in with dad and we no longer lived under the same roof. But even if I lived a thousand miles away, my mother would always know if I was hiding something.

"I met someone."

"In Dènaud? Baby, that's fantastic. What's he like and, most importantly, how does he treat you?" I could hear the excitement dripping from every syllable. My mother was a literal fool for love and believed that it was every person's natural state of being.

"He's wonderful. I mean, except for the fact that he lives here."

"Well, that's just geography, sweetheart. Look at your stepfather and me, we made it work. But what's he like?"

"He's tall, handsome, kind, honest, and he has a big heart."

"I like to hear that. I don't like what I'm hearing in your voice though. And don't tell me that it's just distance."

My mother should consider a career as a clairvoyant; she'd make a killing.

"I don't know." I lied.

"Yes, you do."

"I think he wants something from me that I'm not sure I can give him."

"Oh baby, I'm sorry this is so hard for you. This should be a great time for you both, discovering each other and daydreaming about the possibilities." I simply smiled into the screen at the side of my face. My mom was such a hopeless romantic. Of course she'd think this way.

"I need to go momma."

"It was nice to hear from you. And I'm looking forward to meeting your new friend."

"We'll see. Bye and love you."

"Love you too."

***

We'd gone to town to shop for supplies earlier this morning, and now we'd been preparing for the better part of the day. We'd just finished up with the table settings when the doorbell rang.

"Who would come by this early? We told them five thirty!" Megan shrieked as she started to rearrange the silverware for the third time.

"Calm down, I'll get it." I was halfway towards the door when I was cut off by Adrian coming down the stairs.

"That's okay, I got it," he said as he took a few very long strides to get to the door ahead of me.

When he opened to door, I expected to hear Tabitha's voice as I was certain she didn't think we could be trusted to host a dinner all on our own this evening. We'd invited a few people who had been instrumental in making our stay so comfortable in Dènaud over for dinner as a thank you.

But it wasn't Tabitha's figure that stepped through the

door.

"Hello, Verity," Mayor Grant said as she entered, slipping past Adrian but not before planting a kiss on his cheek.

She had her hair slicked back into a tight ponytail, and she wore a black bodycon dress that hugged each curve of her figure. She'd clearly dressed to impress. The question was who for? *Did that dress receive the proper approvals from city council?*

"You look amazing." Adrian said, not hiding the way his eyes traveled all over her body.

"Mayor Grant, I'm sorry I wasn't aware that you'd be attending our little soirée tonight," I said while giving Adrian a sharp look out the corner of my eye.

"Oh, I hope it's no trouble. I didn't want to miss out on the festivities and was so happy when Noah invited me," she practically purred as she handed a bouquet of wildflowers to me.

"Well, the more the merrier. We're all happy you could make it," I managed to get out before trying to examine the flowers in my hand with appreciation.

If her intent was to get a reaction out of me, I wasn't going to give her that. I turned and headed towards the kitchen to fetch a vase for the flowers. Noah hadn't mentioned anything about inviting the mayor to me.

I recognized that after our steamy session in the bathroom just over a week ago, we'd stopped avoiding each other, but nothing had really been resolved. We still hadn't confirmed what we were to each other, or rather, I hadn't opened up to him yet about my feelings. I was still sorting them out, I told myself.

But I couldn't help being somewhat ticked that he would invite his ex to our dinner with things still up in the air between us. I mean, what was he playing at? I wasn't the jealous type usually, but I also didn't want my hand to be forced into doing or saying something before I was certain.

"They're over here, Verity. In this cabinet."

I hadn't realized that the mayor had followed me into the kitchen. Before I could make it to where she stood, she'd pulled a vase from the cabinet and headed towards the sink to rinse it out.

"I don't mind doing that. You're a guest after all," I said, reaching for the object in her hands.

"Nonsense. I practically lived here, so I think I can handle washing out a vase."

Turning her back on me, it appeared that I'd been summarily dismissed. *Unbelievable. I've got to talk to Noah.* But I bumped into Adrian instead as he, Cole, and Booker were carrying in bags of ice from outside.

"Woah, where are you guys going with all this ice?" I watched their ice train cut through the kitchen when Megan joined us.

"Mayor Grant? I, I had no idea. Oh my goodness. It's so

wonderful that you're here," Megan said before she was hit with the realization that she hadn't made a place setting for the extra guest. "Oh my God!" And then she turned and ran back out the way she'd come.

I shook my head as I caught up with her pulling another plate out of the buffet. Luckily, Noah had a home for hosting so there was an abundance of stemware, plates, and the like.

I was taking the extra champagne flute from Megan when I felt an arm encircle my waist.

"Hey, Beautiful," came that voice from behind me. It still gave me chills that ran up and down my spine. And those arms closing around me. I was tempted to wriggle out of his embrace, but the best I could do was to make myself rigid enough that he took the hint and moved himself around to stand before me.

"Noah, we're still trying to get everything together here," I said, not hiding the impatience I was feeling.

"What's wrong?" He asked. His energy switched to worry.

I shook my head and pursed my lips, adding a shoulder shrug for good measure. I attempted to step past him and follow Megan who had disappeared from the room, but I still had the stemware in my hand and Noah moved so that I couldn't pass.

"Nothing's wrong. Everything's fine," I finally answered when he wouldn't let me pass him for the third time.

"Then why don't you want to talk to me?"

"Because I'm busy, and we've got guests arriving soon."

"Vee?"

"Noah, don't," I managed to say as he reached for the side of my face with his hand.

"Okay, I'm at loss here. We were fine up until just now, what the…"

"Noah, it's so nice to see that you kept some of my suggestions about decorating the place. How long did it take for the wallpaper to come in? I know it was back ordered when we'd announced our engagement."

My eyes shot up then, right at Noah's face as he scrunched up his eyes like he was experiencing pain. When he opened them again, it seemed like he was trying to communicate something without using words, but I'd closed up my eyes and my ears to him by that point.

"Leona, what are you even doing here?" Noah said.

"Nice to see you too, Noah. I was invited, silly goose," she laughed. *That's it. I was done.*

"Noah, let me pass, please," I said as I tried and failed once again to move past him. This time he held up both arms to block my way, but wisely didn't touch me.

"Is something the matter?" Mayor Grant's voice was weirdly high-pitched. I hadn't noticed it before.

"Leona!" Noah shouted.

She hadn't even fully entered the room where we were

standing, but her presence was overwhelming the space.

"I need to get out of here." I was beyond ready to be anywhere else but with these two. But Noah wouldn't let me go.

"No, wait. I mean, stop. Leona, you leave," Noah blurted.

"Why are you telling her to leave? You invited her," I couldn't believe my own voice. It sounded as if I was defending the fact that she was here. *I think I'm going to be sick.*

"Me leave, why? And why are you so mad? Wait, did you forget to tell her that we were engaged Noah?"

I knew that even with her hand on her chest, that the mayor was faking her shock at Noah's omission. In fact, I think she came here counting on the fact that he hadn't told me. But it still hurt. *He hadn't told me.*

"Would you just stay out of this?" I tried to address her as calmly as I could.

"Why don't you just get out of Dènaud," she said.

"What the fuck did you just say to my cousin?"

Everyone's gaze shifted to the front door where Tabitha, Headley, and another couple were standing with two small girls who'd just clapped their hands over their ears.

But the real focus was on the figure coming up the stairs behind them.

"Sheree?"

I SPIED Noah and Sheree at one corner of the long picnic-style table, looking as thick as thieves, laughing in between bites of their food. Mayor Grant was on the complete opposite side of the table, sandwiched between Adrian and Megan, having a markedly less animated conversation. She seemed to be staring daggers over at either Sheree or Noah or both.

I was Switzerland, placing myself between two little girls, Stassie and Quinn. And we were all in between their parents, Ogden and Maeve, who thankfully seemed to have gotten over the shock of their children outing them earlier by announcing that "they always covered their ears when there was swearing at home," after Sheree's explicit entrance.

Headley had arrived *sans* spouse because his wife hadn't felt up for a huge dinner and was also nearing the end of her pregnancy. We found out later that she'd forced him to come out and be social for a change. It was their second baby, but Marigold had experienced some postpartum depression after the birth of their first, so he felt a little guilty leaving her on her own. But as the night progressed and the drinks flowed, he loosened up.

Our little group of "fun" was rounded out by the arrival of Callie, who was doing her very best to annoy Booker with the help of Cole.

"Ahem. Everyone, I'd like to take a moment from all this wonderful food to say a few words to thank our hosts for the evening. Megan, Adrian, and Vee, we couldn't have imagined a better summer without all of you here and thank you for the warmth you've brought to Clarence House. Cheers."

Noah wasn't an overly loquacious speaker, so this was just the right amount for the night.

When he used the nickname he had made for me though, I noticed Sheree beside him mouthing the word like an echo in my direction. And she was dramatic enough to have caught the attention of everyone at the table, including the mayor. I raised my eyebrows in response, hoping that would keep her quiet for the time being. I was wrong.

"Yes, thank you Adrian, Megan, and Vee," she'd emphasized the nickname as everyone raised their glasses once again and she shot me a wink.

Looking over at Noah, I could see a bit of pink staining his cheeks, but that didn't stop him from staring directly at me with a broad smile.

Pushing my chair out and placing my hand on my glass, I'd almost made it to a complete erect position when I was interrupted.

"Yes, it's so lovely that you've made our little town your home away from home. And I know I'm not just speaking for myself when I say that you all will be missed," Mayor Grant didn't miss a beat. It wasn't even her house or her dinner. She was a freaking guest, but she still felt the need to speak like she was at the head of her own table. *This woman was incredible.*

No one at the table rose a glass except Adrian, who only half-heartedly took a sip from it because he already had it raised in front of his face.

I simply smiled as I finished standing. "You're right, Madam Mayor, we've had an extraordinary time here with you all, and this dinner is just a small way of showing our appreciation for how much we've appreciated being accepted and supported over these past few weeks." And then I hurriedly took my seat. I never bothered looking in Sheree's direction. I knew she was staring at me wide-eyed for not standing up for myself more. Thankfully, she didn't say anything as one person after another stood to raise a glass and say a few words.

As Tabitha began to speak, one of her granddaughters pulled at my arm. "I thought your name was Verity. Why did Uncle Noah call you Vee?"

"It's just a nickname. Do you have a nickname?" I asked.

"Yeah, stupid head," said the other sister.

"Girls," came mom's strong rebuke from the left.

"Sorry," they said in unison. Apologizing was clearly a habit of theirs.

After a period of time had passed, I felt another tug at my arm. This time from the little girl sitting on my other side.

"Yes?"

"Uncle Noah has been staring at you for the longest time. Are you two boyfriend and girlfriend?" This question elicited an "oooooo" from the other sister, which triggered a bout of hysterical laughing from both.

"Girls!" A much sharper tone from Ogden.

"Oh Oggie, they're just having some fun. What do you expect from eight-year-olds?" Tabitha chimed in. "Girls, let's go outside and get some fresh air with grandma."

"Ma, smoking isn't going to give them fresh air," he countered.

"Hush. Girls, come with grandma." And with that, Tabitha and the girls popped up from the table to head outdoors.

"I'll help clear the table." Booker announced, and Megan giggled before heading off in the same direction after picking up a few plates.

"Cigars, gentlemen?" Headley announced to the table.

And before you knew it, the table was down to just Sheree, me, Callie, the mayor, and Maeve. Noah lingered behind when all the guys headed towards the back porch, but after a quick whisper from Sheree, he finally left. *What did she say to him? And why were they so chummy suddenly?*

Sheree rose and came to take up the now empty seat beside me.

"A cigar sounds nice. If you'll excuse me ladies," the mayor announced as she slithered out of the dining room.

Once she left, Maeve was the first to speak. "What a bitch!" Sheree couldn't contain her laughter, and I just stared at Maeve. She'd been so prim and proper the entire evening and the words were said with such venom.

"Whoa! Story time," Sheree said, once she stopped laughing.

"There is a story, but I'm not sure I'm the one who is supposed to tell it," Maeve responded looking over at me tentatively as she spoke.

"I'll tell it," Callie blurted. But Maeve's look to her seemed to make her do a rethink and she got up instead to head outside in the direction Tabitha and the girls had gone.

"What?" I said after a considerable amount of silence had hung between all of us.

"What do you mean 'what'? Why are you letting that woman make googly eyes at your man and command attention in his house?" Sheree sounded off.

"I don't want to talk about this now," I said. I wasn't ready for this conversation yet and particularly not when I'd only just met Maeve for the first time tonight. She'd think I was nutty, and besides, it appeared that she may be close to Noah if her kids were calling him Uncle. So I didn't want to say too much or the wrong thing in front of her in case it could get back to him.

I gave Sheree the look that said "not now," and to my surprise, she heeded the warning and tried to help me pivot away from the sensitive topic.

"Well at least the food was good," she said.

"And the company was *almost* good," Maeve laughed.

"I like her," Sheree declared, placing a hand on Maeve's arm.

"I like you too. I've never seen Leona's mouth shut so fast as when you walked up those stairs yelling," she replied.

And we all started laughing.

NOAH

THE ROOM fell silent as Leona sauntered in the slightly ajar door. It was clear that her presence had changed the energy in the room. And it was also very clear that she couldn't have cared less.

"Madam Mayor," said Headley, who was the first to find his manners and greet her formally. Ogden had nodded his head in her direction as well. I was tempted to call her by her first name but opted for a less familiar address instead: "Mayor."

"Guys, we're in a private home in a private space. There's no need for all these formalities. Each of us knew each other long before I took office." She scanned the room, but there weren't any takers. No one was interested in playing best friends with Ms. Leona Grant.

So, when her eyes came to rest on me, I moved from where I was standing by the window and started making my way towards the small mini bar across the room.

"Can I get anyone another drink?" I asked.

"None for me, I've got to drive back tonight," Headley replied.

"Same." Ogden had been nursing his own drink for too long anyways. And he was a notorious light weight.

"I'll take my usual, Noah. You know what I like," Leona said as she lightly touched the back of my neck with her finger. That was it. I was done playing nice with this woman.

"Leona, I need to talk to you outside." And before she could even reply, I had already returned my glass to the counter and was heading out the door.

Avoiding the hallway that led to where Verity and the other ladies were still gathered, I made a beeline straight for the front porch.

"Noah…" Tabitha was in the midst of putting out her cigarette when she saw me walk out with Leona directly behind me, so she didn't finish her sentence. She instead turned and called the girls over out of the rocking chairs and quietly headed inside. But not before giving the cold shoulder to Leona.

"I swear that woman never liked me," Leona said once the door closed behind them.

"Don't make this about Tabitha."

"So, what should I make this about? You? Verity?" She leaned up against the porch railing and smoothed the side of her dress with her hands.

"Leona, why the hell are you even here? And don't say that you were invited because we all know that is nowhere near the truth."

"I'm sure I don't know what you mean," she feigned ignorance.

"Dammit Leona. Verity is none of your concern. I am none of your concern. So why don't you just call it a night. You look ridiculous saying all those things to try and make a problem where there isn't one."

"Oh, come on, she would've eventually found out that we were engaged anyways," she said.

"Yes, from me. Not from you."

"Noah, what's the big deal?"

"You really can't see it at all, can you? You will never ever change."

I was completely done with this conversation as there was no getting through to her. But when I had already turned around and was headed back through the door, I felt her grab my arm. I wasn't quick enough, and frankly speaking, I wasn't expecting her to kiss me. And that's what she did.

I immediately pushed her away from me and wiped my mouth with the back of my hand.

"Oh fuck! Excuse me," said Megan as she hurriedly backed up the way she'd just come and practically ran away from us.

"Get the fuck out," I said as I tried to remove the rest of her red lipstick from my mouth.

She looked at me and simply shook her head before

stepping down the porch and heading over to the waiting SUV. I'd never been so happy to see the taillights of a vehicle moving away from me down my driveway.

Once inside, I made a quick detour to the bathroom to add some soap to the lipstick-removal process.

***

"But why aren't you staying here with me tonight?"

"Because I just sprung up to surprise you little cousin and I'm not going to burden you and your host by assuming space in his home just because I decided to come see you on a whim," Sheree was sitting on the edge of my bed. "Besides, you and Noah need your privacy."

I was about to respond when there was a knock at the door.

"I brought a fresh set of towels for Sheree," Noah offered a set of still-warm white, fluffy towels. I took them from his outstretched hands.

"She's not staying," I replied dryly.

"Now Sheree, we already spoke about this at dinner. There's no way that I'm going to let you stay in that matchbox those two are calling an Airbnb. Cole and Booker don't know anything about running a business. You'll stay with us, of course.

You're Vee's family and that settles it," said Noah. It was obvious he wasn't taking no for an answer, and no sooner had he dropped off the towels than he'd also returned minutes later with Sheree's suitcase. "There, now if you ladies need anything at all I'm just next door."

Closing the door slightly, I walked with him into the hallway. "Thank you for tonight and for letting my cousin stay."

"Of course," he paused before speaking. "Verity, we need to talk about what Leona said…"

But placing my fingers on his lips I simply shook my head. "Not tonight, okay."

He placed his arms around my waist and lowered his forehead against my own. His breath smelled faintly of tobacco and scotch. When I thought he was going to let me go, he only tightened his hold, squeezing me to his chest, his lips just above mine.

"Okay but promise me that you'll hear me out. No letting your mind run wild."

"Promise." I delivered a light peck to his cheek and tried to move away, but he pulled me back towards him roughly and pressed his mouth on my own. His lips parted and he pushed at the crease with his tongue before inserting it into my mouth. Everything in me wanted to return that kiss, and so I encircled his neck with my arms and pushed up on my tiptoes for the kiss to deepen.

When we finally broke apart, we were both trying to steady our breathing without success. I stepped back into the room and pressed my back up against the door to close it.

I was thankful that Sheree seemed to have gone into the bathroom and didn't see my chest heaving. Placing my fingers to my lips, I could still feel his warmth and taste him.

"You're in love with that man," Sheree said, walking back into the room in her trademark pink fluffy headwrap and a towel wrapped around her body. "And don't deny it."

I started removing my clothes to throw on a pajama. Sleeping in a negligée next to Sheree wasn't appealing, so I opened the armoire to grab another set of Noah's top and bottoms to sleep in.

"Is that what you came all the way here to say? And I'm so happy to see you, but why are you here?" I turned towards her retreating frame going into the ensuite.

"Auntie said you were sick, and she was worried. And oh yeah, we both agreed that you're in love."

"Will you please stop telling me what I am? I can't believe you two."

I could hear the water running so I knew she'd jumped into the shower. I finished getting undressed. Later, Sheree emerged from the ensuite in her towel and had already begun to brush her hair into a wrap style.

"Oooh please, please do mine too." I couldn't do a proper

wrap to save my life. My curls always wanted to be the main event, so I could never get my strands to lie flat enough.

Sheree stopped with her hair half wrapped and no hairpins in it, so her long dark locks immediately fell to her shoulders. And then walking over to me, she began using the Denman brush in my hair. I loved the way the pointy bristles felt against my scalp. It reminded me of when she used to braid my hair as a kid.

"Whose is this?" She said pinching a piece of the T-shirt I had on as I got comfortable sitting on the floor while she sat on the bed above me. It was clear that she was trying to draw some connection between my feelings for Noah and me wearing his clothes.

"Whatever, Sheree."

"Why are you so hard-headed? That man clearly feels the same way about you."

"What are you even talking about? And what were you two talking about at dinner?"

"What else? You." She pulled a clump of my hair to the side and angled my head so that I had to look up into her face. "Why are you fighting this?"

"Because what I'm feeling scares me. It's intense. And I don't trust myself to make the right choice."

"Noah isn't Chris, Verity. Not by a long shot. Noah is sincere and clearly invested. Chris didn't have an honest bone in his entire body."

At the mention of my ex-boyfriend, I felt my insides tense up. I hadn't let that pain resurface since my arrival in Dènaud, and it was the greatest peace I'd felt in a long time. And even though Chris had written a chapter in my life's book more than three years ago, it was still a painful one. He was one of my professors in whom I'd placed a lot of my trust, but it turned out I wasn't the only student he was sleeping with and making ridiculous promises to. Coupled with my dad's illness, the demise of that relationship had nearly pushed me to my breaking point.

"You're definitely a supporter of his. Damn, you just met him," I said.

"Bitch, I'm here, in the flesh! And you know I don't do small planes. I love you and I'm your supporter," she said, shaking her hand with a handful of my hair, once again.

"Ouch. Why is your love so painful?"

"Sometimes it just is. But that doesn't mean you can just block it out, Verity."

I leaned my head against one of her thighs and took a deep breath. "I know. I just don't know if my heart is ready for that kind of trip again."

"Don't miss out on something great because of one hurt. Noah isn't your past." And then, leaning over my head and shoulders, she enveloped me inside of her arms.

VERITY

"ERICKA, I THINK I'VE FOUND SOMETHING."

"Your face is so serious. Do we need to bring the whole committee together for this? And what about Megan and Adrian, do they know?"

"Not yet, I wanted to be certain first."

"You're making me nervous. What's going on, Verity?"

I moved a little closer to my laptop screen; I'd chosen to arrange a video call with my thesis advisor this morning and was taking the call in my room for some privacy.

"There's an anomaly within the archives that we reviewed. It's more like a discrepancy. The digital version of the municipal regulations and codes governing elections states that the incumbent's next of kin can be installed as mayor if he or she dies during the election process where that candidate has won but hasn't yet been inaugurated."

"Okay, I follow so far."

"But the archived files contain a completely different process. If an incumbent or other candidate becomes incapacitated in any number of enumerated ways, one of which is death, and wins, but isn't inaugurated, then the runner-up becomes the new mayor."

"It must be an oversight, right?"

"I thought so, at first, but the digital regs and codes

haven't yet been ratified. And I've reviewed the minutes and the audio of the council meetings—there just isn't any record of the change being agreed to."

I could see Ericka's mind spinning a mile a minute through the screen. That's what she did when she was hit with a challenge, and we'd had many along our journey together as advisor and advisee. But this was by far the biggest. If what I had uncovered was correct, then Mayor Grant should never have assumed the role of mayor when her father died. And the runner-up should've been the victor coming out of that election.

"Ericka? What do I do?"

"Give me a minute to think," her voice was serious.

"I mean, this could have a ripple effect that could undermine all the works she's performed from that office since her inauguration and possibly jeopardize any upcoming projects too. And if it was done intentionally, well…"

"Verity, I need you to do something for me."

"Oh my God, the pipeline," I almost whispered.

Dènaud was a town of varying degrees of contradictions. On the one hand, prior administrations had gone out of their way to ensure amity between its townspeople and the surrounding First Nations community. It was a reflective model that was a mirror to other communities nationwide in terms of restoring a mutual setting of respect and partnership.

Not only did the communities share a water source, but

they also co-inhabited a space that was earmarked for installation of a natural gas pipeline that would increase the nation's output by nearly thirty percent. It meant billions of dollars in revenue and countless number of jobs.

But the First Nations community was against the installation of the pipeline, and it'd caused a rift during the tenure of Leona's father that had carried through during her term in office. The pipeline had been a sidenote to the larger issue of electoral system research, which was my thesis focus, but it was still incredibly impactful.

"Verity!"

"Yes."

"Take a deep breath and calm down. Now I need you to keep this to yourself. I mean it, not even Megan or Adrian. I need to make a few phone calls to some contacts that I trust in the energy sector and possibly even the prime minister's office. This could have implications right up to the top. So we need to keep this between the both of us for a while. Okay?"

I trusted Ericka. She'd been my fiercest defender when the university wanted to disenroll me after I took an extended leave of absence from my coursework following the death of my father. And she'd fought hard to ensure that I secured enough funding to even be able to be here. Nothing within this project would've been possible without her support and advocacy. So, if she told me to wait, then that's just what I was going to do.

"Of course. I'll wait to hear back from you."

"It's going to be all right," she said.

"Promise?"

But I saw the uncertainty reflected on hear face. The only thing that I knew for sure was that no matter the outcome, Mayor Grant was going to have yet another reason to dislike me.

AFTER MY CALL with Ericka, I headed downstairs to join the others for breakfast, which was nothing less than downright awkward. Megan had been the life of the party last night, but for some reason she was completely silent at the table this morning. I gave her a few questioning glances and she pretty much just ignored my efforts to engage. *Very weird.*

Adrian had disappeared soon after the mayor left last night, and she'd left without saying goodbye to anyone I might add. But seriously, that last part was probably for the best. Especially given the information I was currently sitting on.

She'd made such a point about "being invited" and inserting herself into our dinner and the conversations, it seemed a little strange that she'd just up and leave without a single word to anyone. Or perhaps she had spoken to someone. That someone was just not me or any of the other women last night. *Did she speak with Noah last night? Was he keeping it a secret? Were there more secrets other than the fact that they'd been engaged?*

I felt sort of guilty myself that I had this potentially very damaging information about a place that he called home and I had to keep it a secret. At least for the time being. But I'd reasoned that somehow what I was keeping from him and what he had kept from me wasn't the same thing. And it hadn't affected the way I acted towards him. *Or had it?*

Noah, on the other hand... he'd been a little more dominating towards the end of the night, especially with that kiss out in the open, in the hallway. I mean it wasn't exactly as if we were sneaking around like a couple of teenagers or anything, but I could feel the pull towards his room after he'd left my toe's curling with how he'd possessed my mouth with his.

"Earth to Verity. Where'd you go?" Sheree had poked me in my side to get my attention.

Grabbing myself I tried to smile. "It's all good. Just thinking." To that response, Noah looked over at me with concern on his face and then pulled my hand into his lap.

"Hey, you promised," he said shaking his head slowly.

I patted his hand reassuringly and then went back to eating. Looking across at Megan, I tried smiling in order to make her do the same, but she was still avoiding my eyes.

"Did you have a good time last night, Megan? Your quiche was a hit." I smiled at her again.

"Yeah, it was great. I think I'm finished." And when she rose from the table without another word, I wasn't surprised to see Booker get up too and follow her out of the room.

"What's going on? Did something happen?" I looked to

Noah first, but he simply shrugged his shoulders.

"Long night, I guess," he offered.

But I wasn't satisfied with that. I made a mental note to go and talk with her later.

***

Noah was determined to show Sheree absolutely everything that Dènaud had to offer, so for the rest of the day we were treated to a whirlwind tour of the town and surrounding area. Although, we didn't go back to the special place only he and I had visited. Which was fine by me as I wanted to keep that memory to ourselves.

At one of the final stops, we ran into a couple of the police officers who we'd met the night that some men had broken into Clarence House. Noah introduced them quickly to Sheree before one of them asked me how I was doing "after everything that happened." I tried to brush it off in front of Sheree before Noah escorted us the short distance back to his truck before returning to have a few more words with them.

"Verity, why is your man talking to those police officers? And what did that cop mean when he asked how you were doing? I'm missing something." Sheree sounded concerned but a bit pissed off as well.

"It's nothing really. There was a little incident not too

long ago, and he was probably just being kind by asking. You know it's a really small town," I said, but I could already tell that she wasn't buying it.

"Girl, if you don't start talking, I'm gonna hit my speed dial button and call your mother," she threatened with a look on her face that said she would do just that.

"All right. Fine." So I told her everything, staying a little light on the details and avoiding the attempted burglary at Clarence House. Adrian no longer wore the scars, so there was no need to say anything further about it.

"I smell bullshit. There's still something you're not telling me."

But Noah was approaching the driver's side door, and I looked at her with a face that pleaded with her to drop it for right now. Surprisingly, she didn't push any further. *Man, everyone is acting out of character today.* But when she pinched me on my hip by reaching her arm through the center opening, right before Noah could see us through the window, I knew that there was no way she'd be dropping it that easy.

***

Sheree was headed back home this morning as she'd taken only a couple of days off work to make this trip. We'd wanted to visit the next town over for dinner last night, but I

198

think the sightseeing coupled with the amount of travel Sheree had done in such a short time had drained her. She was out like a light, snoring softly before I crawled into bed to go to sleep.

No matter what, though, I was gonna wake her ass up in thirty minutes because I needed to spend time with my cousin before she left later. *And she could damn well sleep on the plane.*

Noah had some business to attend to in the bunkhouse, so Sheree went upstairs while I stayed outside to admire the view from the front porch while he headed off in that direction.

A dark SUV pulled up the driveway just as I was making my way inside. Stopping to turn, I wasn't really in the mood to have any type of interaction with Mayor Grant, but she would've already seen me at the door. And I wasn't so mannerless that I could pretend I didn't see her and just walk inside. So I waited until the vehicle came to a complete stop and the door opened. But the person I was expecting wasn't the person that stepped out of the vehicle.

"Were you waiting for me? That's sweet."

"Adrian. You're riding in style these days," I said.

"It's nothing. Just an early morning meeting."

"Isn't that the mayor's SUV?"

"Are you jealous?"

"No, ride around anyway you want, Adrian," I said, hoping he got the double entendre. My eyes hadn't missed the fact that he was wearing the same clothes he had on last night.

I turned to enter the house, but his hand caught mine before I could finish getting through the door.

"It's not like we both aren't having a little bit of fun on the side while we're here."

I quickly pulled my hand out of his. "I don't know what you're doing during your time here, nor do I want to know."

I started walking down the hallway towards the kitchen.

"Verity. Verity!" Adrian called from behind me. Thankfully he didn't grab me again.

But I'd been so focused on getting to the kitchen that I hadn't realized how closely he'd been following me. When I stopped short, he collided into my back and then brought his hands to my waist to stop me from being propelled forward.

Just then the door off the kitchen opened.

"What the fuck is going on?" Noah practically shouted.

And before I could stop him, Noah had a handful of Adrian's shirt and pushed him back with such force that I fell to the ground. "Ahhhh!" I couldn't help the outburst; the floor was cold and hard.

"Verity," Noah said, forgetting about Adrian and crouching down beside me.

But the position left him vulnerable, and Adrian flew towards him, knocking him to the ground. My eyes widened in disbelief as the two of them rolled around, each struggling to get the upper hand. But just as Adrian was getting ready to throw the first punch, a glass broke somewhere behind us.

"Stop it! The both of you, just fucking stop it now!" screamed Megan. Everyone stopped to look over at her. She had a second glass dish poised over her head, ready to be thrown against the floor, if needed.

Both men straightened themselves up and moved a reasonable distance away from the other. Noah was at my side in an instant, even though I'd managed to help myself up in the commotion. And at that moment, Sheree walked into the kitchen rubbing her eyes, and in her bare feet, before she stopped short looking down at the broken glass.

"Okay. Seems like I might've missed something," said Sheree with all sincerity. When no one spoke, she adopted her auntie voice. "Um, hello, seriously start talking. Anyone."

"I saw Noah kissing the mayor last night," Megan blurted out, like a painful secret she'd been keeping for a long time.

All eyes immediately went to Noah, and he was looking straight at me. I gave it a couple seconds to see if he'd have some type of explanation because I knew that Megan wouldn't lie about something like that.

But when he simply lowered his head, I had my answer. I didn't even need to look at anyone else's face. Adrian was probably laughing to himself, and Sheree was likely trying to figure out how she could fashion a shiv from the broken glass beneath her.

I, however, was done. *This carnival ride could continue without me.* Ignoring everyone, I walked past Sheree to the front door. I needed some fresh air, and the night air would do just fine.

"Vee," Noah said, sounding almost like he was wounded.

"Don't, Noah," I shouted, without even turning around.

I knew instinctively that Sheree's protectiveness would kick in and she wouldn't let him follow me.

I reached the bottom of the steps before the first tear fell.

I IMMEDIATELY wanted to go after her, but Sheree had convinced me that she needed some space to collect her thoughts. Sheree's her cousin—her family—and she knows her better than I do for now. So I listened to her. But I'd been waiting for over an hour and was getting more and more worried.

The summer months still meant longer days, and nightfall was hours away, but this wasn't ground that Verity was overly familiar with, and she was upset. If I'd seen her cry, I probably would've just ignored Sheree and ran after Verity.

God, I hope she's not somewhere crying.

"She's still not back?" Megan and Booker reappeared in the front room where I'd been held up since she left. Megan had come on her own to offer an apology for the way she'd blurted out her statement earlier, but she was still adamant about what she thought she saw. She was being protective of her friend. I could understand that.

I shook my head *no* in response.

"This is getting silly now. We should really go out there and bring her back," Booker said.

A part of me agreed with him. But what if she needed more time? It was my fault. I should've talked to Verity last night after everything happened. I could've told her about the kiss too. She deserved so much more than to be humiliated the following day.

I'd asked her to trust me and to make me promises, but I hadn't been honest with her. And added to that, I could kick myself for not seeing how manipulative Leona was being last night. I should've known what she was capable of.

Verity was gone. And I'd been a coward and a fool.

I wanted to see her. Hell, I *needed* to see her. Without saying a word to either Megan or Booker, I stood and shoved my hand through my hair as I placed my Stetson atop my head.

"I'll come…" began Megan, but thankfully Booker pulled back on Megan's arm, so the rest of her sentence just got swallowed up.

I gave him an appreciative look and headed outside to my truck. I drove around my property several times. Verity was on foot, so she couldn't have gotten very far. And she'd only ever explored beyond the fence line with me by her side, to my knowledge, so I didn't think she'd venture off into the forested areas alone.

But she was upset. But she wouldn't put herself at risk by going out there alone.

After calling Booker and Sheree separately for the third

time to find out if Verity had returned, and hearing the same answer, I knew I needed some help with the search.

Booker and Megan went into town to try some of the shops and restaurants where she liked to go sometimes, while Adrian and Cole drove in Cole's truck to the sites they'd used for research purposes, like the library. Sheree stayed at the house just in case she returned, and Tabitha offered to keep her company while we were out searching.

It was going to be dark in less than a couple of hours and Verity had been gone nearly an entire day now.

I'd put a call into Dan to give him a heads up that I might need some support from the department if we hadn't heard anything from her by nightfall. He tried to give me the standard "24-hour missing person" line, but he could tell rather quickly that I wasn't in the mood to entertain it, so he promised to send a squad car out to the house.

Here I was racing back to the house to make sure that I was the one to meet with the officers upon arrival. I didn't want to scare Sheree or the others. I just wanted to take certain steps and err on the side of caution rather than waiting.

But pulling up the driveway, I realized that I was already too late. Tabitha and Sheree were both on the front porch, the latter with her hand over her mouth as the officers, one male and one female, spoke to her. I didn't know either of them.

The female officer had her hand on Sheree's shoulder as I

was began walking up to them.

Dammit, why were their car lights still flashing? Why were they even on in the first damn place?

"Mr. Sawyer, I'm Officer Menon and this is my partner, Officer Griffin."

I'd tipped my hat to both, but still wore an expression of confusion on my face.

"We understand that you filed a missing person's report for one Ms. Verity Reynolds earlier today?"

I heard Sheree exhale sharply behind him.

"I didn't file a report, I simply made a call to Dan Gregoire at the precinct to suggest that we might need some help to find her if she wasn't back by nightfall," I answered.

"Were you the last person to see Ms. Reynolds today?" Officer Griffin paused her movement on Sheree's shoulder briefly as she looked at me.

"We all were. She was here this morning and then she was upset and left sometime after breakfast," I said.

"But then you left the house a short time later to look for her and she hasn't been seen since?" Officer Menon chimed in.

I looked first at Sheree who had clearly been crying and then back to the officers. Something felt odd about their questioning.

"I've been out searching for her, yes. But no, I haven't seen her. I thought she'd be back by now."

Now Tabitha was rubbing Sheree's back who had begun to cry once again.

"And you're certain you haven't had any type of contact with her over the last few hours?" Officer Menon continued to press.

"I'm sorry, but what is going on?" There was a still calm that sent a chill up my back. And we were in the middle of a heatwave. "Tabitha?" I asked. She too had begun to shed tears.

"They found some of her clothes, and it looks like there was a struggle," Tabitha blurted out before Sheree started to fall towards the floor.

On instinct, I ran towards Sheree and picked her up before placing her into one of the rocking chairs. She'd quickly regained her wits and placed both of her hands on my arms to brace herself. Then, looking into my eyes, she could barely get the words out.

"Find her," she said with a voice so hoarse it sounded as if she'd been screaming. I gave her a reassuring squeeze before pulling myself upright to turn my attention back to the officers.

"Tell me everything you know," I demanded.

"I'm sorry, Mr. Sawyer, but we can't do that." Officer Menon sounded as if he was truly apologetic.

"What the hell are you saying, man? Verity is out there somewhere, and I've just heard that she may be hurt badly, but you don't want to say anything?" I said struggling to contain myself.

I started to approach the officer standing at the bottom of the steps, but the female officer got to me first and placed her hand into my chest. I just looked at her.

"I know that you're upset right now, but trust me, this isn't the way to go about things," she added.

"Noah, please," said Tabitha, the voice of reason.

I didn't have a rational thought in my head, especially not after hearing that Verity might be injured. But when I felt Sheree squeeze my hand, I knew that I needed to calm down and focus.

"Fine. What can you tell us?" I pinned my gaze to the male officer.

"As I explained prior to your arrival, there were some articles of clothing that were found, which we now have a positive identification on," Officer Menon said, looking at Sheree who was still somewhat slumped over the arm of rocking chair. "And yes, there appears to have been some sort of a struggle given the condition of the clothing; and there was some blood in the area where the clothing was found."

"Oh my God," Adrian said as he approached with Cole. Megan and Booker weren't too far behind. In all the commotion, I hadn't noticed their vehicles pull up.

"You mentioned that she may have been upset when she was last seen earlier this morning?" Officer Griffin took over.

"Uh, yes. She was upset. She may have been crying," I

answered, barely a whisper.

"Do you have any idea what she was upset about, Mr. Sawyer?" My head was becoming too muddled to recognize which officer had asked the question.

"She found out he was cheating on her," Adrian offered.

It couldn't be helped what happened next. Before I could think, I descended the steps and punched Adrian square in the jaw. Watching him fall to the ground was the most satisfying moment amidst all the chaos. Adrian, to his credit, got back up on his feet quickly and was poised to retaliate.

"Just what the hell is going on here?"

We both stopped to turn towards the speaker.

"Dad?" I said, almost breathless.

"Oh my goodness! When did the both of you get back into town," Tabitha exclaimed, rushing towards my mother.

I was feeling a bit disorientated given the circumstances with Verity missing and my parents' sudden appearance.

"Noah, what's gotten into you?" My mother was already walking towards me with her hands reaching for the sides of my face.

"Son?" I heard my dad say.

"Dad, Mom, there's not a lot of time to explain. But you know the students that were staying with us during the summer, well one of them has gone missing. I just got here, so I know just about as much as you do," I said hurriedly, after pointing out

Adrian and then to Megan.

"Well, if these are our guests, then why did you hit him?" my father asked.

No one responded to that question.

"Perhaps we should take this discussion inside?" said Officer Griffin.

"I'm not gonna just stay here and do nothing while Verity is out there alone and probably beaten up or god-only-knows what," I said to no one in particular as I started towards my truck.

"Mr. Sawyer, as I told you already, we've made certain discoveries and we're just at the beginning of our investigation. It does no one any good for you to go out there and possibly interfere. I promise you that we're doing our very best to find her," she continued.

"Noah let's do as the officer says and try to get to the bottom of this." My father had his hand on my shoulder at that point.

Somewhere deep down, I knew he was right, but it didn't make it any less difficult to hear.

I looked over at my truck, parked idly at the top of the driveway. I was somewhat blocked in anyways, and I'd been looking for her for hours on my own without any success.

Turning back towards the house, I reluctantly followed the others inside.

NOAH

BY NIGHTFALL, the house had been taken over by the local police, and there were rumblings about enlisting the help of the RCMP detachment just off the reservation as well as the First Nations police force.

I don't really remember when the call was finally made, but as I watched Chief Miller giving orders to the additional officers who had arrived within the last hour, I overheard him mention that he was awaiting word from the First Nations police chief.

There was a makeshift command center outfitted in my living room. Megan and Tabitha had commandeered the kitchen and were serving drinks and cold sandwiches to those gathered, including a few members of the community who had volunteered to search at first light but had stopped by to get their marching orders for the morning.

Adrian had left with my cousins to get more supplies from the town grocer who'd graciously stayed open late to accommodate a very rushed request, so we'd be able to keep all the volunteers fed throughout the process the following day.

I'd wanted to put my foot down and keep Callie from coming over, but our parents had returned unannounced and, besides, she considered Verity a friend, so there was no stopping her. She'd fallen in step with everyone else though and even my parents were helping by making up the extra rooms just in case we needed to house first responders or volunteers.

This community came together in a crisis, and I felt my heart expanding at the knowledge that they all cared as if Verity were one of their own.

"Noah, do you want a coffee? Or something to eat?" Tabitha asked, but I could barely muster a headshake.

"You've got to eat something, dear. You'll be no good to Verity if you don't take care of yourself," she added while placing a reassuring hand on my shoulder.

I knew she was right, but I just couldn't bring myself to consume anything or think of anything other than bringing Verity home. The guilt I felt at having let her leave in the first place was gnawing a pit in my stomach.

"She's right, you know son," my mother chimed in. *Where had she just come from?* I almost couldn't handle the look of concern on her face on top of everything else.

"I know, Mom. I know," I reassured her. But she didn't look convinced.

"Chief Miller knows what he's doing, Noah. They will find her—and soon."

I didn't share her confidence in our chief. I was about to provide Tabitha and my mother another soft brush off, when I noticed that Chief Miller and some First Nations' police officers having an animated conversation by the front door. It appeared as if Miller was trying to redirect the officers back out of the house to take the conversation to the front porch—that put my feet in action as I walked briskly towards them.

"What's going on Bryan?" I'd dispensed with the formalities. He was in my house potentially discussing details about a woman who deeply mattered to me. Hell, she was the woman I loved. I didn't have time to let the realization of that self-confession affect me. "Tell me what's happened," I asked in a way that bordered on a demand.

"Noah, I need you to let us do our job now," he tried to disengage me from the conversation, but it was too late for that.

"Dammit, Bryan!" I choked out the words. I didn't care who heard me or what the repercussions would be.

"Mr. Sawyer, we think we may have found her," said the officer closest to Miller, but not without a hint of annoyance in his voice at having been muzzled in the first place. "We've received a garbled SOS message from an area just on the outskirts of the reservation. There's no cell service or any other utilities out there. It's pretty much wilderness. But the description provided of the injured party matches the description we have for one Ms. Verity Reynolds."

He'd finished speaking, but I was already grabbing my hat, pushing my way through the door. "Address?" I said gruffly.

"Noah, listen to me. It's not a place that we can get to easily." Bryan looked as impatient as I did, but most likely for a different reason. "There's been some unrest in that area lately because of the work to commence on the pipeline. And the area has been filled with protestors setting various booby traps and such," he tried to continue but was interrupted by the First Nations' chief of police who had just joined the conversation.

"Allegedly, chief. I know you meant to qualify your accusations and not cast dispersions on certain citizens simply exercising their inalienable right to peacefully protest." He'd meant it to sound like a question but also a condemnation of Bryan's words.

I couldn't have cared less in the moment. "I need to know where the fuck she is! Now!" I'd lost it.

"You can follow me out there. I'm Chief Rainwater," he said and offered me his hand.

I looked at it before shaking his hand briefly. "Under different circumstances, chief, as you can imagine, but at the moment I really need to get to Verity."

"Of course," he replied and began to move.

"I'm coming with you." I heard from somewhere at the end of the hallway, and then I saw a burst of curly black hair speed by me. I knew that diminutive size matched with the stern voice. She wasn't asking.

"Fine, Sheree, but I'm unsure of what state we'll find her in," I said. I'd been raised on a ranch and knew I needed to prepare her for whatever may come.

"Fuck that. I'm going" was her only reply.

"Well, okay." Chief Rainwater headed out first and left with one of the other First Nations' officers.

I sprinted with Sheree close on my heels towards my own truck, and I could see when we pulled off down the driveway that Chief Miller was driving behind me with another squad car tailing him. It seemed like a lot of firepower for an excursion to this remote area, where clearly someone already had the wherewithal to radio for help. It was unlikely that Verity was in any immediate danger, although I didn't yet know her condition.

There was something else at play here, though. I looked over at Sheree with her steely determined glare out the front windshield.

What had I gotten the woman I loved, and her family member, involved in? And why had the Miller's truck and the rear squad car behind me suddenly turned on their flashing lights?

VERITY

MY THROAT was so sore. I didn't—or rather couldn't—open my eyes, and I just had this feeling that with every swallow I was doing irreparable damage to my throat.

I felt hot, practically sweating. My body had been wrapped up in some type of thick blanket, and I was lying down on my back. At least I could feel that. I tried moving around a bit to see if I could loosen the tightness of the wrap around my arms.

"You're waking up. That's good." The voice sounded like a man and didn't sound threatening, but it was still an unknown sound attached to a stranger, so my body tensed up.

As I tried to put some distance between myself and whoever's voice that was, I recognized that my movements were extremely limited by whatever was encasing my body. *Was I tied up somehow?*

"You are safe here. No one is going to hurt you." At least this person sounded convinced of what they were saying.

I, on the other hand, needed to come up with a plan. My mind was running wild as I tried to determine the last thing I could remember. There'd been that terrible revelation by Megan in the kitchen, and then I'd stormed out. Yes, I'd walked off down the driveway and started towards the main road before everything went dark. *What happened to me after that?* I was drawing a blank.

"Please," I managed to push out of my mouth. The resulting pain was excruciating. I couldn't even use my hands to rub my throat, although I doubt that would've given me any relief. Then, instead of my own fingers, I felt someone else's rubbing a warm salve onto my throat. My initial reaction was to struggle against the bonds that were my blanket, but I couldn't deny that the instant that mixture hit my skin, relief washed over me.

After a brief period, the pain almost completely dissipated, and I could feel the exact moment when I knew that it would be safe to talk again. I had no such confidence in my eyes though, and so they remained closed.

"Where am I?"

"You're at my place. I live here, most of the time anyways," he offered with a slight chuckle. *How could he think to be funny under these circumstances?*

"Why?" I didn't want to push my voice too hard, so I limited my words.

"I found you near the riverbank. You looked like you were in some trouble, so I brought you back here."

"How did I get there?" I'd likely only have a couple more words left in me before needing to rest my voice.

"I'm not certain. It's not as if this place were easy to find. But I suspect you were brought here. And given the state you were in, I think you were placed where you were on purpose."

He stopped talking completely at that last statement. I felt a sudden chill set in right down to my bones, even in this hot box of a cocoon I was in. I couldn't trust my eyes at this point and was just barely able to rely on my voice, but my ears didn't deceive me. *Those were sirens I heard.*

There was some swift movement by the individual who had been at my side only moments ago. And when I felt the cool night air rush into the space, I pushed my face further away from the blanket's edge to absorb as much of it as I could and to make sure that I was seen by whichever first responder was about to come through that door.

But it wasn't a first responder.

"Verity."

Noah.

AS SOON AS we started making winding turns along an unpaved road through a darkened area, I had a sense of where Chief Rainwater was leading us. I hadn't been out this way since I was a child. During the time when my grandparents had been around, the communities around Dènaud were very amiable with each other, including many families on the reservation.

There was one family that we used to visit; the father was a good friend of my grandfather's. I remember many fishing trips with them and their grandchild, a boy who I became fast friends with. We were almost joint at the hip during our times together.

We pulled to a stop outside of what looked like a cabin with a flat roof and a smokestack that emitted from it a dark cloud that I could make out even in the dark. Climbing out of the cab, we were instantly hit with the smell of something burning that wasn't unpleasant, but very strong.

The area was still thickly overgrown with brush and trees like I'd remembered. To an unfamiliar eye, no changes would be detected. But I could tell that there were some scant efforts at modernization: a septic tank just off to the side of the structure and a well out front with what looked like a battery-powered pulley.

The other vehicles had all arrived and people began to exit them and make their way towards where we were standing out front. No weapons were drawn, and there was no hint that there was a need to be on alert for impending danger.

This wasn't a rescue; it was a retrieval.

Verity wasn't in any additional danger, but I was still desperate to know what condition she was in.

As much as I wanted to charge headfirst into the cabin if Verity was inside, I was trying to keep my calm for her sake and for Sheree who stood wide-eyed by my side. It didn't take but a moment for Chief Rainwater to begin knocking gently on the front door of the cabin.

I was racking my brain to remember the name of the boy who had befriended me way back then. Perhaps he still lived in the area.

"Samson," Chief Rainwater said and immediately all my childhood memories of this place came flooding back.

"Chief, she's inside," the tall figure who appeared at the door said. His body nearly filled the entire doorframe. We were about the same height and build. When he made eye contact with me, I knew that there was a glimmer of recognition there, too.

"It's been a very long time," he said and offered his hand to me as I walked to him.

"Very long. This is Sheree, Verity's cousin." Sheree didn't

say much of anything as her eyes were already searching beyond us to where her cousin lay just hidden from our direct line of sight.

"Come in. She's still hurting, but it'll be good for her to know that you're here," Samson said, ushering us both in.

The place wasn't big enough for everyone, so I was happy when Samson turned the door after saying a few words to the others to remain outside.

I recognized the covering that Verity was in. Made of natural fibers, it was a blanket purported to have healing capabilities. She was wrapped up pretty snug so that only her head and a part of her neck were visible, but I could tell that she'd been well looked after.

Sheree knelt alongside her on the other side of the pallet she was on. "Verity," she whispered.

I knew she could hear us and felt our presence then as tears started to escape the bandaging around her eyes and began streaming down the sides of her face.

I looked at Samson quizzically for an explanation about the bandages around her eyes, but he simply lowered his head, and without words I knew that I needed to speak with him offline about it. Verity didn't know yet about whatever condition her eyes were in.

Sheree saw the look as well and simply pressed a kiss into the side of her face. Verity's head gravitated towards her cousin as their skin connected.

When she turned to my direction it was as if she was expectantly waiting for me to say or do something. Words were failing me. There was so much that needed to be said, but seeing her laying there injured was breaking me. So I simply reached out a finger and traced her jawline.

I didn't expect it, but she turned slightly as I neared her mouth and let her lips graze the tip of my fingers.

Now the tears were my own.

***

It was too late that night to get an ambulance up to the area, so Sheree and I spent the night in the cabin thanks to Samson's hospitality. There wasn't a chance in hell that I would leave without Verity anyway and Samson understood that.

The following morning, after a night to rest and recover, we were finally able to transfer Verity back to Clarence House. Other than some bruises and a nasty gash to her forearm, she had no other injuries that would warrant a trip to the hospital. Our town doctor had made a special house call and confirmed that she could be treated at home.

Samson had done a wonderful job with the preparatory work to immediately treat her. Her wound wasn't infected. Her eyesight would return slowly according to Dr. Orelle. The loss of sight didn't have a direct physical cause, so he concluded that it may be due in part to the trauma she'd experienced. He referred us to a specialist at a hospital in Saskatoon who occasionally had office hours in Wakepa Lake. So as soon as she was well enough, I'd ask Headley to take us.

Until then, she'd keep the bandages on so as not to strain her eyesight too much.

"You need to get some sleep, my darling boy," my mother said as she brought in a change of flowers to Verity's bedside. "She's been fast asleep for hours, and she won't be stirring anytime soon. Go and at least take a shower," she said.

"Do you think the medication dosage is too high? Why hasn't she woken up since we've been back?"

"I put up my nursing uniform a long time ago, sweetheart, but if Dr. Orelle prescribed it, then I'm certain it's fine. Besides, she wouldn't have been able to make that long trip back with you all in the truck without some painkillers. Just let her get some rest," she answered.

When I still hadn't moved, she added, "I'll sit with her while you shower and get something quick to eat. I promise to come get you as soon as anything changes."

Reluctantly I rose and headed out the door. With one last look at Verity, I made quick work of getting into my room and out of my clothing to take a shower.

Upon my return, I noted that Sheree had taken up at her

bedside. My mother returned a short time later with a sausage, cheese, and egg biscuit in her hands. Unwrapping the paper encasing, she handed it over to me with a look that warned that she wasn't kidding around. I took a bite, but it tasted like ash in my mouth. I finished it for her sake and for my own. I was running on fumes.

Sheree started speaking to me the moment my mother stepped back out of the room.

"I have to tell my aunt what's been going on. She's been calling me since last night. I can't hide it from her any longer."

"That's understandable," I muttered in response.

"I also think that we should start making plans to bring Verity back home with me."

I sat up straight with that statement. I could feel every muscle tighten. *There was no way I was letting Verity go.*

"Perhaps we should talk about this another time," I said as I walked over to the windowsill and leaned against it.

She took the hint and dropped it.

***

Later that afternoon, I spoke with the couple of officers who'd stopped by to check on Verity's progress. They didn't have any additional information about the circumstances surrounding Verity's disappearance and injuries, but at least they were staying engaged. I wondered if that was Bryan's doing or at someone else's insistence.

As the squad car pulled away, I saw another vehicle approaching. When the jeep was only a few yards out, I could make out Samson's figure.

"Hello, I wanted to check on my patient and see how the rest of you were doing," he said, walking towards me with a box in his hand.

"She's recovering. Listen, I wanted to thank you again for all your help. If it wasn't for you finding her, I don't know what would've happened." But the both of us knew that I understood what would've happened with long-term exposure to the elements.

Samson nodded. "I've brought some herbs and vegetables from my garden. Thought maybe they could be put to good use." I took the box from him and offered a smile.

"Do you want to come in? She hasn't woken up yet, but I'm sure she'd be grateful if you'd stay a while."

"Sure, I'd like that."

I walked him through to the kitchen, expecting my mother to be in there, but she had probably brought something up for Sheree who was holding down the fort while I was out talking to the police.

My father had gone to the barn with Adrian and Megan. Despite what had occurred between me and Adrian, I was grateful that he'd offered to help. Although, these novices would need a little guidance on how to help out around here.

"If your mom keeps cooking like this, I'm never going to leave," said Sheree as she walked into the kitchen balancing a plate with a coffee mug on it. "Oh, hi…um, I mean hello again," she said.

I didn't miss the slight nervousness in her tone as she addressed Samson. *Hmm. Perhaps there was a way to stall her from leaving with Verity after all.* Either way, whether Sheree liked it or not, I was determined to make sure that Verity stayed right here in Dènaud. But I did really want Sheree to be on my side about it. Especially since Verity hadn't yet regained consciousness.

I excused myself and ducked upstairs to make sure that Verity wasn't alone. Those two could find something to talk about for a bit I was certain. Turning the doorhandle, I made my way to my usual corner of the room to check on the sleeping figure in the bed. But she wasn't in the bed.

"Verity?" I called out, unable to hide the panic in my voice.

Just then I heard the toilet flush and then running water. I rapped lightly on the closed door and jiggled the handle, but it was locked. *The door was locked.* I pulled on it with a little more force.

"Verity, open the door," I commanded. *What if she was in*

there and ended up falling? I continued pulling on the door handle as if I wanted to pull the door right off its hinges.

A positively pissed Verity threw open the door at that point as she struggled to balance herself against the doorframe.

"What the hell are you doing?"

Regardless of her anger, I reached for her and tried to put my arms around her waist to which she rebuffed the action and took a step further back into the bathroom. I was momentarily shocked at her appearance. She'd removed the bandages from around her eyes, and I could see the small cuts around her eyelids now. There was swelling just below her eyelids and the skin around her eyes was a shade darker now with a purplish hue.

"Sorry, it's me. I just got worried when I didn't see you in the bed. When did you wake up?"

"Just a few minutes ago. I had to go to the bathroom so badly," she said, trying once again to make her way past me into the bedroom.

This time when I tried to assist, she let me, bracing herself against my arm. But as soon as she felt the bed with her hand, she released her hold on me and climbed into the bed on her own.

"Oh my goodness, thank God you're awake!" Sheree rushed over to the other side of the bed and enveloped Verity into a hug, which Verity didn't hesitate to lean into.

I felt my heart pinch a little. I stood there awkwardly until

Verity finally addressed me: "Noah, could I talk to Sheree in private?"

I didn't want to even acknowledge what she'd just said. A big part of me wanted to just bend down, scoop her up and take her back to my own room like a caveman. But her waking up was a miracle. And it wasn't a completely unreasonable ask that she have some time alone with her cousin. I just wished that she hadn't been so cold towards me.

"Sure. I'll be right outside," I said.

"Actually, I left Samson downstairs in the kitchen," Sheree added.

I took the hint and turned to leave. This time I didn't turn to take a last look before closing the door.

It was too painful.

I KNEW he'd left the room. It was strange, but a piece of me went through that door when he'd gone. So I was sure that he was no longer in the room.

The bandages were removed, but I still couldn't see anything clearly when my eyes were open. Dr. Orelle assured me that the loss of sight was temporary, but I was still freaking out. In truth, I was freaking out about a lot of things.

I scooched down on the bed so that I could lie flat on my back. It didn't surprise me when I felt the bed shift downwards as Sheree laid down beside me.

"I don't know what I'm doing," I said.

I felt her fingers lightly touch the side of my face. "Does it hurt?" My guess from the positioning of her fingers below my eyes was that she was inquiring about them.

"Not really. Not anymore. Dr. Orelle says that I should regain my eyesight any day now. He said it's just shock." I was answering Sheree with more confidence than I felt.

"From ending up out there in the wild, and also maybe what happened between you and Noah?" Sheree was fishing. I could tell.

"Yes," I'd lied by omission. Noah was something I was struggling with, but there was also what I knew about the town's mayoral race and the cataclysmic impact of revealing that information.

I felt Sheree snuggle up next to me and hold me in her arms. She was smaller than me, so I'm sure we'd look like quite a sight with her entire body hugging my upper body. But I was beyond grateful for the warmth in that embrace. I let it seep into my every pore. I wanted to draw strength and rejuvenate myself from this.

"He loves you, Verity," she said, but I think that she felt my body tense, because she paused before continuing. "I mean it, he loves you in a way I've never seen a man love a woman. And he appears to me to be all in. You should've seen him yesterday when we got the news that you were hurt and in need of help."

"But what about the kiss?" I said, my voice trembling.

"Girl, fuck that bitch. I clocked her trifling ass from a mile away. Noah and I haven't discussed this, but I wouldn't be surprised if she tricked him somehow or just caught him off guard," Sheree said, her body moving around rapidly. She was an animated talker, particularly when she was passionate about something.

"Did she trick him into not telling me that they'd been engaged, Sheree?"

"That was fucked up. He should've told you first. Period," she said.

"See?" I exclaimed.

"See what? That your man has a past he didn't tell you about that doesn't directly affect you because he's no longer together with her?"

"Look, I'm not like you! I don't need to be married by some made up expiration date!" As soon as the words left my mouth, I knew I'd gone too far.

She tried to roll away from me to get off the bed, but I held on to her and wrapped my arms around her waist as I leaned my forehead into her back. "Shit, Sheree, I'm so sorry. I didn't mean to say it like that."

"But you did mean to say it?"

"No! You know what I mean. It's just that, I don't want to move forward with Noah if I still have unanswered questions," I concluded.

"Then ask him Verity," she practically yelled at me.

I could tell that she'd already forgiven me for the remark I'd made earlier, because if Sheree had wanted to really get up out of the bed, she would've kicked, scratched, and pulled my hair until I'd released her. Eye swelling and a bruised body be damned, Sheree didn't play.

Breaking the hold I had around her waist, she turned her body towards me in the bed. "Listen Verity, I'm so glad that you're awake and back with us. I was so terrified. And your mother has been calling me nonstop. I didn't know how much longer I'd be able to hold off on telling her. Your eyes…I mean if auntie saw you like this…" Sheree was rattling off sentence after sentence like her life depended on it. When she finally took a break, I decided to try to get a word in.

"Sheree, I need to tell you something."

"What's going on, Verity?" she asked, but I was still trying to find the words, so I remained silent a little while longer. "Oh my god, what now?"

I needed to have her full attention. This wasn't just about Noah and a kiss with his ex, it was much bigger than that.

"Okay, Verity, what is going on?"

I tried opening my eyes.

"Whoa, wait. You heard what Dr. Orelle said. Don't rush things."

But I'd taken my bandages off for a reason. When I was in the bathroom earlier, it was because I needed to empty my bladder but also because I had begun to be able to make out shapes slightly. It was all still very new and shaky, but not wanting to miss out on this opportunity to test it in front of Sheree, I was pushing myself just a little bit past where Dr. Orelle had said I should be at this stage.

As soon as the air hit my naked eye, they started to water. Nature's protection mechanism I was sure, but still a bit unnerving. My body was doing a lot of things that were catching me off guard. But she was also resilient and self-healing, so I wanted to trust her.

"Can you see me?" I heard Sheree ask as I began to blink rapidly.

"Somewhat," I answered. "You're sort of more like a darkish blob at the moment, actually," I added.

"Well, um thanks for that, I guess."

"No, you know what I meant."

But when I saw the blurred figure before me start to move up and down in spurts, I knew things were fine. Sheree was just laughing.

"This isn't funny you know," I threw a fake punch towards her, although with my lack of depth awareness, I was lucky that it didn't connect.

"Damn right, it's not funny. And seriously, when are we going to call your mother? Auntie is quite literally going to kill me when she finds out how much trouble you were in and that I didn't call her first thing. Come on, you know how she is. She already knows that something is up anyways, so might as well get it out of the way." Sheree sounded as if she would dissolve into hysterics at any moment.

But I couldn't share what was happening with my mother just yet. There would be deep repercussions no matter how I handled the next few moves I had in mind; and arguing with my mother about going back to Ontario or—worse—flying to her in Belize, just weren't options that I could contemplate right now.

Nope, we—which included an unwilling participant, my cousin Sheree, in the plan—could not tell my mother *anything*.

Sheree knew that I was up to something because, from what I could make out, she started to move away from me and was moving to stand up beside the bed.

The reason for asking Noah to leave Sheree and I alone had been two-fold. One, I knew that my eyesight wasn't good enough to be able to decipher between the two of them clearly, and two, I was on the cusp of making certain disclosures to Sheree, so I wanted to ensure that what I said was for her ears only.

"I need to leave this house," I said quickly.

"I absolutely agree! We need to pack you up and head first to Saskatoon to see the specialist and then get on the first flight back to Toronto," she said, without even taking a breath.

But as she was speaking the last words, she began to slow down in response, likely because of my shaking head.

"I'm not leaving for the reasons you think. And I don't want to go too far away from Dènaud," I tried to qualify.

"I'm not sure I follow," she said.

"Something is happening in Dènaud, and I think it's connected to why I can't remember much about anything until Samson found me. And it may very well have something to do with why I'm so banged up."

"Verity, it looks like you were attacked my someone or something," and for added effect she lightly touched the arm that was sporting the gash.

"It's just too coincidental that all these things have been happening around us since we got here, and it doesn't make any sense that I would be found by Samson that far away from here and especially on land earmarked for construction of a pipeline," I rattled off.

"Wait a minute, has more been happening out here than what you've told me, Verity?" Sheree had dropped back down into a fully seated position on the bed now.

And when I still hadn't answered her, she gave me a small pinch on the side of my neck. Probably because it was one of the areas on my body that she knew was uninjured.

"Ouch!"

"Start talking brat, or so help me Verity, I will call Auntie right this very second," she threatened, using that special tone of voice reserved for moments like this when she took on a motherly role with me instead of just being my big cousin. So to put it plainly, she wasn't joking around.

I opened my mouth and let spill the events that occurred during my time since arriving in Dènaud. When I was finished, I wasn't sure if I'd done the correct thing or not. Her silence had me extremely worried. *Would she still tell my mother?*

"Sheree?" It had been getting more and more difficult to make out her shape, and in truth, my eyes were getting a little fatigued being open for this long.

But she didn't speak. She didn't move for a good while, and then with a swiftness which I hadn't expected, I felt her weight pushing down in the middle of the bed as she pulled me into a hug. And then she just held me. We sat there like this for a long time. And after this reaction, I'd contemplated whether to tell her about my suspicions about Mayor Grant and how I thought that all of these things had occurred because of my graduate research on the town.

"I'm so sorry this happened to you," she said. "But Adrian and Megan are doing the same research, why aren't they at similar risk?"

"Noah" was the only word I needed to say.

Things got quiet after that.

"You really think she'd be capable of all this just because of Noah's feelings for you?" she whispered.

"Well, one, I can't speak for what Noah feels and doesn't feel," I shot back in my normal level speaking voice.

Then I felt her pinch me again.

"Ouch! Dammit, Sheree! Stop doing that!" I tried to slap her on her lower body somewhere, but she moved too quickly and jumped off the mattress before I could connect.

"I'm sorry, but you know how that man feels about you,

Verity. It shows up each day in everything he does for you."

"But he lied to me," I countered.

"Look, I'm not going to presume that I know the inner machinations of the mind of that man but what I can tell you is that he was immovable last night. When we were initially trying to scramble to find a way to find you, he was the one who would've been out there all night if it wasn't for the police intervention. To my knowledge, he barely ate and didn't sleep to until you were safe again. Now, should he have told you about his broken engagement to that viper, yes. And should his lips have been anywhere near her slutty ones, no. But you've got to let him explain, Verity. Don't lose something this special over a misunderstanding," she said and returned to the mattress.

Now it was my turn to be in awe. I'd never heard Sheree defend the actions of any man before, and she'd only been around Noah for a couple of days. Her opinion of him must be pretty damn high if a lie by omission and a lip-locking session didn't bring her claws out. And I'd seen those claws before. They were shiny and always on the ready.

She wasn't wrong about the person that Noah presented to me day in and day out. But that only strengthened my resolve to put some distance between us.

"I understand what you're saying, I do. And I appreciate it. But I can't let him know my suspicions because all those things you've said about him are right and I know that if I let him in on my thinking that his instincts would lead him to react. And I can't put him or the other people in this town at risk."

"And what about yourself? Who is going to keep you out of danger while you try and sort all of this out?" she countered.

I paused for a moment like I was giving it some real thought, but the truth is that I'd already decided on a course of action. It would be for the best because it would mean that I wasn't putting my friends in any direct danger. And based on where I was found and presumably left on purpose, the perpetrator or perpetrators wouldn't come after me if I was no longer near Noah. Clarence House was just too much exposure.

"Is Samson still here?" I asked.

NOAH

I WAS just returning from speaking with my father in the barn about one of the fillies we were housing when I received a text from Booker. He'd just gone up to the house and noticed that either Sheree or Verity, or both, were putting some suitcases in the back of a jeep in the driveway.

It couldn't be Verity, I resolved to myself. No matter how she'd felt about us, after everything that had gone on, she wouldn't just up and leave. *Would she?*

Not waiting around to find out, I high-tailed it back to the house, nearly running over Samson who was moving a bag that very much looked like Verity's brightly colored suitcase. I didn't see the look he gave me, nor did I stop to speak with Sheree who was pulling her own bags out onto the porch as I approached the top step.

My focus went directly to the figure leaning against the wall just a bit further down the hall. Movement was based on instinct alone. I could see that Verity's eyes were open, and she was struggling to focus on my approaching figure.

I bent slightly to secure my arm behind her legs and swiftly tossed her back so that I could scoop her up into my arms bridal style. A gasp escaped her lips, but I was moving too quickly for her protests to become any more vocal.

Her instincts seemed to kick in as well as she threw her arms around my neck, and I felt her drop her head just below my shoulder. It could also have been sheer inertia that pushed her into that position, but I wanted to believe that she needed to have her body against mine as much as I needed hers.

One foot in front of the other. I had a one-track mind. And I wasn't stopping until I made it to the other side of my bedroom door.

NOAH

AS I SET HER DOWN on top of my bed, I could feel her reluctance to let me go. But I needed to do some things, so I gently slid her arms from around my neck and placed them on either side of her. Then I went to the door and engaged the lock.

I turned around just in time to see her flinch a little at the sound of the door locking.

Don't worry. I'll take it slow. As slow as I can.

Kneeling before her, this time I didn't remove her hands when she'd placed both on my shoulders. Well, at first she put them on my chest in a manner that made me wonder if she was trying to push me away, but then she slid them up towards my shoulders.

"You're shaking, Vee," I said, placing my fingers on her thighs and moving them in an upward motion to calm her.

She didn't respond to me, but I could tell by the way her head leaned a little to the side and how tightly she squeezed her eyes shut that she was trying to figure out the right words to say.

So we just stayed like that for a bit. Me knelt in front of

her with my fingers grazing back and forth along her thighs, and her very slowly rubbing my shoulders.

You can't leave me. I placed my head in her lap, and her hands moved towards the top of my head. But I needed skin to skin contact, so I began pushing her little sundress, that sat just above her knee, up even further. When it was pooled nicely around her upper thighs, I moved my head and placed my cheek in between them. Her legs were closed, but I swore I could still feel a heat emanating from her. She started to squirm as I began kissing her skin beside my mouth.

First shaking, now squirming. I couldn't have that. So I brought both of my hands up and held her legs still. Applying just enough pressure so that she knew that I wasn't about to let her go. That spurred her to talk.

"Noah, I wasn't going to leave without telling you."

At that statement, I lifted my head to look at her face. Her eyes were still closed. But I could sense her determination. There was something she was keeping from me.

I kissed her deeply and she kissed me back.

My hands had a mind of their own and began to pull her legs apart. I watched her face for any sign of resistance. The determination remained, but she wasn't running from me anymore. I could feel her wanting to reach out to me.

Dammit, what aren't you telling me? I needed answers, and at this point I would take any sound at all from her, even without words.

Slowly, I traced one of her inner thighs with my index finger upwards so that she knew what I was about to do to her. Keeping the other hand occupied by pressing down on her other thigh I could see that her resolve was cracking.

"Talk to me, Verity. Why would you leave me?"

Her head tilted backwards a little so that her eyes were momentarily hidden from me. And when she brought her head back upright, her eyes were open and she bit down on her bottom lip. She was trying to focus on me, but I could sense that she still wasn't quite able to make my image out completely.

"It's not what you think," she replied finally.

I grunted in response. "Not good enough," I said as I took back my index finger, which had almost reached its destination and brought that hand up to the middle of her chest before applying just enough pressure to push her backwards.

When she was lying flat on her back, I crawled up the bed so that I was directly above her and balanced my weight on my forearms so as not to crush her. Leaning to one side, I slid my hand back down her body until my fingers met her core. She was soaking my digits even through her panties.

She'd arched her back at the contact and I could tell that her nipples were hard as rocks jutting up through the thin material of her dress. I couldn't hold off. Taking an entire nipple into my mouth, I rolled the nub with my tongue and sucked on it hard over the fabric.

She hissed her response as her arms flailed and her hands grabbed clumps of the bedspread.

"I can't...talk...when...," she was trying to explain herself now, but it was already too late. I couldn't hear her try and rationalize her leaving me, this house or Dènaud. I didn't care if she had intended on talking to me before she left. Although, there was plenty of evidence to the contrary with the scene I'd just walked up to.

No, the time for talking was done. I put my middle finger into her first, having pushed her panties to the side. *I loved that she wore thongs. It made things much easier.* Then I began pumping in and out of her as my mouth continued to torment her nipple, leaving that part of her dress soaked with my saliva.

She yelped.

I bit her. Couldn't resist that taut little button. And she just kept on writhing beneath me. Every lick, each nibble was deliberate and just hard enough for her to never forget whose mouth was on her right now. Her chest rose and fell multiple times between each finger thrust, and I could tell by the feel of her inside that she was close.

I couldn't take my eyes off her. Verity was beautiful at all times, but she was ethereal when she was about to climax. Her chest pushed up to me while I used my mouth to counter her movement, driving her wild with my wicked tongue.

I needed more flesh. Making a quick decision, I ripped her dress with my teeth which finally exposed her nipple to me. She gasped. I knew she wasn't wearing a bra, but if she were, I would've destroyed that too.

"No….ahhhh," Verity cried out at the exact moment that I'd withdrawn my finger from her core.

Don't worry beautiful. I'm not done with you yet. As she moved to straighten her arched back down to the mattress, I felt her body freeze in place. *She knew what I was about to do.* She felt my hand moving in between us toward my jeans.

"Yes, yes, yes," she said over again.

It was all the encouragement I needed as I continued loosening my belt buckle and unbuttoning and unzipping my jeans in record time, even with her juices coating my fingers. I'd barely had my dick in my own hands before I'd pulled her panties to the side and let her pussy swallow my entire length in one go.

She screamed in ecstasy, and I moaned loudly too. If anyone had been in any corner of the second floor of this house, there was no mistaking what we were doing to each other.

"Fuck, Vee." I almost screamed into the side of her neck having finally released her nipple from my focus.

"Baby, don't stop. Please." I don't know if it was her affectionate pet name for me or the fact that she'd begged, but I was like a man possessed, and my hips really began to move after that. Raising one of her legs over my shoulder, I was determined that we'd cum together.

I vacillated between watching the transformation coming over her face as she got closer to climaxing and the sight of my dick pumping in and out of her in all its veiny glory. I don't think I've ever been this hard.

"Uh, uh, uh, ahhh," she took each hard stroke I gave her. I loved the sounds she made when I made love to her.

The leg over my shoulder was pushed back to nearly the side of her head as I switched my angle for the last few plunges into her sweet heat that pushed us both off the cliff.

I was spasming as I emptied myself inside of her. I wasn't going to waste a single drop.

VERITY

I'D FILLED my suitcase in record time and grabbed a shower with some assistance from Sheree. I could bathe myself, but I didn't want to fall and bust my ass, so she stood watch outside the door just in case.

Sheree met me in the hallway after she'd gone back to her room to get her things and had a quick conversation with Samson.

"Did you see Noah?" I asked.

She sighed loudly, "You're going to have to talk to him Verity. You can't just leave. You must at least explain something to him." I knew she was right but that didn't make it any easier for me.

Samson had come upstairs to help with the bags. Adrian and Megan were still out, so I'd call them and explain things later. I was waiting to hear Noah's voice or to feel his presence, but there was nothing.

"I can just call him when we get there," I said. I was a coward. That was clear.

Taking a deep breath, I could see a vague outline of my surroundings. Thankful my eyesight was improving, I could make out two figures leaving the front room I was standing in. When a figure reappeared, the shape looked like Samson, so I waited patiently for him to come over and help me up. But when a hand went behind my back and the other underneath my thighs, I was startled momentarily.

"It's okay, I can walk myself. You don't need to carry me." But he didn't stop and pulled me up into his chest, hard.

My hands flew to his chest, and I ended up with my arms around his neck to keep my balance. Although it was clear that he wasn't putting me down despite my protest. When he started to walk away from the front door and back towards the stairs I tried to speak up.

"What are you doing? Put me down…"

"No."

"Noah?"

Cutting me off sharply, I think he actually growled at me. And he didn't say another word to me as he walked with me in his arms down the upstairs hallway. We were headed towards his room. I struggled in his arms trying to get myself down, but my effort was so slight, I wasn't even convincing myself.

Once we were inside he put me down on the bed, before going to close the door, then returned to stand above me. *He'd engaged the lock.*

"I…I was going to…"

But he didn't let me finish. "Were you just going to leave here without saying anything?"

"Noah."

"Verity," he said in a low whisper. There was a moment of fear that evaporated in an instant once he dropped down with his arms pressing the mattress on either side of me.

I had no chance to react when I felt his lips crushing mine. He mashed his mouth over my own. A moan escaped from somewhere deep within me as I accepted his tongue into my mouth.

His hands were on me in an instant, exploring every part of me. And I was kissing him back like an act of pure desperation. He pulled the sleeves of my dress down my shoulders, exposing that I wasn't wearing a bra. He latched onto my breast and his entire mouth devoured the nipple while his hand snuck up my thighs to underneath my dress. I was wearing underwear but the gusset was soaked and easily pushed aside by his finger entering me.

Finding his lips again, I had to push his head forcefully back up and away from my chest. I needed to taste him. I needed him. Right now.

"Noah." My voice sounded like I was struggling to not only speak but also to breathe.

"I know," he said. And without any further prompting, I heard him messing with his belt, pulling his zipper down.

There was no way we'd get to removing my panties quickly enough to satisfy the lustful pace we'd set. I shivered as his fingers grazed the lips at my apex.

I focused on that particular sensation, and I lost my mind when I felt him pull my panties to the side with his fingers and thrust into me in one swift movement.

"Oh…ahhhh."

***

He was still inside of me when he let down my leg and rolled me on top of him. My insides were still quivering at his presence there, and I was in no rush to let him go. We both breathed heavily, trying to gain our balance.

Thank God I was on birth control. We'd just had sex without a condom. But I knew we were both clean based on conversations we'd had with each other.

Noah moved one arm from around my waist to rest his hand at the back of my head. It was clear that he wasn't going to let me get up. I tried moving, thinking this positioning would inevitably get uncomfortable for one or both of us.

"I'm not letting you go," I heard him say into my hair.

"Clearly," I smiled into his neck. *Could he feel that?*

"No. You are not leaving Verity," he couldn't have been clearer at that point.

"Noah…" I tried to interject.

"If you're going to tell me that after all that, you think I'm just going to let you walk out on me. Out of my life?" his voice cracked at the last words from his mouth. Then I felt him shaking his head against me.

He began kissing the skin just between my shoulder and my neck. Then returned to sucking it slowly. And he was getting hard again. I could still feel the way my body had been stretched after the lovemaking session we'd just finished. *And now he wanted round two?*

He flipped me on my back and took my breath away with an open-mouthed kiss. Only then did he pull out of me.

As soon as his tongue found its way into my mouth, I knew I wanted him again. *I guess I was going to be sore outside as well as inside.*

This time he tore away the panties and hurriedly pulled down the remains of my dress. I helped to kick the materials off the side of the bed. Taking off his own shirt with one hand over his back, he stood briefly, and his jeans practically fell to the floor having been weighed down by the belt I guessed.

Then before I knew it, Noah had turned me over on my stomach and pulled me down to the edge of the mattress where he now stood behind me.

He entered me swiftly and with a force that propelled me to the position I knew he truly wanted, butt high in the air and my face down into the bed. I could feel that he must have a fascination with watching how our bodies met because he was driving in and out of me slowly, while he kneaded my backside. I loved the feel of his strong hands on either side of me.

He guided me back and forth with ease because we'd already generated so much wetness between us.

I felt him lean his weight into me.

"I want to hear you say it Vee,"

I could barely catch my own breath, so I had no idea how he was speaking so clearly.

"Say what?" I managed to garble out.

"That you're not going anywhere," he added a thrust to emphasize his demand.

"Ah, Noah…"

"Just. Say. It." He was getting more primal. I'd never experienced him like this before. It should've scared me, but I just felt myself getting more turned on.

"Mmm, mmm," I couldn't form words. What he was asking of me was impossible for so many reasons.

And as if he'd just given up getting any response, he thrust deeper and deeper, all the while putting more of his body weight onto me until I was flattened underneath him with my stomach on the bed and my legs squeezed together. The feeling of him entering me this way was causing me to free fall.

I almost missed the feel of his power behind me when my butt was higher in the air but then he slid a hand underneath my thigh and pushed it up as far as it could go. I was stretched so deliciously.

He hadn't slowed down the pace, just the pressure. Then he ramped up the intensity so much, driving me further and further into the mattress, that he had me screaming out his name. I'd turned my head so that it was slightly muffled by the sheets, but I felt him turn my head with his hand in my hair.

"No, just scream," he commanded as his thumb found my clit.

And I did. As my orgasm finished tearing through me, I finally realized Noah's plan. He was going to *fuck* me into submission.

I might be here for it.

I'D LEFT HER lying in my bed. I'd put her to sleep.

After watching her eyelids flutter and the soft way her lips opened and closed as her breath escaped, I realized that I'd better get out of this bed before she woke up and realized that she'd just made love to a man obsessed. *There was truly no way in hell I was letting her leave this house today. Shit, maybe not even this room.*

Closing the door behind me, I adjusted my jeans and shirt as I walked barefoot down the hallway, I could sense that the energy in the house was a little off. Almost like there was someone on edge in it. And sure enough, as I made it to the bottom landing of the staircase and peered over into the front room that was just adjacent to where I stood, I glimpsed Sheree sitting with Samson and my parents.

Sheree's head turned towards me immediately as I descended the stairs. But there was no accusation in her face; in fact, she raised her eyebrows at me and gave me a little smile. Almost like we were privy to some inside joke together.

Samson sat rather stoically as if he didn't truly want to be there but was staying out of an obligation to someone. His proximity to where Sheree was sitting seemed to suggest that she was the reason. He also said nothing to me. My mother looked a bit uncomfortable, in a way that I'd never seen before.

"I'm going make us all a little tea. Does anyone want tea?" she asked but was already halfway out the room before anyone could respond.

My father looked me straight in the eye and stood up. I had him by a couple of inches, but my father's aura always made him the biggest man in a room no matter what. I could feel myself caving a little, like I'd need to explain myself if he asked. Thankfully he didn't. He simply tipped his head towards me and headed off in the same direction as my mother.

Our lovemaking wasn't something I was ever going to be ashamed of. I wanted Verity to scream and be completely uninhibited with me. *With me and no one else. Ever.* But I realized that my desires had taken over and would likely cause her a little embarrassment when she faced these people.

My intention had been to grab a glass of ice water or homemade lemonade from the fridge to replenish Verity's body. It was the least I could do since I was solely responsible for dehydrating her. Just the memory of it was making me hard again. I could still taste her.

But bumping into my flustered mother and stern father in the kitchen had zero appeal to me. So, instead, I grabbed some bottles of water from across the room in the bar and started to make my ascent back upstairs. I'd almost gotten to the middle of the stairway before I overheard Sheree talking to Samson.

"Well, I guess that takes care of that. We aren't leaving after all," she had tried to whisper, but I caught every word.

Damn right.

***

She was still asleep when I re-entered the room, so I left the water bottle by her bedside and stripped down quickly so that I could resume my position lying beside her naked. I desperately wanted to place my hands on her body again, even if it was just to spoon her, but I didn't want to risk waking her up.

Having no idea where her head would be at when she woke up, I didn't want to end up arguing over her attempt at leaving, especially not after what we'd just done with each other.

I could hear Samson's jeep starting and heading off down the driveway from just outside of the window. I had no idea whether he'd gone alone or if Sheree had gone with him. Secretly I was hoping for the latter. I liked Sheree, a lot, but having Verity to myself without any distractions and no co-conspirator able to assist her in leaving was the only thing I played out in my mind.

Suddenly there was movement beside me. *Shit. Here we*

go. Verity was beginning to stir. It had already begun to get dark and without any of the room lights turned on I relied on the movements she was making in the bed to guess whether she was really waking up or just stirring lightly.

"Mmm, Noah?"

"I'm right here, Vee," I replied, placing my hand on her shoulder and gently letting it glide up to the side of her face.

I felt her turn her lips into the palm of my hand. I bit my lip trying to keep from lowering myself on top of her again. I'd already depleted her I'm sure and the last thing I wanted to do was to hinder her recovery in any way.

Her movement in the sheets had caused warm air to escape from underneath us. The sweet smell of sex and sweat hit my nose all at once and made my mouth water. My other hand slipped around her waist to bring her closer to me. She didn't resist physically.

"Noah, we need to talk," she said.

I couldn't stop caressing her waist and that sweet dip before her hip, but I didn't speak so that she knew I was listening. And I pressed into the top of her backside with my fingers possessively as I grunted my response.

"I really wasn't going to leave without first speaking with you. Everything has just been happening so fast and all at once. I didn't know how to say things to you so you wouldn't get upset. I'm not leaving Dènaud, just Clarence House. I'm going to stay with Sheree at Samson's for a bit while I finish up my work. I'll be in touch daily of course, back and forth, especially since Adrian and Megan will be remaining here. But I need to do this to finish everything. Okay."

She was rambling and it didn't sound as if she was going to let me get a word in edgewise, so I was surprised when she ended her speech by saying "okay." Although it didn't sound like a question. She wasn't asking me. She was telling me.

That simply won't do.

I contemplated how to respond to her, but I felt myself getting more and more frustrated. She wasn't giving me a reason for leaving that made any sense at all. *Was she leaving to stay with Samson? Why? Was it me? Had I done something to make her feel as if she could no longer stay here?*

I knew that my parents showing up had been a lot, and with everything else that had been happening all around us it was like the icing on a very complex cake. But I'd done everything I possibly could to ensure that she would be comfortable here. Or maybe she was still hung up on the stuff with Leona?

"I'm sorry. I am. I should've told you how far Leona and I had gotten in that relationship. It was dishonest of me, and I apologize. I never wanted anything to come between us. And honestly, Vee, when I met you, I knew that nothing I'd had before could even compare. But that's no excuse for not being completely transparent in the first place. That was my fault. And that kiss, I'll take responsibility for that too. I shouldn't have even left an opening for her to be able to do something like that. I messed up, Vee, but that doesn't mean I deserve to lose you."

I needed her to know how badly I'd fucked up and that I wasn't running away from my part in all this. There was no excuse for me not telling her right away about it. It probably could've diffused a situation that was only made worse by the fact that I'd kept it from her.

Now I was rambling. I felt her move underneath my hands, and I grabbed her around her waist with a little more force than I'd intended.

"Ahhh, wait. Noah, I wasn't moving away," she said.

I released her immediately but kept my hands close to her skin. And then she moved towards me. I had to hold myself back, not wanting to frighten or hurt her.

"I'm so sorry," I said, bending my head down slightly.

Surprisingly, she reached out her hand and began rubbing the back of my head and down my neck. But there was no way she could've felt me lower my head, because it wasn't on the bed or pillow.

"Verity?"

"Mmm," she replied as she continued stroking my neck.

I reached over her to flip on the light switch at the bedside. The light was soft, but as soon as my eyes adjusted, I could tell that she was trying to complete the same adjustments as well. She was blinking somewhat rapidly, and her eyes were watering, but as she moved her face closer towards mine, I could just tell.

"You can see me," I whispered.

She nodded her head and began crying fully now. I grabbed her into an embrace and rolled her atop me.

"Oh, Vee, thank God."

I'D MESSED this up, completely. Here I was, wrapped up in this man's arms and feeling the safest and the most cared for than I had in the longest time by someone that I was developing deep feelings for, and I was trying to leave him.

But you were doing it to keep him safe.

Feeling the way his chest flexed underneath me, or the way his muscular arms encased me while he held me between his very strong thighs, I had to chuckle to myself.

I was trying to protect him.

But it wasn't just the physical. Noah had a traditional mindset that appealed to me on so many levels. Yes, I knew that he'd support me in whatever endeavor I decided to pursue, and he just wanted to be there to take care of me. He'd already shown me in so many ways that he wanted all of me, heart, mind, body, and soul.

So why did my heart keep fighting against this? I was being loved and I was in love, with Noah. I relished the warmth of being his arms. My cheeks being prickled slightly by his chest hairs. I wanted nothing more than to kiss him repeatedly there. And so, I did. His response was to emit a low growl.

"Mmm careful," he warned.

"What if I don't want to be?" I countered.

He turned me over suddenly, and now he was on top of me. "Believe me when I say that I want nothing more than to be inside of you again. So you just say the word, and I will bury myself so deep you won't wake until the morning when I'll happily do you all over again," he smiled and kissed my forehead and then my cheek. Next would be my lips and then I'd truly be lost.

Some sense was returning, although it was becoming increasingly difficult with that hot appendage of his so close to my own wet core. He could've entered me in an instant now without any resistance. The thought made me shiver. The shiver made him laugh.

"I need to go explain somethings to Sheree and Samson," I said trying to regain my equilibrium.

"Well, I don't think that Samson is here anymore. Heard his jeep peel off some time ago. And as for Sheree, I'm not sure. They were all in the front room earlier."

"They?"

"Sheree, Samson, and my parents," he added, although he looked a little sheepish while doing so.

Suddenly the events of the evening came flooding back to me. Had I screamed loud enough for everyone to hear me. *Oh great!* Now they'd think that their son had fallen for some kind of nymphomaniac or something. I was never coming out of this room again.

"I can already see the wheels in that head of yours churning, but you don't need to worry. My parents will love you. I don't think you've even been formally introduced with all that was going on. Come on, let's get up," he said.

And before I even had time to calculate the ways in which I'd never live it down how much I enjoyed having their son make love to me, he was headed for the shower.

Meeting the parents, this was going to be terrifying. But honestly, with everything that had already gone down so far, I couldn't imagine things getting any worse for me. *Yes, I was a sexual person, and I was falling for their son. I was an adult, what was the big deal?*

I tried to keep that top of mind as I joined Noah in the shower. It was supposed to be a quick one, but once he got behind me and hooked one of my knees over his forearm, I found myself trying too hard to stay quiet as my breasts slid up and down the beautiful, tiled interior as he entered me from behind.

And when I'd ignored Noah's second demand that I just scream, he covered my mouth with his hand and ground me into the wall until I was a blubbering mess into his palm.

I managed to keep my bandage from getting wet by hooking an arm outside of the shower door. It also gave me great leverage to throw myself backwards and take Noah even deeper.

And Noah gave me no mercy, as he held me up I crumbled under force of my own orgasm. He wasn't too far behind me.

Damn, this man had stamina.

All in all, a one hundred out of ten experience.

Once we were both satiated and clean finally, we dressed and headed downstairs hand in hand. I was practically starving after having been "dicked down" so much, but my mind was also on Sheree. She was sipping on something in the kitchen across from an older woman I presumed was Noah's mother. She had hair just like Callie's that hung straight down her back and was peppered with flashes of grey.

"Hi, I'm…" but Noah interrupted me.

"Mom, this is my Verity."

At the word "my" I turned to look up at him, but there wasn't a hint that he'd done anything wrong. In fact, he seemed the happiest I'd seen him in a while.

Now if the word "smug" could be attributed to anyone, it would be Sheree who cast me a knowing glance.

"Well, it's more than a pleasure to finally meet you, Verity," she said, taking me by both hands and pulling me gently over to the island.

I shot Sheree a look that promised a painful experience if she didn't behave herself, but what more could I have expected from my own family? *This was Sheree we were talking about.*

"Glad to see you both finally coming out of that

room. Thought we were going to have send in a search party," Sheree smiled over the rim of her cup as she took another sip.

"What are you talking about? Everything is fine. Right, Noah?" I turned towards him looking for backup of any kind.

"More than fine. We were just, ah, making up for lost time," he remarked.

"And you've got your eyesight back I see. Good job," Sheree added with a wink and a thumbs up to Noah. *Useless. The both of them.*

I could feel my cheeks heating up as I turned back to Mrs. Sawyer. "Oh, don't be embarrassed, dear. Noah's father used to 'make up for lost time' like that almost every day when we were your age," she added and turned towards Sheree with a smile.

Sheree raised her coffee mug towards Mrs. Sawyer like she was making a toast, and they both dissolved into a fit of laughter. Noah was unusually quiet suddenly.

"Sir," he uttered. His eyes were directed at the screen door as an older gentleman stepped through the doorway with what appeared to be a shotgun. Having never really seen a weapon that large up close, I hesitantly took a few steps backwards until I hit Noah's chest.

"Oh Kristoff, you're scaring the poor woman," Mrs. Sawyer said as she handily relieved him of the weapon and walked out of the room. The silence she left behind became sort of deafening.

"Seems like I missed out on something," Mr. Sawyer said. "There was a mountain lion I was trying to scare off near the perimeter," he added when the stiffness in the room still hadn't dissipated.

"Dad, I told you that you don't have to do that anymore. The ranch hands will take care of things like that. Besides, there's something more important right now," Noah said. Then he put his arm around my waist and pulled me into his chest. "Verity, this is my father, Kristoff Sawyer."

I held out a hand in greeting towards him, and he wiped his hand on the side of his pants before taking it. He looked a bit apologetic at first, which I didn't fully understand until I felt his large, calloused hand swallow mine. When I went to release his hand, he held me steadily for a few awkward moments before he finally let go, and Noah pulled me backwards by my elbow.

I looked over at Sheree who also had her eyebrows raised. *What was that about?*

"Well, it's been a long day already. Mel, are you ready for bed?" Noah's father called out before tipping his head towards us and beginning to walk out of the kitchen.

I turned around in Noah's arms as I watched his father's retreating back. As if sensing my disappointment, Noah leaned down and kissed the top of my head.

"Don't worry, it isn't about you," he offered.

Okay? That still doesn't help at all.

"Samson helped me bring our stuff back upstairs, so I guess I'll be heading off too," Sheree said with less ceremony than expected, as she too tried to step by us towards the staircase. She only briefly looked back when Mrs. Sawyer reappeared, gun-less in the hallway. "There you are Melody, headed up?"

Melody? Oh, uh huh... how did my cousin and Noah's mom get on a first name basis? How much time had we spent in Noah's bedroom?

I was just about to follow them both up the stairs and tried to press away from Noah, using my hands on his shoulder. Something was up between those two and I wanted to figure out what it was. That and I wanted to talk to Sheree about the executive decision she'd made to keep my things here and let Samson leave without us. But when I felt Noah's grip tighten around my waist, I knew that the conversation would have to wait. He pulled me back in front of him so fast that I had to steady myself with one hand against his chest this time.

"Hey," I smiled.

"No running off. I just got you back. Do we need to go back upstairs so I can remind you of all the ways I can get you to submit to me?"

"Noah," I gasped and playfully swatted his upper arm.

"Sounds like a yes," he turned suddenly as if to march with me back up the stairs.

"Okay, all right, fine. Come on, I'm hungry," I said

exasperated.

"Me too," but his look made it clear that he wasn't talking about food. He began to crowd me. My response was to simply point to the covered plates warming on the stove top.

"Fine I'll eat here, first," he said as he went for the plates.

I hadn't missed the inuendo dripping from his last word.

I HADN'T even closed the door behind me when Sheree poked her head out of the ensuite with her toothbrush hanging out of the corner of her mouth. "What are you doing in here?" she asked.

"I'm going to bed," I replied. I was too tired for this.

"Um, but why are you *here*, in this room?" she countered, wiping some errant toothpaste from the side of her mouth.

"Sheree, this is my room," I replied. *Honestly, what was this girl on?*

"And your big swinging dick is next door," she said with a devious smile.

"Oh my goodness, Sheree, don't call him that," I felt like a kid in school that had just stamped her foot because her parents wouldn't buy her something in the store. And from the look of pure elation on Sheree's face, I could tell that she wasn't buying my act at all. It was time to drop the façade. "I'm just getting a pajama," I answered finally.

Sheree just rolled her eyes and returned to the bathroom vanity. She turned around and did a run and jump into the bed before pulling the covers up over top of her.

"Don't even give me that look," she said in response to

my pout. "I don't know who the two of you think you're fooling,"

"I thought you'd at least miss me a little. After all, you did come all this way just to see me. But I see you chumming it up with Noah first, and then his mom, and let's not forget Samson. Girl, what was that about?" I took a seat on the corner of the bed.

"Girl, bye." She tried to give me the brushoff, but I wasn't backing down.

"Sheree?" Now I was trying to put on my auntie voice. It was a lot less convincing. After a few moments of her not answering me, I put one knee up on the bed and moved into my stance to pounce on top of her to get her to finally acquiesce.

"Hold it. Don't you dare. Save that ramping for your man. I don't need all that energy in here tonight," she said with a serious tone, but I could see the smile forming at the side of her mouth. After another pause, she finally opened up: "Samson and I waited for a bit and talked for a bit. We even went out and walked around for a bit. And then when it was loud and clear that you weren't exactly fighting your way out of this place, he finally just left."

"A bit? You walked and talked for a bit?" My eyebrows were nearly up to my hairline at this point. Sheree was never coy about anything, especially men, so this release of very little information was uncharacteristic and exasperating.

"Listen, I didn't come down to Saskabush to find love, so whatever you're thinking, just forget it," she tried to dismiss me and the topic of conversation with a wave of her hand. She was clearly finished with the conversation.

"Okay, okay, I'll stop," I said. Solid plan because like I've mentioned in the past, Sheree don't play, and I didn't relish heading back over to Noah's room with more bruises and inexplicable scratches.

I couldn't help but laugh internally. though. Sheree had a heat seeking missile most of the times and was never afraid to approach a man, anywhere, anytime. But she seemed to be acting shy when it came to speaking about Samson.

She couldn't be blamed at all for having a crush on him. He was tall, crazy good-looking, and he had an air of mystery about him. Imagine living and surviving all the way up in that wilderness on one's own. Although, he'd offered to take us to a different home on the reserve that he shared with his grandfather. It was sufficiently hidden away and could've provided the perfect coverage for me to continue with my work without any further dangerous distractions.

But that plan had been thwarted. In a good way of course. I didn't want to be away from Noah any more than I wanted to be recovering from my injuries.

I'd realized something about my feelings, and at some point, I would need to tell him. *Right?* Sheree would've already told me to tell him. But I didn't want to rush this. It was enough that I hadn't left. And I was sleeping in his bed.

Geez, I hope he didn't wander down here asking me to hurry up. I was listening for any noise in the hallway, as it was just us and Adrian on the floor tonight. Megan was sleeping away, again.

"But for real, I'm proud of you, little cousin," Sheree said out of nowhere. My look of confusion probably spurred her into explaining in a little more detail. "I know you, and sleeping beside that man instead of in here with me is a very big deal."

"Well, his parents already know more than enough about our sex life, so what's the difference?" I tried to sound flippant.

"Don't do that. Nobody here is judging you," she said as she moved a little closer to where I was kneeling on the bed.

"Except Noah's father. He couldn't get out of the room fast enough. And, as a matter of fact, neither could you or his mother. Is there something going on that I'm not aware of?"

"Noah's mother loves anyone that loves her son. She told me as much. Apparently, he's really been talking you up to them, so she was dying to finally meet you. And as for Mr. Sawyer, well something tells me there's more to him than meets the eye if you know what I mean."

"No, I totally don't. I'm super confused right now," I said while shaking my head.

"Go talk to your man, Verity. Stop shopping for answers

here when you have a man next door who desperately wants to give you everything. Trust me, just talk to him," she said finally reaching me and grabbing the sides of my face with her two hands. "Now get out. I need my eight hours or I'm going to be useless. And I'm flying back this afternoon, so I'll be heading to the airport later this morning. If I stay here any longer, I won't have a job to go home to," she said as she turned to head back under her covers.

"But what about me? And Samson?" I pleaded.

In truth, it was only a fake kind of pleading, and I had to move quickly to get out of arms reach when she spun around and lunged towards me. Thankfully she stopped short of coming down off the bed. But I'd gotten the reaction I deserved and a piece of me was glad that she would no longer be around and therefore no longer at risk of getting hurt.

"I told Auntie that you'd be calling her as soon as you wake this morning. I was light on the details about what's been happening around here, so I suggest that you are too, although I promise you that it's not going to matter. She sees and knows all," Sheree rolled her eyes just as I did. "And I might think of coming back sometime before you leave. We'll see."

I couldn't help the grin that lit up my face. She ignored me and tucked herself back under her sheets. I was almost halfway out the door at that point.

"I'll see you in the morning. Goodnight, Sheree. And

cousin, I love you," I said, closing the door behind me and having not changed into any pajamas or carried anything out of the room with me. *Who was I fooling?*

"Three little words, Vee, that wasn't so hard," Sheree said just before the door closed, and putting all the emphasis on Noah's nickname for me.

With my back to the closed door, I looked down the hallway towards Noah's room. *It shouldn't be that hard. She's right.*

***

We had just enough time to grab a coffee and some delicious pastries, which were brought over by Tabitha. She'd found out that Sheree was departing today and wanted to drop by to say goodbye.

I thought that Tabitha was also going to be her ride to the landing dock where Headley would meet her for the transfer to Wakepa Lake, but I was wrong. I shouldn't have been surprised, but it was still a little shocking to see Samson's hulking form walk through the kitchen entryway before we'd finished eating.

"Good morning," he said. He was an early riser, and you could tell by the crisp, deep tenor of his voice. Not a hint of sleep anywhere in it.

"Morning," I said while shooting a quick wide-eyed

glance over to Sheree. She ignored me.

There was a smattering of other greetings from around the room as we all continued to tuck in. The kitchen was slowly filling up as a couple of the ranch hands stopped by as well. I'd been told that nearly the entire community had stepped up to volunteer to help find me. I felt a little guilty that my disappearance had caused such stress but was immensely glad that no one else had been harmed trying to help me.

I had a call later with my thesis advisor, Ericka, to get some clearer directions on how to approach the discoveries that I'd made. My heart and mind were completely on edge, as I hadn't yet disclosed to her this latest incident.

I knew Ericka, she'd likely tell me to pack my things and come home immediately. But I just couldn't do that. Not anymore. These people had shown that I meant more to them than just a visitor, and I would be there for them, too. Even if it meant delivering some news that may throw their town into chaos. I couldn't just let the news come out and then turn tail and run. And I couldn't just turn my back on Noah, either.

Suddenly the half-eaten Danish in my hand didn't seem like such a good idea anymore.

"You, okay?" Noah asked as he placed a protective arm around my waist. I simply nodded and gave him a smile. His grip tightened slightly when we heard a commotion coming from the front of the house.

"Is she back there?" was all we heard before a frazzled looking Mayor Grant came barreling down the narrow hallway, made narrower by the fact that Adrian seemed to be trying to hold her back without any luck.

When she finally reached the kitchen, the target of her wrath was unmistakable. If her eyes had been daggers, I'd be bleeding out on the kitchen floor.

Noah pulled me behind him. "Leona, what's the meaning of this? Why are you here?" Noah asked. His tone contained a warning though.

"Did she tell you what she's working on? That she's trying to undermine the results of the election and boot me out of office? Huh? Tell him! Tell him what you're up to! You have so many fucking secrets this one!" her voice continued to rise as she took another threatening step in my direction.

Noah was standing fully in front of me now, and the mayor was practically blocked from my view. I brought my hands to his waist to try and move around him, but he wasn't budging.

"Do I need to change my flight?" Sheree piped in as she stood and began circling from behind the kitchen island where she'd been sitting across from Noah's mother.

Mayor Grant's eyes darted quickly over to Sheree's location, and finally realizing who the others were in the room, she dampened her rough demeanor slightly.

"Melody, Kristoff, I, I'm sorry. I heard you were back and..." she stammered. Seeing the mayor caught off-guard was a new one.

Kristoff was the first to acknowledge her by walking over towards where she was standing. "Leona," he interrupted and nodded a greeting while everyone else in the kitchen remained silent. "Now what's going on?"

"Dad, I'll handle it," Noah tried to interject.

"It seems as if something Leona has to say affects us all, son. So perhaps it might be better if Verity provides a little more clarity to the situation," he said directing that last sentence towards me with a look that was meant to challenge.

"I, I can..." I tried to say, but Noah cut me off and stepped back simultaneously. His actions moved my body backwards as well.

"No, no. Leona, you don't just barge in here and make demands of anyone. This isn't your house," Noah's voice was steadily rising.

"It used to be," she smarted.

"It *was* going to be," Noah corrected her. "But it never was a home we shared together. And you know this," he lowered his voice to a level that made the hairs on the back of my neck stand up.

"Really, Noah! Really! For her! She's been nothing but trouble since she arrived, and now she's tearing our town apart.

Are you just going to let someone like her do that to us?" The mayor had placed the emphasis on the word "us," so it wasn't clear whether she was talking about the town or her and Noah.

For my part, I really was done caring. *Now if I could just get around Noah, I could straighten this woman out.* But no sooner had the thought cleared my head than I noticed a quick movement of dark curly hair out of the corner of my eye.

Sploosh! Sheree emptied an entire vase of stale flower water on top of the mayor's head. And it was a lot of water. She was drenched from head to foot. Even I caught a bit of the backsplash.

Mayor Grant opened her mouth in surprise and almost looked like she wanted to shriek, but nothing came out. That almost seemed worse. Adrian retrieved the vase from Sheree who stood off to the side, satisfied. She'd made sure that not a drop of water hit her.

We all stood in silence for a moment as the mayor tried to rearrange her matted hair away from her face, which now had eyeliner running down it. And it was just at that moment that Megan and Booker decided to make an appearance.

"Ahhhh, yeah, okay," was all Booker could manage.

No one else seemed to know what to do next. It was Megan who retrieved a kitchen towel from the stove handle to hand to the mayor. Mayor Grant snatched it out of her hand with such force that Booker had to steady Megan before she fell forward.

Oh, that is truly it! I shoved Noah's hand out of the way and walked towards the dripping wet mess that was the town's mayor, pointing my finger in her face to make sure I had her attention.

"You follow me," I ordered. And I didn't stop to look behind me as I marched towards the front door.

I WAITED until we were a little distance from the kitchen, outside, and nearly back to the SUV that she'd presumably arrived in.

"Oh my g…" shouted someone from the rolled down rear window of the SUV.

"No! We're talking here!" I returned with just as much volume. I recognized the mayor's assistant as he immediately drew his face back into the vehicle and rolled the window up.

"Oh, this ought to be good," Mayor Grant came to a stop before me, placing her hands on her hips. She'd managed to get to the last step of the porch without slipping on the wet spots she created wherever she put her feet down.

"First of all, I don't owe you any explanation concerning the work that I do or that of my colleagues. But I notice you're putting particular attention on what I'm doing." I wanted her to receive every bit of the accusation threaded into my words.

"You think it's going to be that easy to come in here and tear apart everything that I've done for this town? Everything that my father did for this town?"

"I have no intention of tearing anything apart. I'm

reporting on mine and my colleagues' findings, and whatever happens after that will be up to the appropriate stakeholders," I finished.

The mayor's face scrunched up into a scowl. "Look at the fancy graduate student, with your fancy words. Your little school project isn't going to change anything. This is so much bigger than you could possibly imagine," she said, now moderating her voice. Perhaps she no longer wanted an audience for what she was currently disclosing to me.

"Then why come over here and accuse me of something I'm not capable of doing, according to you?"

"Just who in the hell do you think you are?" Mayor Grant snapped as she managed to make up the distance between us, putting her face right up to my own. "I can't wait until Noah finally sees through all your bullshit to see who you really are."

I'd been waiting for this.

"I'll tell you because you're clearly acting like you don't already know. I'm the woman that Noah chose. I'm the woman he loves. And I love him."

I watched as her face contorted at my announcement. Clearly she'd been aware of the first part, but that last part seemed to catch her a little off guard.

I continued, "So don't go poking your nose around in places where it doesn't belong." I took another step towards her, even though there wasn't really a full step there, until our noses were nearly touching. "And another thing, stop showing up at this house as if you own the place. Noah and you aren't anything anymore sweetheart, so the next time you want to stop by, call first. Or better yet, don't," I said as I brushed past her and headed up the stairs to return inside.

As I pushed through the screen door, Mayor Grant finally let out that shriek.

***

I returned inside the house to everyone standing pretty much frozen in place back in the kitchen. Noah was the first to approach me, and I could tell from the way he let his eyes roam up and down my body that he'd been expecting much more than just two women having an exchange of words.

"I'm totally fine, I promise," I said.

And with that reassurance, he finally released me from his grip, and the conversation pretty much resumed back to normal, as it was right before the mayor had burst in. It was almost as if everyone was content that I'd handled her myself and that she was no longer around. All except Noah's father, who had excused himself from the room not too long after I'd returned. Catching Sheree's eye roll and head shake, I felt better about not reading too much into his action.

"Listen, I have to jump on a call," I said to Noah, but it

landed like more of an announcement, since practically everyone's attention turned towards me. "I'll be about thirty to forty minutes, I think. Sheree don't leave until I get back," I said. Sheree mock saluted as I patted Noah's hand and jumped up from the table to head upstairs.

Back in my room, behind the closed door, I was glad for a little solitude. I hadn't meant to make such an admission to Mayor Grant. Especially when I hadn't even clearly communicated my feelings to Noah. I was thankful that it didn't seem as if he'd heard anything. *We needed to talk, though.*

I dragged my laptop across the bed and readied myself for the call. Not surprisingly, Ericka wasn't the only face that popped up on my screen. There was also the dean of my department, Dr. Kennedy, and two other members of my thesis committee, Drs. Cane and Whittier. The latter two were external to my university, having simply been the foremost subject matter experts on federal, provincial, and municipal law and rural governments, so I began to piece together how Mayor Grant may have been privy to my findings.

After a brief introduction, the committee members and my dean essentially extolled the greatness of the findings to both academic and national interests. And that while the resulting disclosure may cause difficulties for the current sitting mayor, the value of it extended beyond Dènaud and had broader applications to the proper functioning of all levels of government nationwide.

"I don't know. I just don't want to hurt anyone," I managed to say.

"Verity, I know this is much more than you thought of when you made your initial proposal to go to Dènaud," the dean offered. *Understatement of the year, buddy!*

He continued, "But if this isn't handled properly, it could create a greater mess down the road. As it is, it's almost certainly going to create a domino-like effect where you are. From what I've been told, the federal government is already making some moves to head off any resistance to the pipeline being built. But there are at least two motions in the works for an injunction to stop the pipeline, so things in Dènaud are likely soon to start getting some national press attention. Perhaps it makes sense for you all to come back home while this mess gets sorted out."

Now that's not what I wanted to hear at all. And I'd already begun to shake my head on the screen for all to see.

"Verity, this is serious. They're talking about deploying more law enforcement and maybe even troops if the estimates on the number of protestors headed for that area are true. I must agree with the dean. It makes sense for you all to come home," Ericka finished.

"And what are the people here supposed to do?" I countered.

"Perhaps hope the mayor steps down of her own volition.

And that at least one of the injunctions goes through so that all sides can take a step back to truly determine what's best for this community and the nation," Dr. Whittier said.

There was silence on the call at that point. I looked at the screen to make sure that no one was accidentally muted, and they weren't.

"I know you might feel like this is in some way your fault," Ericka said.

"Isn't it?" I felt like I already knew the answer.

"Not at all. Things like this always come out. The injunction will likely be issued because the authorization came from a municipal official that had no actual authority. Come home and let this blow over. In all likelihood the pipeline will go forward later, once they've sorted out their election *faux pas*," the dean added.

"Not necessarily," I countered. "The runner-up would be installed, and from what I've heard, he would never make an agreement for the pipeline to continue. This matter could be tied up in court indefinitely as a result."

"All the more reason to leave, Verity." Ericka was still pushing.

"I can't just abandon the community. I'm staying. I'm not sure what Adrian or Megan will want to do, but I want to see this through." There, I couldn't have put any finer of a point on it.

"Fine, but you realize that the university will likely have

to put some measures in place and have you sign a waiver of some sort as to liability," Dean Kennedy said.

"Dan?" Ericka almost shouted. These types of interactions were typically where people's titles were used often, so Ericka calling the dean by his first name was unusual. "We can't do this. Verity?"

"She understands the risk, Ericka. Now let's take this offline. Verity, we'll be in touch." And with that, Dean Kennedy signed off. In quick succession the others trickled off the line as well. Ericka was the last to go as her cellphone began to ring incessantly. She gave me one last look through the screen with a forced smile before her square disappeared.

What had I just gotten myself into?

I needed to be upfront with Megan and Adrian. And Noah.

***

Just as I'd thought, Adrian and Megan were keen to stay also. We'd all developed ties to this community and not seeing this through with them wasn't an option. As I couldn't hold off on talking to Noah any further, I'd asked him to take us to "our" place that afternoon. He'd been more than happy to oblige, even packing us some sandwiches.

Sheree had decided to push her flight back one more day,

and I didn't even ask where she'd be spending her evening as I noticed her walking towards Samson's jeep as we were leaving.

When Noah and I reached our hidden oasis and got to the place where we had removed our shoes on our first visit, I bent down to roll up the legs of his jeans.

"You didn't have to do that," he said with a grin.

"I know. I wanted to," I said. I'd remembered how last time the hem of my dress had remained clean while his pants had gotten dirty around the area closest to his feet.

I shouldn't have been surprised when he retrieved a picnic blanket and basket from the rear of his truck before taking my hand. We walked hand in hand as I admired the canopy above us. Soon these leaves would change colors, fall, and eventually provide no cover at all. My heart ached a bit at the fact that I wouldn't be here for it. I'd be back in Ontario, prepping for my defense. I squeezed Noah's hand a little tighter.

"Seems like you have something to tell me, Vee," he said when we reached our picnic destination, and he began spreading out the blanket before us.

"I do, I just don't know how to say it."

Noah reached out to turn my back towards him and lowered us both down to the blanket. I immediately leaned into the solid warmth of his embrace. *I wanted this always.*

"Well then, why don't I start first," he said before placing a kiss on the spot just behind my ear. I stilled for a moment and then turned slightly so that I could face him.

"No, not this time," I said shaking my head, but still with a smile on my face. He looked as if he was about to argue with me, so I placed a lone finger against his lips.

"You've said a lot. In fact, you've been saying it all, and I haven't been fair to you," I said quickly. Then I took a few moments to try and find all the right words.

Noah took that moment to lower his face towards mine and draw my bottom lip into his mouth. He nibbled on it and then gave the same attention to my upper lip before releasing my mouth and sitting back to look at me.

How could this man command me with just a kiss?

When he moved to kiss me again, I put my hand on his chest. That garnered a look of disappointment and a bit of fear perhaps.

"Listen, Vee, if this has all been moving too fast for you…"

"I love you."

"…I'm not sorry about that."

I THINK I misheard her. *What did she just say?*

"Say it again," I said as I placed both hands on either side of her face and she twisted her body towards me. She smiled at me and then let her tongue run along her bottom lip before she spoke again.

"I love you, Noah Sawyer."

"Oh again, again!" I couldn't contain myself.

"And what about you?" she asked, pretending to be shy.

I kissed her then. But no regular kiss. No, I took her lips into my mouth first and then aggressively pushed past her soft barrier with my tongue. All the while holding the sides of her face so that she couldn't move in any direction other than the one I wanted her to. When we finally broke apart, she was trying to catch her breath. We both were.

"I think I've made myself very clear. Verity Reynolds, I am so in love with you, and I always will be," I added.

Then I helped her to face forward once again, with her body following the motion. And when I had her between my legs and her back against my chest, I slowly began to pull up the hem of her dress towards the middle of her thighs. I loved that she was so fond of wearing dresses. It made occasions like this one all the better.

When her dress was nearly up to her waist, I slipped my hand underneath the material and began sliding my fingers over her sensitive nub through her panties. She jumped with a start before my soft whispers calmed her.

There was no escape for her. She was completely at my mercy as I pushed aside the cotton material covering her core and strummed her slick inner folds like she was my personal string instrument. I wanted her to feel every slight touch of my fingers. So, placing my free hand underneath her leg, I propped her leg over my own for that extra stretch. I'd contemplated moving her other leg in the same way but wanted to take things a bit slower.

When she'd finally adjusted to the way it felt to have what I was doing to her exposed to the nature around us, I went in search of her nipple. Flipping the strap of her dress to one side, I pulled down the top enough to expose one of her full breasts. Pushing and trapping her head to the side with my own, I began the slow and steady assault on her node. I wanted it rock hard, so I pinched and stretched it until it was so.

"Do you know all of the things I want to do to you, Vee?"

She just shook her head in response. So I offered her no words as a follow up. But she couldn't mistake what I did next. Taking my hand away from her chest briefly, I opened my belt and pants and then lifted her up at the waist so that I could lower her slowly onto my fully erect penis.

"Ahhhh" she said as I stretched her further, guiding her up and down, with me fitting snugly inside of her. She took over and using her hands to prop herself up against my thighs she began controlling the pace at which I pumped into her. This left me free to tease her clit and continue torturing her nips. It was like our bodies were completely in sync.

There were no words— neither of us needed them to communicate what the other was feeling—but we were both vocal. It was probably the loudest I'd ever let myself be, but we were isolated in the woods with no one around to hear us. No one around to hear her. The thought of that made me thrust upwards into her a little harder, which yielded the result I wanted and so desperately needed. I could tell by the chokehold she had on my dick that it wouldn't be long now.

Verity must have been feeling the same way about the isolative nature of our surroundings. She was completely uninhibited and seated herself right to my balls while she pulled down the top of her dress to expose her mounds that bounced higher and higher as I rammed myself up into her.

Now I just wanted her to come. And I needed to hear it. So, taking the power from her, I placed my hands on either side of her slim waist and peppered her with strokes, again and again without a pause. *She was going to cum. Hard.*

And cum she did. *She was a squirter.* The feeling of bringing her so roughly to the precipice made my juices explode inside of her too. I held her with both arms pulling her in at her waist to my chest as her channel spasmed and trapped me inside of her.

When she finally stilled, I pulled out of her and felt the wetness beneath us as my seed spilled out of her.

"I'm never going to get tired of this," I managed to say from behind into her hair.

"Mmm, me too," she said. The sounds of sleepiness already tinging her voice.

She turned over so she was facing me and I pulled the picnic blanket over the both of us until we were wrapped inside of it like a burrito. A few minutes of shut eye wouldn't hurt either of us. And then perhaps I'd get to make love to her once more while looking in her eyes before we headed back to the house.

With that solace, I closed my eyes while holding, wrapped in my arms, everything I treasured in this world.

***

I heard it first, but the way that Verity's body tensed beside me let me know that she was also awake and had heard the distinct sound of a branch breaking nearby. Almost as if someone or something had stepped on it.

I'd packed my bear mace with me, so I wasn't concerned about a large animal peeking in on us. Not wanting to scare Verity, I pushed my hand into the basket to locate the canister and then rested my arm above the cover to be ready. We couldn't stay in the reclined position that we were in if we were going to be confronted by wildlife, so I slowly raised up and helped to pull her up beside me as well. Just as we were about to get up on to our feet, I saw something move out into the clearing before us. Or rather someone.

"Found 'em" I heard him say. He was probably an inch or two taller than me, but he was mostly skin and bones. But what he didn't have in mass, he more than made up for with that shotgun he had strapped to his chest.

He hadn't pointed it at us yet, but from the look on his face I was certain that he wasn't just out hunting.

Sure enough, three more men, each one looking rougher than the next, lumbered into the clearing. All large and suspicious looking and all armed—there were two who didn't have any guns, but it looked like one had an ax and the other a sledgehammer. I sat up a little straighter, trying to shield Verity behind me as she grabbed on to the back of my shirt.

"Gentlemen, can I help you with something?"

"Get up," the one with the shotgun said.

It was definitely not a space for argument, so I simply turned slightly to help Verity with her clothing and then made sure she was still behind me when we were standing before them.

The sun was going down, so we were mainly relying on the light of the sunset. I knew we'd be plunged into complete darkness before too long.

"You, you come forward," the second one had a handgun, and he not only pointed it at us but was also motioned with it as well as though he wanted Verity to come over to him.

Not happening. I held Verity behind me.

"She's not going anywhere." I sounded a lot more confident than I felt. He had a shot gun and I had bear spray.

"We just want to talk with her. Nothing too serious. Now come on, darling, you don't want to get your boyfriend shot, do you?" he said tauntingly.

"Noah," Verity whispered. I could feel her hands trembling while she still clung tightly to my shirt.

"We can talk right here. What do you want to talk about?" I said, while holding my hand up to try and diffuse the situation. *That was about as much as they'd get from me.*

"Go take her," the handgun guy said to the others.

As they approached, I began to move backward while holding Verity close to my torso with the other hand. *If I could just get back to my truck, I had my own answer in the form of steel to deal with these guys.*

When the two men got close enough, I pushed Verity out of the way and swung at the one with the sledgehammer as he wasn't in any type of fighting stance and knocked him out cold. The one with the axe swung first and sliced the air with it, but I pushed back in order to avoid getting hit and Verity hadn't been ready and was still too close. She fell to the ground with a thud, and I nearly tripped over her legs extended before her. The fool with the axe took that as his opportunity to grab one of her legs. She screamed but kicked him so hard that the axe fell from his grip and he landed on his backside on the ground.

"Enough of this," said one of the gun holders, and he let off one shot in the air to signal his exasperation.

I'd been trying to help Verity and immediately brought her into the circle of my arms, pulling her into my chest as I showed my back to the area where the gunshot had gone off. I was bracing myself for another gunshot, this time probably into my back, when I heard but didn't feel another loud bang.

The resulting groan let me know that the intended target had been hit, and I turned over my shoulder to see the man holding the handgun now holding his bleeding hand. The one with the shotgun had both hands in the air now and was trembling so bad that the shotgun was at risk of falling at any moment.

"What the…" I didn't get to finish my sentence.

"Are you two all right?"

"Dad?"

I couldn't have been happier to see the old man. He

stepped forward into the dimming light of the evening and grabbed the shotgun away from the one and then kicked the handgun away from the other.

I turned towards Verity and held her away from me slightly to ensure that she was all right before rushing over to where my dad was now standing, never removing my arm from around her shoulders.

Lights and sirens in the distance were music to my ears.

***

Later at the station, I'd made sure that Sheree and Megan were there to comfort Verity before finding my father by the water dispenser.

"Thank you for what you did for us tonight. How'd you even know that we were there?"

He took a big gulp of water before answering. "You forgot that I was the one that showed you that special place. The place where I took your mother before we got engaged."

"Oh yeah," I said.

"I overheard Verity ask you to go there and when you still hadn't made it back before it started getting dark, I thought I'd just go out and make sure that everything was all right. I saw the truck those guys used parked near to yours when I drove up, so I called the police and went in search of you both," he said. Then he leaned over a little further and said, "don't tell your mother." And to that I just smiled and placed a hand on his shoulder.

Removing my hand before things took an awkward turn, I was surprised when my gaze landed on Hex Tanner being brought into the station. He had a jacket thrown over his hands in front of him, but he was definitely handcuffed. As he passed by, he offered a sneer and not much else.

Just then, I caught the eye of Dan as he was headed from the breakroom back to the front desk.

"Hey man, what's going on?"

Dan looked around briefly before starting. "Turns out there might be a connection to all the happenings concerning Ms. Reynolds back to Mr. Tanner," he practically whispered. "It's still an ongoing investigation so that's all I've got for now." And he moved swiftly into another room, so no follow up questions could be asked.

"Shit," I said to myself as I turned to look over at my dad.

His face carried the same look of surprise.

I needed to see Verity.

VERITY

TO SAY that I was in a state of shock didn't do my feelings enough justice. And then, to top it all off, I watched as the mayor walked briskly towards where I was sitting in between Megan and Sheree. I didn't think I could take much more.

I felt Sheree sit up a little straighter beside me and noticed that the mayor slowed her approach considerably in response. When she was only a few feet away from us, she began speaking.

"I heard what, what happened, and I just wanted to come and see if you and, and Noah were all right," she seemed to have developed a slight stutter. Her attempt at being clueless wasn't convincing.

"I'm sorry, but didn't you already get dealt with already? Sheree spoke up first, but I was done letting other people fight my battles.

"Why are you here? Did you have something to do with what happened tonight? Someone could've been killed," I was on the verge of screaming, but Sheree's hand on my thigh and

Megan's on my shoulder kept me in check.

"Nothing like this was supposed to..." then she stopped speaking and just started shaking her head.

To her partial reveal, I was on my feet and almost nose to nose with the mayor. My stomach was in knots. I couldn't believe that things had gone this far. I had so many follow-up questions for her, but I couldn't collect my thoughts fast enough.

"What the hell is going on here?" Noah's booming voice carried across the room. "Get away from her," he commanded as he brushed past the mayor and came to stand before me.

"Noah, I didn't know. I, I couldn't stop..." she stuttered again. And instead of fighting through it, she simply turned on her heels and headed in the direction that Noah had just come from.

"Hey, come here," Noah said as he turned and pulled me up into his arms again.

I watched the mayor's retreating back over his shoulder and somehow couldn't drop this nagging feeling. Not that I wanted to hear anything from her tonight, or ever really, but her sudden onset speech impediment really did get in the way. *I'd never noticed or heard it before. Strange.*

"Noah, we need to talk about something," I said quickly. The mayor's appearance had reminded me that I hadn't been completely open with Noah about what was going on with the research, our findings and what the university had advised each of us to do.

I didn't want a repeat of a situation where he heard this from someone else, so we took over one of the interview rooms and I asked Megan and Sheree to give us some privacy while he and I chatted for a while.

"I think you should go back," Noah said.

"What?" I was having a hard time registering his words.

"They're right. I mean look at tonight. I can't keep you safe, and if things are only going to get more dangerous, then I don't want you in the middle of it, Vee," he pleaded.

"There's no way I'm leaving. I'm not leaving Dènaud, and I'm not leaving you."

He paused for a moment before resting his forehead on top of mine and placed his finger right below my chin. There was an electric current passing between us that was immediate.

"Oh God, Vee, at this rate I'm gonna end up locking you up in my room at Clarence House until this all blows over," he said.

I smiled. *Shit, he looked serious.* "As much as I would love to be your little captive, I've got work to do and so do you," I tried to laugh it off. "Now take me home Noah Sawyer."

"Yes ma'am," he said, delivering a quick kiss to my lips.

NOAH

THE POLICE had agreed to come out to Clarence House the following day with any additional questions, and I completed the identification process of the assailants alone. I didn't want Verity to go through anything further tonight.

"Has your dad already gone," Verity asked just after we'd seen off Sheree and Megan in Samson's jeep. Sheree and Samson had been together when we'd sent out the distress call to meet us at the station and had picked up Megan on their way to us. "I can't thank your dad enough for being in the right place at the right time. How'd he even know we were there?"

"I'd forgotten, but he'd actually brought my mother there right before they got engaged," I replied hastily. I regretted it almost immediately as I saw Verity's demeanor change suddenly. And I knew the reason why.

"I never took her there, Vee," I added.

"What?"

"Leona, I never brought her there," I repeated.

"But you were engaged to her," Verity pushed.

"My dad told me that's actually why he'd come in search of us, because he'd known that I'd never taken Leona there, and he'd overheard when you'd asked me to take you back to that special place."

"Oh," she replied. I could see her inner glow growing as

the corners of her mouth turned upwards.

I reached over and pushed the center console up so that she could be seated right next to me; I intertwined our fingers and placed our hands into her lap.

"Like I said before, I'm not sorry if this is going too fast. With you, it's forever, Vee."

I'd put my life on the line for hers tonight. I wasn't going to leave anything unsaid. I wanted her to feel the same way too, but my expression of those feelings wasn't going to be dependent on what she would say back to me. But I also didn't want there to be any doubt.

I wasn't surprised that we rode in mostly silence for the rest of the way home. And when we got inside my bedroom, I let her curl up into my chest and held her tightly until morning.

***

I was staring at my phone when Verity began to make soft breathing noises beside me. I hadn't released her at all throughout the night, and now my arm, which had fallen asleep several times already, was beginning to produce those sharp prickling things that told me I needed to shift my positioning. But when I tried to roll my arm into a different spot, it only spurred Verity to burrow deeper into my chest. I rested my lips against her temple.

"I've got to get up, but I don't want to," she murmured, sleep still clear in her voice.

"Then don't. Let's just stay here, like this," I said, making a point to rub myself up against her as I threw my leg overtop both of her legs.

There was no mistaking how I'd woken up this morning. It wasn't completely stiff just yet, but it wouldn't take more than a thought to make it so. I desperately wanted her to open her eyes so that I could get the 'all clear' from her. A quickie before I left for the stables would surely makeup for the loss of her by my side today.

"I wish I could, but we need to get through some of the paperwork sent over by the university and I need to go into town," she barely whispered that last part, but I'd heard it.

"No," I said and rolled away and stood up from the bed before she even knew what I was doing.

"You can't tell me no, Noah," she said, but it sounded like she was trying to convince herself and not the other way around.

I turned and dropped one knee back onto the mattress as I lowered my face to within an inch of hers. "I will keep you locked up in this room, Verity, if you even think about leaving this property without me by your side. Do you hear me?"

"Noah! Come on, be reasonable," she said as she climbed out of the bed to follow me to the ensuite.

"This is me being reasonable. I'm telling you what I will do beforehand, so we don't have any misunderstandings," I finished.

She tilted her head to the side as she stood behind me. I watched her reflection in the mirror and raised my eyebrows as far as they would go, trying to keep my focus off her naked body. *I'm not budging on this.*

Turning, she walked away from me back into the room, but when I saw her picking up clothes off the floor where they'd been strewn the night before, I jumped into action. Picking her up in my arms, I placed her back onto my bed as gently as I could, and when she tried to get up again, I held her in place. Raising one knee out of the knelt position I'd been in, I moved my head until she was staring directly at me.

"I'm not playing around, Vee. Last night we were both held at gunpoint, and I'll be damned if I let anything like that happen again. You're getting ready to sign off on some liability waiver from your school and you think I'm just going to let you walk out of here! Fuck Vee, come on," I hadn't meant to get this worked up, but the circumstances really gave me no choice.

And her response let me know that I'd finally gotten through when she placed both of her hands on my shoulders and then she kissed me. Anytime our lips met I always wanted more from her, but this time I just needed her to hear me and understand where I was coming from.

"Okay," she said.

"Okay?"

"Yes. I won't leave without you," she said.

My shoulders dropped as I pressed my head in between her breasts. *She smelled so good.* I inhaled deeply. We were both very naked and all I wanted to do was push her backwards onto the bed, but a knock interrupted us.

"This better be good," I almost snarled.

Throwing on my jeans, I was more than a little surprised to see Adrian on the other side of the door. At first, he didn't speak, and I'd only opened the door a crack, so I turned slightly to ensure that he didn't have a clear view into the room to see a very naked Verity behind me on the bed.

"Mayor Grant is downstairs, and she's with the police," Adrian said, looking as if he wanted to say something further but stopping himself.

Just as I was getting ready to fire off a round of epithets at the fact that she'd dared to show up unannounced once again, Verity appeared beside me fully dressed in what she had on from the night before. I disliked the way that Adrian's gaze immediately went to her, and he appeared to be having his own difficulties with the knowledge that she was in my room this early in the morning. *This guy was either really thick or just couldn't take the hint. She's mine.*

"Adrian, what do you mean Mayor Grant is here? Why?"

Verity directed the question at him.

I wish she'd just let me handle this interruption. It was fucking hot watching her set Leona straight yesterday, but I didn't want Verity to have any more unnecessary run ins. And I'd wanted to tell her that I'd overheard every word she'd said, including how she felt about me, but hearing her say the words to me herself later that evening was better than I could've imagined.

"She's just come from the station. Seems like she may have given some important information to them for their investigation against Tanner," he stated.

"All right thanks, we'll be right down," I said as I closed the door in his face. Turning to Verity, I ran my index finger underneath one of her dress straps.

"Noah, this is incredible news. Maybe she'll resign and we can finally put all of this behind us," she said. I could hear the hopefulness dripping from each word.

"Perhaps. But I don't know why she'd come here to make that type of an announcement. And with the police," I added. "Something's up and I don't like it. If I asked you to stay up here and to let me meet with Leona on my own, what would you say?"

I didn't need to hear her answer; the look she gave me said it all. Wrapping her arms around my neck, she pulled my head down into a kiss, and this time, we both took it deeper.

I was breathless when we finally parted.

"I love you, but I'm not staying up here. So please don't ask me to," she said. Then I watched as she opened the bedroom door and took a step out into the hallway.

I had no idea what awaited us downstairs but being the support she needed was the only thing I'd ever want to be.

When she reached her hand back to take my own in hers, I sensed a little calm settle in the center of my chest.

I shouldn't have given into it.

THE LAST THING I expected to see when we reached the main level of the house was the mayor sitting inside of the front room and my cousin Sheree handing her a cup of anything, much less tea. But that was the scene, along with the presence of Noah's parents, two police officers, Adrian, and Megan.

My eyes widened more and more with each step, and I could see Sheree's facial expressions flitting back and forth as well. *Something was up.*

"Mr. Sawyer and Ms. Reynolds, we're sorry to have to barge in on you again, but we need to clarify a few things with Ms. Reynolds in furtherance of this investigation concerning her disappearance the other day," the first officer said.

I didn't recognize Officers Menon and Griffin, but Sheree and Noah would later explain to me that they were the responding officers when I'd first gone missing.

Officer Menon kept on speaking. "Ms. Reynolds, we have a few questions we'd like to ask you if that's all right?"

I simply nodded my head, still unclear as to how the mayor fit in with all of this. *And why was Sheree serving her hot tea? Had she poisoned it? Was she getting ready to throw a pot of boiling hot water in her face?*

"If you'd prefer, we could use another room for some more privacy," said Officer Griffin as she looked around at everyone present.

"I don't have anything to hide. We can do it here," I answered quickly.

"On the night in question, you'd been upset about something, isn't that, right? Something one of your friends had seen Mr. Sawyer do?" It was framed as a question, but it seemed a little accusatory and completely superfluous at this stage. I was almost tempted to roll my eyes in response. *Why on earth were we going back to this?*

"I doubt that the reason for my disappearance is relevant here unless you suspect Noah of doing something to me, so why don't we get to where you really want to go officer," I was tired of this run around.

I felt Noah's hand press lightly into my lower back and I gave him a reassuring look before refocusing my attention on the last officer to ask me a question.

"We're aware of the circumstances regarding your abduction Ms. Reynolds. Mayor Grant has offered an explanation for the occurrences that day," Officer Menon offered.

My gaze immediately fell on the mayor. Everyone else in the room seemed to already be privy to what she was going to say, oddly enough, so when she admitted to purposely kissing Noah, only he and I had any real reactions.

Noah tightened his hold on me.

"Why?" I asked the obvious question. "Why would you do something like that?"

And I still didn't understand why Sheree was remaining so calm. I knew that the police presence alone wouldn't have kept her off the mayor unless there was a good reason.

"I needed to make you leave. I was trying to get you to go," she said, and suddenly she was in tears.

And Sheree was rubbing circles into her back. *Okay, I think I must be high.* Shaking my head in her direction, I couldn't believe what I was seeing or hearing.

"I don't understand. You abducted me to keep me away from Noah?" I had to keep myself from shouting.

"No, it wasn't just that. A piece of me did want you to leave for selfish reasons, but that wasn't all of it. Hex Tanner was behind my getting installed as mayor after my father died. He and my father had been in some type of business dealings that were dependent on the pipeline going in, so when my father died unexpectedly, Hex helped me into the office to make sure that things could carry on *status quo*," she paused. And that's when Officer Menon continued speaking.

"As it turns out, Hex Tanner needed her to find a way to muzzle you and your findings concerning her appointment as mayor. And when their prior actions didn't push you out of town, she manufactured a way to get you to leave once and for all. But turns out, Hex wanted to take it a bit further, and when you stormed away from the house the next morning, he'd hired someone to abduct you," Officer Menon completed his stream of disclosure seemingly without a breath.

I could feel myself becoming more lightheaded by the second, so I reached for the back of a chair and graciously accepted Noah's help to sit down. Sheree was by my side in an instant and grabbed one of my hands. The mayor continued to look over at me with tears in her eyes and a genuine look of regret. Something I'd never seen in her before.

"I'm sorry, Verity. I didn't realize that he'd take it this far. And what happened with you two last night, I knew I had to say something before, before..." she couldn't finish what she was saying.

I wasn't expecting Sheree to go back over to her, but I did catch the disparity in the fact that she had no one beside her while she was obviously falling apart, while I was sandwiched between my cousin and the man I loved, each holding on to a part of my person.

"Why would you get involved with something like this in the first place Leona?" The harshness in Noah's tone of voice made me flinch.

"I, I, love this town, and I loved my dad. I didn't want..."

"It seems as if Hex Tanner and the former Mayor Grant had some less-than-ideal business dealings with one another. Their commitment to the pipeline had been fueled by their interests in carving out a larger drug trafficking route that extended from the Northwest Territories into a corridor that led south into the northern United States. There's a joint taskforce on their way up to Dènaud that includes a partnership between the DEA and RCMP. Apparently, it'd been in existence for years and was how Tanner had generated most of his wealth." Officer Menon finished.

I felt sick to my stomach. How could something so small that we'd been working on be turned into all this? The room was quiet for some time after that particular disclosure. Even if someone had wanted to say anything, it was difficult to follow that up.

"With the mayor's resignation and ultimate cooperation in this investigation we should be able to send Hex away for a very long time," Officer Griffin finally added.

"And what about her part in all of this," Megan demanded as she pointed in the direction of the mayor with a forcefulness that quite frankly shocked everyone.

"The prosecutor's office is aware of the situation, and I'd imagine that her cooperation will likely be taken into consideration. But a crime was still committed. Many crimes actually," Officer Menon added.

There were another few moments of uncomfortable silence.

The mayor stood up at that point. "Well, that's all I really came here to say," she said before walking in the direction of both officers as they all turned to head towards the front door.

Before she crossed the threshold, she turned inside the doorframe with one more sad look at Noah and then me. "I am truly sorry for everything that happened. Neither of you deserved this and...I wish I could take everything back." With her head bowed she turned toward the open doorway.

"Wait a minute. I have something to say," I said, using Sheree's hand to steady myself before walking over to where Leona stood.

I paused for a moment, uncertain of my steps suddenly. But then I felt a hand spread across the small of my back and I knew it belonged to Noah.

I could tell from her gaze that the mayor hadn't missed his action and there was an added sadness that I saw behind her eyes. Up until that point, I'd still been angry at all the craziness I and everyone else had to endure, but somehow the sting went out of it at that moment. I still had so much and she was about to lose everything, including the one person she never truly had.

"Thank you for coming forward, Leona." I said as I let my hand graze her upper arm. It was the only thing that felt right to do or say at that moment.

The room was truly silent then, and the mayor left out the door with both police officers trailing behind her.

***

With the drama having died down after Mayor Grant stepped down and Hex Tanner remaining behind bars with his bail application denied due to him being a flight risk, a state of normalcy started to return to Dènaud. The news coming out of Dènaud had also dispirited many protestors and far fewer numbers showed up to protest the pipeline than original estimated.

True to her word, Sheree had returned for one further visit before my stay came to an end, and from the looks of things between her and Samson, I was pretty sure that she'd be a regular visitor from here on out.

Megan and Booker decided to spend some time getting to know each other better and taking full advantage of her freedom, Megan extended her time away from returning home, to travel to more places across the country and the United States with Booker by her side.

After the mayor's confession that day at Clarence House, Adrian apparently showed up for support as she was being booked down at the station for her alleged misdeeds. Noah and I were just so happy to not have to deal with Adrian's interference anymore, so we literally paid him no mind for the rest of the time I lived at Clarence House.

The prosecutor did take her cooperation into consideration, and she received probation instead of jail time due in huge part to the fact that she'd kept very detailed records of Tanner's schemes. She'd even turned over some information that incriminated her own father, which she'd found in his office after he died.

My thesis defense was a complete success and much of our work made it into numbered exhibits in the case *R v. Tanner,* the criminal court case against Hex Tanner.

Which brings me to today, waiting at the Wakepa Lake dock for Headley, my ride back to Dènaud. I wasn't supposed to come back today. In fact, it was Noah who was supposed to come visit me now that I'd finished my defense, but I couldn't wait for whatever ranch business he had to complete before he'd get on a plane to Toronto. We'd talked about alternating visiting each other, but knew that long distance wasn't ideal. So here I was, headed to surprise him. Only Tabitha and Headley knew about my arrival, so I was hoping that it would truly catch him off guard.

The plane ride with Headley was shorter than I remembered from the last time, and Tabitha was there to greet me with trusty old Gray by her side. I still wasn't a fan of Gray, but we'd figured out a way to co-exist. I could manage provided he didn't get too close, lick or jump up on me. So after a calm greeting where I gave him a few pats on the head, he rode in the back, and I sat up front with Tabitha.

"We have surely missed seeing you," she said as she squeezed my hand closest to her.

"I've missed you all so much too," I replied.

Everything looked about the same as we made our way towards Clarence House. The trees no longer had any leaves and there was a definite chill to the air.

"How has he been?" I asked, knowing that I'd just spoken with him that very morning and hadn't led on that I was on my way to him.

"Missing you, you know how it is," she remarked as we turned onto his driveway.

As we came closer to the house, I noticed that there were a large number of vehicles parked around the driveway and several folks standing around outside in front of the house. There was a banner hanging from the porch that said, "Welcome Home Vee," but it swung a little too low for anyone to stand under it safely.

I turned towards Tabitha with a look that begged to know what was going on. But she made a motion like her lips were sealed and hurriedly jumped out of the car. When I finally got up the nerve to get out of the vehicle, I noticed quite a number of faces were turned squarely in my direction.

I smiled a little more awkwardly than I'd intended and began making my way slowly over to the porch. The faces weren't all known to me, but they all had the same thing in common: they were all smiling sweetly at me. If I was a less optimistic person, I'd have thought that this was a pivotal moment in a horror film. But I kept up appearances and continued to smile as I passed everyone by, hoping that I'd see that one familiar face that I'd missed so much. Then I'd bust his chops over how he'd found out I was coming and why there were so many people around.

As I began to place my left foot on the bottom step, the screen door suddenly opened, and Noah's parents walked out. I was almost ready to greet them when I noticed another figure coming out just behind them.

Momma?"

I was just about to have a heart attack when I glimpsed Sheree standing hand in hand with Samson off to the side by the rocking chairs with a smiling Callie holding one of Tabitha's granddaughters.

"What, I, what…" I managed to let out.

I looked to my mother as though she was the source for making all things make sense, and she nodded her head upwards in a way that indicated that I should turn around.

And when I did, I turned to see Noah, down on one knee before me.

"Verity Reynolds, my Vee, will you marry me?"

My legs were already in motion to get to him.

"Yes!"

Epilogue

NOAH

I ROLLED OVER and pressed my hand against Verity's cheek. I'd slipped into bed early this morning after finishing up the daily morning routines over in the barn, leaving the ranch hands to figure out the rest on their own.

I always showered after coming in from the barn, and I always made sure the water was piping hot so that my body would be as warm as possible when I curled up next to my beautiful wife.

She made it easy for me on mornings like this, scooting her body backward into my embrace and even lifting her hips so that I could put an arm underneath her and encircle her waist. Inhaling deeply, I listened to the soft suckling noises before looking down at a scene that never ceased to amaze me.

Our son, Christian, with his pinkish lips wrapped around one of Verity's nipples as she cradled him in her arms. And by the sounds of it, I'd made it just in time for the beginning of his feeding because, as usual, he was ravenous. He was a Sawyer after all, and Verity had been unaware, but soon found out, that Sawyer offspring were always big. He'd weighed nearly nine pounds at birth.

Now, I knew that Verity's nipples could take some application of pain, but she never would give me a clear answer as to whether the pain was greater when our little Christian was feeding and would accidentally bite her or when I'd purposely do it. She'd just play hit me or try to change the topic.

Not that I minded sharing with my little man. Verity's breast milk tasted so sweet to me, and from the sounds our son made, it must have been like Heaven's nectar to him too.

I loved our lovemaking while she was pregnant, especially when she was full-term and in need of my assistance to spur along labor. The memory still replayed on a reel in my head from time to time: holding her hips in place with one hand and placing a steadying hand on her back to create a small arch while I entered her from behind.

But being able to bring her to orgasm alone in the missionary position, even without clitoral stimulation, had been an amazing development in our sex life post-pregnancy once she'd been cleared to resume having sex. Giving birth had somehow heightened her libido and intensified her orgasms. And we'd been fine in that department anyway, but her willingness to explore more positions while pregnant and me worshiping her post-baby body had not only increased both of our freedoms in sexually pleasuring one another but had also taken us both to a new plateau of understanding about what makes us both responsive to each other.

Even as I watched Christian getting his morning feed in, I had never been more attracted to this gorgeous woman whom I'd somehow convinced to be my life partner.

"Good morning. Whatcha doing?" Her voice was soft so as not to wake up our son whose long lashes made minuscule movements as his eyes remained closed.

"Just watching our little man get his breakfast in," I answered while attempting to snuggle even closer to her. Her body was soft and perfect against my hard body. It was as if they were made at the same time and for one another.

"Mmm," Verity sighed deeply.

This was our perfect start, even though I'd been up for hours. The day didn't really begin until I held her in my arms and watched her give our son the liquid gold that would make him big and strong like me one day.

"Oops, sorry, not sorry," I smiled as I leaned over her ear to continue whispering. My body was having its normal reaction to her proximity as well as the overall scene in and of itself.

Verity as a mother to our child was sexy as hell. Even when she couldn't bear to wear anything other than sweats, maternity sports bras, and her favorite holey sweater, it took a lot for me not to be overly handsy with her or to pin her against a wall every chance I could get. It was like she'd become even more attractive to me—if that was even possible.

"And what do you plan on doing with that, Mr. Sawyer?" I loved it when her tone was playful, as she rubbed her backside suggestively on my ever-growing erection.

"Anything you want me to Mrs., or sorry, I mean Dr. Sawyer," I quipped, giving her earlobe a little tug as I opened my mouth and traced the underside of her ear with my tongue. I reveled in the feel of her shivering in my embrace.

"Careful, not yet, and I don't want to jinx anything. Besides, I've got a very long way to go," she offered.

But I was having none of it. It had always been her intention to pursue a doctoral degree once she'd completed her Masters. And even after we'd found out that we were having a baby, that path was simply delayed but not abandoned.

"I'm so proud of you, and I can't wait until all of your dreams come true," I said, a little more loudly than I'd intended.

We both froze up a little when Christian's little cherub frame began to stir, and his eyelids began to flutter. But thankfully, he didn't awaken, so I watched as Verity carefully put her fingers just under his little chin, I heard the satisfied pop of his mouth dislodging from her nipple. This little one could sleep through almost anything, except my voice at a normal level, so I was careful to lower my octave as I whispered more sweet nothings to Verity as she moved our son to the bassinet attached to our bed frame.

"My dreams have all already come true," she said.

I think my heart just skipped a beat.

When she turned over towards me, she was beginning to lower the threadbare tank top she typically wore to bed for easier feeding and to keep from overheating, but I stopped her. I loved the look of her swollen nipples after feeding and how the nodes around her darkened areola stood at complete attention.

There was still a bit of breast milk sitting in tiny beads on the nipple that Christian had just left, and the peak glistened with his leftover saliva. I looked into Verity's eyes for permission, and when she gave me a simple nod, I dove in. Latching on to her breast with my mouth, I trapped her nipple with my lips before swirling my tongue around it. My hand was busy squeezing the other breast gingerly so as not to mess too much with the balance of its contents as compared to the other that I was licking currently.

Raising up on my elbow, I pulled my arm from her side and pushed it underneath her to offer her more support from behind, then I drew my fingers across her chest from her breast down to her belly button. Hearing a soft gasp told me that I was headed in the right direction.

Thankfully, Verity didn't feel the need to sleep with bottoms next to me and preferred either her own tank tops or sometimes one of my own. I loved the latter the most because they were always more than twice her size and her full breasts would always be exposed, their heaviness impossible to hide and sometimes even her nipple would poke through an armhole or the collar.

I listened for any movements of our son but took my time putting one finger and then another into his mother. I knew she was biting her lip because my line of sight was the side of her face as her chin drew upwards and the back of her head pressed further into the topside of my arm.

Then I turned my hand to palm her as I simultaneously worked her clit feverishly with my thumb and continued pumping away with my fingers, increasing my pace as I felt her tighten further around them. I pushed another finger inside of her, and she turned her head into my neck to muffle her scream. The resulting explosion released her silky fluid all over my fingers, and I let them linger inside of her as she convulsed beautifully but removed my thumb from her sensitive node.

Once she'd returned her head to its normal position, I removed my fingers and placed each one that had been inside of her inside of my mouth as she watched.

I felt how soft the inside of her palm was as she went to draw her hand down the side of my face.

"I love you so much," she said.

"I love you too."